AWFUL
BUT LAWFUL

A Law Enforcement Tale

Bob Country

Fulton Books, Inc.
Meadville, PA

Published by Fulton Books 2021

ISBN 978-1-63860-980-3 (paperback)
ISBN 978-1-63860-981-0 (digital)

Printed in the United States of America

CONTENTS

CHAPTER 1

An Introduction to Me

I think the vast majority of us want to do the right thing. In today's age, the definition of what that might be can be problematic; however, in my mind it is generally what we can be proud of at the end of the day. Regardless of your age, race, religion, sexuality, etc., it is what you know that your mother and father can see and for which say aloud, "That's how we raised him!" From a political perspective, I was a conservative individual raised by liberal parents with liberal siblings, so I was something of a black sheep growing up, but I shared my family's sense of fairness and acceptable behavior. One should never steal, cheat, or lie (unless we were playing Canasta, in which case deception is expected).

God was center stage in my life growing up. As the son of a minister, I went to church every Sunday and usually several other days during the week or on weekends. Being raised in a church helped me to see how people should treat others and, as the Good Book says, "as you wish to be treated." This seemed like sage advice to me, and I believe it was foundational in shaping my sense of fairness.

I loved football and can remember seeing my first football game on a black-and-white television as a very young man. I recall the game was played between the Dallas Cowboys and the Washington Redskins. For whatever reason, I chose the Redskins as the team I wanted to win the game and was sorely disappointed when the Cowboys put a proverbial licking on the Washington team. I played football as soon as my parents would allow me and sat on the bench the first year. After that, I was a starter on every team I played with until my freshman year in college. That final playing year taught me that professional football would not be a part of my eventual career. After I had injured one of my knees in the last organized game I would play in, the team's orthopedic doctor asked me if I envisioned myself playing professionally. I had seen stronger and faster players in college and knew I could not compete at that level, so I honestly answered him, "No." He then asked me if I wanted to be able to walk when I turned fifty years of age. I took his point and quit playing organized football that day.

Football served to enhance my sense of fairness and served as an example of how one should behave. Sure, there were those who broke the rules, but when they did, they usually got penalized for doing so. Of course, there were always those who purposefully sought advantages, but it was my belief that those who played with dignity and honor would prevail. For the most part, that bore out to be the truth in the many games I played and watched throughout my lifetime. While many of us can attest that we favor certain teams and disagree vehemently when the referees make a call against our chosen group, we all agree that we have to abide by those decisions of the some-times-fallible zebras who are only trying their best to get it right.

While growing up, I did not know what career path I wanted to take, but I had a strong sense that I wanted the law to be part of what I would eventually do. Upon finishing college, I joined the United States Army Reserves and decided that as a military occupational specialty (MOS), I might like being a military policeman (MP or Ninety-Five Bravo). I would later learn that the primary job of an MP was to guard stuff. Long hours of boring nothingness interspersed with more hours of boring nothingness.

I was attached to the 320th MP Battalion stationed in Saint Petersburg, Florida, upon my release from basic training and MOS schooling in Anniston, Alabama. When I reported to my First Sergeant, I requested that he release me from my reserve obligation and allow me to return to active duty. The First Sergeant listened to my request and then made one of his own. He asked me to give him six months in the Reserves, and if I still wanted to go full duty, he would sign the necessary paperwork. I never made that second request.

Several of my fellow Reservists were police officers in surrounding cities, which added to my curiosity concerning a possible career in law enforcement. I applied at several cities and counties in the Tampa Bay area. There was a lull in hiring at that time in law enforcement, so it took me almost a year and a half before getting a job offer. While I was waiting and hoping to be hired, I became quite proficient in short-order cooking. I worked my way up in a restaurant to the point of Sous Chef and actually took a cut in pay to become a police officer.

My starting pay entering the police academy in August 1988 was $6.05 per hour during the time I was in training. Once I graduated and began working on the street as a full-time officer, my pay was raised to $10.12 per hour. I still worked in the Army Reserves, and for a weekend, my pay as an enlisted private (E-3) was approximately $50 for the entire weekend. Once I began working as a police officer, I could "moonlight," making $13 an hour cash on my time off. It did not take me long to figure out that I probably should not re-enlist. As a retiree, I wish I had stayed with the military so that I could have cheaper medical benefits, but as a young man, I was more about instant gratification.

I was somewhat naive entering the world of law enforcement. I honestly believed, as I was raised, that everything was fair and everyone was honest (for the most part). I distinctly remember sitting at a convenience store on a night that I was required to ride with my corporal during training when a vehicle limped into the parking lot. There was a flat tire, and steam was rising out of the radiator, with severe damage to the front of the car. Almost simultaneously, the police dispatcher called out a BOLO ("Be On the Look Out"), reading off the tag of the suspect vehicle that had fled from the scene of a serious-injury traffic crash. The driver got out of the car after parking it in two spaces and stumbled into the convenience store. My corporal looked at me and said, "What do you think?"

I responded, "The tag she read out was off by one digit," and went back to writing my report.

Almost instantly, I realized what a foolhardy response I had given and jumped out of my car to make the arrest. But I honestly meant what I had said...for a minute.

Fast-forward in my career, and I had the opportunity to join the department's first Community-Oriented Policing (COP) squad. Most of the veterans did not want anything to do with signing up for the new squad or the concepts concerning COP, but I had about six and a half years on the department and definitely wanted to advance. This appeared to be the perfect opportunity.

The first six and a half years, I worked the area known in the department as the champagne district. While I stayed in the same district, I moved to an area in that district for the COP assignment that was predominantly public housing. It was the largest public housing unit in the city, and as a comparison, I worked one homicide in my initial assignment in six and a half years and worked approximately twenty homicides in the COP assignment during my four years there. Halfway through the COP assignment, I was promoted to corporal and given the job on the COP squad (supervising what had been my peers). That was not typical when one was promoted, but my superiors had a well-placed trust in my ability to lead, and I did not disappoint.

My COP assignment was dissolved, however, and I was moved to a street-level narcotic unit (known as QUAD, or Quick Uniform Attack on Drugs). Both the military and the police love their acronyms! We worked in plain clothes, driving ordinary-looking civilian vehicles, and attempted to make arrests of street-level drug dealers. If we stumbled upon large quantities of narcotics or arrested a street-level dealer who could provide information on someone moving "heavy" weight (defined as a kilogram of cocaine or more, fifty pounds of marijuana or more, or more than four grams of heroin), we were required to bring in one of our Vice squads (made up entirely of detectives, with a sergeant overseeing the squad). In contrast, my QUAD squad was made up entirely of officers, with one corporal (me, who was the equivalent rank of a detective) and a sergeant supervising.

I spent a little over a year on the QUAD squad and only left when I was promoted to sergeant. I toyed with returning as a sergeant, but I was offered a job as a Field Training and Evaluation Program (FTEP) sergeant before the QUAD sergeant offer came in. While the person offering me the FTEP sergeant was merely a lieutenant and the person who offered me the QUAD sergeant was a Deputy Chief of Police, I stuck with my sense of honor as I accepted the first offer before the second offer was made. The Deputy Chief held a grudge to the bitter end and likely cost me additional promotions for a period, but I could look myself in the mirror and know that I had done the right thing.

Being a police sergeant was the most gratifying position I held during my law enforcement career. When you showed up to a scene, everyone knew you were the one in charge. Your people looked to you for answers, and the public knew you were the one to take care of business. As an FTEP sergeant, I was allowed to pick who worked for me. My corporals and I were very conscientious of who we put on our training squad. In my latter years and even now in retirement, I take great pride in those training officers who went on to excel within the department (two deputy chiefs, a major, a captain, two sergeants, and several corporals/detectives at last count).

I took a test for lieutenant and was on the eligibility list for promotion. The list was good for two years, and just as the list was about to expire, we got a new Chief of Police, who wanted to reorganize the department. What that meant for me was that everyone left on the eligibility list would be promoted to lieutenant. I had fallen in love with my sergeant position and was not enamored with the politics at the rank of lieutenant and above (we called them "the brass," and it was a disdainful term for the rank and file). I talked with my wife, sharing with her my skepticism and that I was considering turning down the promotional offer. My wife listened (as she always did) and then made a very salient point. I had been through a class with all my fellow sergeants on the promotional list and was not really impressed with their desires to continue to climb the organizational ladder (at almost any cost). My wife asked me, "Which one of them do you want to work for?" Her point was well-taken. I took the lieutenant position when it was offered to me, vowing to make sure that all those over whom I had influence would be protected from "the brass," which I was becoming a part of.

I was a lieutenant for almost eight years (the second-longest stretch in my career at any rank; I was a patrolman for eight and one-half years before promotion to corporal). I spent most of that time on the midnight shift in patrol and thoroughly enjoyed myself. As our Chief of Police would say about me, "He's the chief of police on the midnight shift. I can rest at night knowing he's in charge." The buck stopped with me on most things. The trick was learning what needed to be pushed up the chain. I cannot tell you how many times I or one of my subordinates was a complete idiot while sleeping after a shift, but as soon as I was awake enough to speak to the brass that same day, we became consensus All-Americans.

At one point, a major who liked me (and whom I liked) told me that I should come to day shift if I wanted to be promoted to captain. I liked the thought of making captain and running my own sector, but I told my wife I feared my brash and to-the-point mannerisms would not fare well on day shift in the land/time of the brass. We discussed it, and she reminded me that given our children's hectic schedule, such a move would allow her more time with our kids. I am all about family and what is best for mine, so I gave up on the familiar and comfortable assignment I had grown accustomed to in an attempt to move up in my organization.

My initial response to the day shift was shock at how lazy a lot of the patrol officers appeared to be. The department had begun a "shift bid" process that was based on tenure and allowed officers to pick when, where, and for whom they worked. The specialty squads were still handpicked, but not the average patrolman. When I had first started on the department, you worked for the sergeant you were assigned unless or until you were promoted or asked to join a spe-cialty squad (as I had been in going to the COP squad). The end result of the shift bid process was that the senior patrolmen ended up on the day shift and the rookies were primarily on midnight shifts. The rookies were more eager to get involved in proactive police work, while the veterans preferred to answer the calls as they came in and otherwise occupy themselves during downtime. As someone with the drive to attempt to do his best every shift, I was driven nuts by the day shift's outward appearance of laziness!

Captains had a group of lieutenants work for them. Most of the lieutenants knew that we were nothing more than the captain's corporal—meaning, we got to do the things that the captain wanted done but that he or she did not want to do him- or herself. To further complicate my transition to the day shift, my captain knew that I was very good administratively. On midnights, I was able to choose the time to accomplish my administrative tasks and spent roughly half my time in the office, with the remainder spent on the street, interacting with my people. On day shift, the captain kept me busy most days, and weekends were the rare time I got to spend with my people.

The problem with not spending time with your people is that you must rely on the interpretation of others regarding what is happening outside the police buildings. For most of the brass, it had been so long since they had spent any time responding to calls for service that they would rely on sometimes-untrustworthy sources (or those with an agenda) *or* they would pull the old "The way I used to do it" spiel. I tried to keep my feet grounded in reality by going out and seeing issues for myself. It paid dividends in the long run for me because those who worked for me knew I would not be deceived by anyone with a self-serving plan. They also got to see firsthand how I operated.

After a little more than a year as a day shift patrol lieutenant, I was asked to take, design, and lead a new specialty team as a "Tactical" lieutenant. The department formed squads of "Rapid Offender Control" officers, who worked in plain clothes, driving civilian-type vehicles. The reasoning was that the old QUAD officers were purely interested in narcotic arrests and were missing the links to property crimes. That assumption was correct. By combining the former QUAD resources with the Street Anti-Crime sources (SAC, which dealt primarily with prostitution), the department was able to address narcotics, prostitution, and property crimes in conjunction with the department's property crimes detectives. The results were a success.

When promotions were imminent, everyone knew it well in advance. I was the most senior lieutenant on the department with the best chance of being promoted. There were three openings, so the likelihood that I would get one of them was strong. Just prior to the announcement concerning who would be picked, I was asked if I would take a position on the statewide training commission. It was quite an honor, and I was happy to accept. My major at that time joked, "Let's hope that isn't the booby prize." After that prophetic comment, I had something of an ominous feeling concerning my promotional chances.

I worked on the commission for eight years during my employment with two different agencies. There are nineteen commissioners authorized by state law to be on the commission. We would meet quarterly at revolving locations in the state for four days to get the commission's business done. One of the commission's legislative mandates is to oversee all the training for law enforcement and correction officers in the state of Florida. The other mandate was to sit in a quasijudicial position over the certifications of all Florida law enforcement and correction officers. While the former mandate was what I loved most, the latter was what consumed the vast majority of the commission's time.

The staff of the Florida Department of Law Enforcement (FDLE) ran the operations of the commission and were among the most professional bureaucratic staffs I had ever been associated with. They briefed me prior to my first commission meeting, and I was given a voluminous amount of material to read prior to that meeting. I was told to worry primarily with the "A tabs and B tabs" because most of the discussion would center on those cases (there are tabs A through M, but most of the cases are in the earlier tabs). At that first meeting, I was the new guy who said nothing as I was soaking in the entire atmosphere and attempting to learn. The staff attorney had told me that due to the Florida Sunshine Laws, commissioners were not allowed to speak about pending cases outside of the open meeting room, where everything was open to the public.

At my very first meeting, I saw that former sergeant Ernie George was the chairman of the commission. I must admit that I am something of an admirer of the man, whose "From the Desk of Ernie George" column in the state Police Benevolent Association's (PBA) monthly newsletter during my rookie years served to inform all of us in the state about what would get your certification yanked and how to avoid trouble (seemingly common sense, one would think). Mr. George was (and probably still is) one of the champions of the rank-and-file law enforcement and corrections officers in the state of Florida.

At that very first meeting, everything went pretty smoothly as I watched the process unfold. True to form, the vast majority of disciplinary cases that were discussed were from the A and B tabs. Even though all the commissioners wore suits with ties, I began to get the sense of who was from management and who was from labor based upon the statements made and the voting patterns that began to emerge. Close to the end of the meeting, an M-tab case was called and I scrambled to pull the tab up on my computer screen. I must admit that I had not read the entire case because of what I was told, and I was amazed at what unfolded in the next few minutes. The case involved a law enforcement veteran who had tested positive for the use of cocaine. The typical resolution of such a case was the revocation of the officer's certification.

At the beginning of the discussion, the case appeared to be headed toward its prescribed resolution. The FDLE attorney presenting the case (who acts as the prosecutor) suddenly got a "reality stricken" look on his face as the tide began to turn (as I simultaneously began to realize what was happening). The FDLE attorney interrupted the move toward something less than revocation by saying, "Commissioners, if you believe that this man knowingly consumed cocaine, then follow the commission's precedence in revoking his certification. If, however, you believe we haven't proven our case, then please just throw this one out! But for God's sake, don't split the proverbial baby!" It was an impassioned plea, and one I will never forget, as I sat there in utter disbelief. My fellow commissioners ignored the FDLE attorney's advice and voted to impose a period of suspension on this officer. When they called for the vote, I said the only word I uttered publicly during that meeting. When asked if anyone opposed the commission's recommended disciplinary action, I sat forward in my seat and said very loudly and very clearly, "Nay," into the microphone in front of me. Everyone looked at me as if seeing me for the first time.

After the conclusion of that first meeting, I was greeted by several of my fellow commissioners and commented to one of the obvious union representatives, "Boy, that went pretty fast." He smiled at me and acknowledged the speed through which the cases were handled, saying, "Yeah, most of these are worked out in advance." I was shocked by his candid admission that these cases were being discussed by my fellow commissioners in advance of the actual meeting and in violation of the direction given to me by the FDLE attorney assigned to the commission concerning the Florida Sunshine Law.

I also learned a lesson from that first meeting: never again would I show up without having read every word of every piece of material given to me. That was something that bothered me at my regular position on the police department and something I would take with me to the commission. We had many passionate arguments during commission meetings over the coming years. For some reason, the union representatives wanted to lower the penalty for the consumption of illicit drugs by those holding law enforcement or corrections certification. I felt (and still feel) that the public we served had the right to expect that those responsible for overseeing prisoners and those responding to their homes for domestic disturbances, for example, were not high on marijuana while at their respective jobs. Prior to my arrival on the commission, Ernie George had championed second chances for sworn officers arrested for driving under the influence (DUI) in their personal vehicles with no injury to others, which used to be automatic revocation. A second DUI is now automatic revocation. I believe that was a just and fair reversal of the past practice of automatic revocation for first-time offending officers.

Over a year after I left the commission, one of my fellow commissioners, who was retiring, called me to tell me that at one of their recent meetings, a union representative made the comment that if I was still there, he would be confident that at least I would read all the material associated with the case being considered. All the commissioners knew that regardless of my seemingly management position, if the materials did not support what was being alleged by law enforcement or corrections management, then I would not support any type of disciplinary measure.

One of my best friends on the police department got gravely ill, and I was asked to fill in for him while he fought cancer. I was an acting captain for a short period, and after my friend's death, I was reassigned to the midnight shift without any real explanation. I thought my promotional chances were over, and I spoke with my wife concerning my feelings on the topic. My wife was worried that I would not be able to adapt back to the midnight shift because of the strain put on one's body by changing sleeping patterns. The first time I had been a lieutenant on the midnight shift, I would come home from work at 6:30 a.m. and wake my kids to get ready for school. After taking them to school, I would rush home and sleep while my wife worked. Later, I would pick them up from school and bring them home for homework, then dinner with my wife and children prior to leaving for work. This next go-around, my son was in college and my daughter had her own car to get back and forth to school. All I had to do was sleep between shifts. Much easier!

Determined to not let the disappointment over my failed attempt for promotion negatively affect my work attitude, and resigned to the fact that I had probably advanced as far up the ladder as was my destiny to go, I dived back into my assignment with great enthusiasm. My major asked me to surreptitiously attempt to help one of my midnight sergeants with a personal issue, and I did my best to assist without letting him know what had been requested of me. The next ten months went by smoothly, with me enjoying my assignment as much as I had previously done as a patrol lieutenant. I was quite surprised by the telephone call I received late one October afternoon from the Chief of Police informing me that I had been selected to be one of her next captains. I would finally get the opportunity to lead my own patrol sector.

I worked for five majors in three separate sectors in each of the three patrol districts in just over four years as a captain. I learned quite a lot about how the department operates, a vastly large array of personnel issues, and just how much I enjoyed my job. To be sure, there were times I questioned my decision to advance past the rank of sergeant, but in the end, the answer I always came back to was that my decision had ultimately been the best one. Unlike most of the captains before me, I remained heavily involved in the work at the primary level and even assisted in some arrests (though those were further apart and less frequent than when I was a lieutenant). Besides my love of the actual work, I was determined to remain grounded in the reality of the backbone of the department (patrol) and not let the rarified air that the brass breathed infect my decision-making. I learned to argue politically and became quite adept at maneuvering within the administrative environment.

My majors were each unique and each had his or her own ways of doing things. I adapted to each one's personal preferences, and to this day, I can call any one of them to have a mutually satisfactory conversation about life in retirement. My development of both personal and professional relationships with each of them led me to the next chapter in my professional life after my retirement from my first law enforcement job.

CHAPTER 2

Failing Retirement

One of the majors I had worked for in my first law enforcement job (we will call her Rosa Truth) had taken a job in another, smaller city in Florida as the Chief of Police. She had asked me if I might be interested in working for her again in this new city. She explained to me the challenges she was facing and her plans for the future of her department. She told me what she was looking for in a staff-level position she intended to create and that I would have to apply for the job if I was interested. I told her I would get back to her after I spoke with my wife about the possibility.

The month I retired, my daughter, who was my youngest, graduated from college. My wife and I had diligently worked at ensuring that our children had a better start than we had in life, which meant that they would both graduate college without any student loans and with a reasonably reliable car. After meeting that goal, we felt that we could comfortably retire in a new state that was more affordable, with a more distinctive change in weather (we were both tired of being hot all the time). I retired in May, we sold our house of almost thirty years in June, and we bought our retirement home in July. During our conversation of my returning to law enforcement work in Florida, the fact that we would live apart in different states was definitely a con for me doing so. In the end, my wife convinced me that it would be okay for me to continue to work because we both felt I had more to offer and this would be the perfect opportunity for me to do so.

At one of the first public functions we attended after I had made the decision to apply and then was offered the job in the new city, my wife jokingly told someone that I had failed retirement. That began our running joke for years to come. After I was hired, but before I arrived at the new agency, the senior staff and I had a telephonic discussion of the reorganization of the department to accommodate the new position that was being created. I have since joked that the chiefs gave to me the oversight of all the jobs that they really did not want to do. I was the department's only major in charge of most things administrative, which included the detective division, the training unit, the forensic unit, the recruitment unit, the internal affairs unit, the property room, the accreditation unit, the field training unit, the records unit, the department's mobile field force, the defunct special weapons and tactics team (SWAT), the honor guard, the crime analysis unit, and the armory.

I arrived in the latter part of August of that year and began adapting to my new agency and my roles within it. I had a lieutenant assigned to me (we will call her Sabrina Powers) who was very charming and very meticulous in her writing. She had previously been in charge of Internal Affairs (IA), and she attempted to get me up to speed on the active as well as previously active but still relevant cases. At first blush, she appeared to be hesitant and not so trusting of me. Of course, that might be explained with her being a veteran law enforcement officer at her agency and my being an outsider brought in to be her superior without any firsthand knowledge of her agency. The other possibility was (and is) that she had worked her entire career for an opportunity to fill one of the upper-level management positions and there was some professional jealousy in my having come from the outside to seemingly thwart her chance. There was a similar feeling with most of the people I met, and I knew I would have my work cut out for me convincing them of my intentions as well as the reputation of being fair that I had earned at my previous agency.

After a few interactions with Lieutenant Powers, and after reading several of the internal affairs cases that she had authored, I quickly realized that she had a habit of overexplaining her position in writing while jumping to her own conclusions in investigations rather than allowing the facts to speak for themselves. In the state of Florida, an internal affairs investigator is not entitled to an opinion concerning the case he or she is working on when reporting his or her findings. The case summary should provide the reader the investigative findings and contain no personal feelings regarding the outcome of the case. Ideally, there should only be the facts for the decision makers to review in order for them to determine the proper outcome of the case. There was quite a bit of agency history in the internal affairs files, but I decided to let my interactions with people be the basis for my developing relationships rather than rely upon some past case, regardless of the outcome.

One of the first tasks Chief Truth assigned me was preparation for the upcoming department reaccreditation. It was a daunting task for any individual, one that was meant to be a dedicated position for a full-time employee who did nothing but prepare for two years. The previous accreditation manager had left the agency under a cloud, and it was later determined that she had purposefully sabotaged some of the supporting documentation necessary to meet some of the standards. It was surmised that this was likely done because of that manager's dissatisfaction with the department. The natural choice to replace her was Lieutenant Powers, whom the previous accreditation manager had reported to, and Chief Truth reassigned her to Deputy Chief Alex King to work solely on reaccreditation since it was scheduled for four months after my arrival at the agency.

While I was somewhat relieved to see Lieutenant Powers reassigned, I did not relish what it meant for the Internal Affairs Bureau. Since I had no experienced individual as replacement for the lieutenant, I would have to assume the lead until I could train a new investigator. I chose an extremely capable and seasoned detective (Felicia Direct), who would ultimately become accomplished at the task, but she and I had to have several long conversations as well as work our way through several cases before she reached a level of competency that did not involve direct oversight. There is a distinct difference between investigating criminal cases involving civilians and investigating police officers. A wholly different set of rules exists, called the Police Officers Bill of Rights, as well as legal standards, such as the Garrity rule, that must be followed, and failing to follow them can land an investigator in deep trouble.

As part of my introduction to the agency, I needed to understand the various operating systems and software used by the agency and the people within it. There was one Information Technology civilian lady who took care of all the department's technology needs (we will call her Bright Action). There were supposed to be two civilians, but the guy that worked there before I arrived left under a cloud (was allowed to resign in lieu of termination). Ultimately, the city agreed to fund three positions due to the volume of work just prior to my departure from the agency, but in the meantime, Mrs. Action attempted to do the work of three. When I was attempting to understand who all had access to the internal affairs files, I found out that two sergeants that were currently in patrol had access, a patrol sergeant that was currently administratively relieved from duty had access, and Lieutenant Powers, who was now in accreditation, had access. After consultation with Chief Truth on who she wanted to have access, I immediately removed all these individuals' ability to access these extremely sensitive files. Literally within two minutes of my having done this, Lieutenant Powers darkened my doorway rather nastily telling me that she still needed access to those files for accreditation purposes. I professionally responded, telling her to just send me an email detailing which files she needed and I would supply them to her once any sensitive information was properly redacted.

I was provided an executive civilian secretary (Molly Mad), who was excellent at her job, but she was secretly dating (not much of a secret within the department) one of the current deputy chiefs, Deputy Chief Wily Trust. This made it difficult for me to have confidential conversations regarding department matters without risking the start of rumor. I was grateful when the opportunity arose to have my secretary moved to another part of the building so that "the walls have ears" was not a real concern.

My initial detective sergeant (Al Simpson) was a salty veteran with skepticism running deep in his veins. He would agree to handle things to my face but would not accomplish them when my back was turned. To get him to take care of what I wanted done, I had to stay on him, routinely reminding him of my direction. I had never been one to give away my problem employees and did not seek to be rid of this one, but when Deputy Chief Trust suggested he be moved back to patrol, I did not object.

Chief Truth asked me to review the assigned/referred cases in the department. Like most of the tasks she had planned for me, this was not small. I had spent twenty-eight years learning one operating system for reporting in one department, and I needed to quickly get up to speed on this department's computer system. This resulted in some very long initial days on the department, but since I was living by myself while my wife was getting our retirement home in the state of repair she desired following its purchase, I could afford to be out late. I would typically arrive at work between 0630 and 0730 and would not typically leave until 1800-ish.

One of the signs of a good supervisor is delegating work to subordinate employees that can help the employees understand the supervisor's overall direction and relieve some of the pressure of too much work on that supervisor. I tried that with the Chief's initial direction to review all the assigned cases, but that reluctant detective sergeant ran too much interference to get any meaningful information. I was inundated with many other requests from the Chief (I kept a running list on a legal pad, which she added to almost every staff meeting, and there were two of those per week), so I prioritized that request as lower in the scheme of things. I was eventually given two sergeants (Jacoba Faithful and Felix Frank) in the detective division (one for each district) and a lieutenant (Whit Singer) to oversee them. Lieutenant Singer was also put over the records section, the property room, the crime scene technicians (forensic unit), and the criminal analysts.

My property room was kept by a very capable civilian employee (Hardy Cane) with years of experience at his job. He was very conscientious and had a very good organizational system for the most part.

One of the main problems was space. The department was outgrowing the allotted space for storage, which made it difficult to house all the property that was being submitted. Furthermore, retention schedules were not being met. Departments in the state of Florida are allowed to dispose of property after certain lengths of time, and this had not been done in quite some time, which only added to the problem.

Even though I had a lieutenant to oversee the records unit, I had to pay close personal attention to this area because of the sensitivity of the information housed there. Florida state statute chapter 119 covers the state's Sunshine Laws and more specifically covers the requirements regarding public records requests. There is a game that has been played by activists seeking an easy payday, and it involves catching an unsuspecting and ignorant-to-the-intricacies-of-the-law agencies for failing or refusing to fulfill a public records request. This can be very expensive and embarrassing for any agency caught in this quagmire, and the tendency is to release too much information to overcompensate for the fear of being caught in a trap. The city's activist population was almost overwhelming, given its relatively small size and the fact that my civilian records supervisor (Ida Shy) was not a strong personality. Mrs. Shy was deeply religious and very prim and proper (comparable to the proverbial librarian). She professed her ignorance to the law early on and her surprise that people would actually try to trick her. We had to have routine meetings and impromptu office visits to get through a week (and sometimes just one day). It was tiresome but necessary.

The department's training unit was headed up by Sergeant Ethan Quick, who had multiple years of experience in tactical operations, the detective division, and patrol. He worked full-time keeping the agency up-to-date on contemporary legal issues and practical training and was constantly looking for opportunities to bring additional training to our personnel. He had a street crimes detective reporting to him part-time to help with training (Walter O'Reilly), and there was a dedicated full-time recruiter (Officer Damond Loyal) who also assisted with training.

When I arrived, there were only two civilians in the department's forensic unit, and they were extremely busy throughout their shifts. The overtime hours being generated by this unit justified hiring another civilian position, which we ultimately got approved prior to my departure. Staffing that position to include finding additional transportation (fully stocked van) was an adventure in prudent spending for a department with very little resources.

The department was authorized one hundred and twenty-six sworn positions, and when I arrived, we had twenty-six vacancies. Officer Loyal was constantly processing new applicants, and during my two-year stint at the department, we hired thirty-six officers. When I left, there were seven vacancies. The problem was (and still is) that the department could not compete with the surrounding agencies' salaries. So we would hire them and get them trained. After two years, the outside agencies would lure them away for more money. The gap between three years on and ten years on was very large. It will continue to be a problem for the agency until the city's management decides retention is important.

At my first law enforcement agency, there was one captain (out of twelve) that was placed in charge of the agency's field training and evaluation program. I was that captain and was very proud of all that we accomplished while I was in that position. I correctly identified in advance a potential issue for the city that was about to lose a very large number of personnel to retirement. I came with a solution to the upper management, and my plan was implemented. It swelled our training ranks from three dedicated training squads to six dedicated training squads, and we kept the department adequately staffed during this time of intense hiring and training.

Chief Truth knew about the job I had done at our previous agency, and she put me over the field training for her department. One of the first things I did was request copies of training jackets (records compiled by training officers to document what training each rookie received). Lieutenant Powers had previously been the staff member in charge of the FTEP, and she brought me the requested records. After reading through several, I recognized some immediate shortcomings that would need to be addressed. One glaring example was the lack of information, and another was the poor grammar in these files. Rather than hear excuses from the lieutenant, I asked to speak to one of the training sergeants who happened to be the lieutenant's husband (Ethan Powers). Sergeant E. Powers entered my office and shrugged off any shortcomings as, "That's the way we've done it for years." I attempted to share with him the civil liability concerns associated with such poor record-keeping, but to no avail. When I asked Lieutenant Powers about her husband's responses, she told me that he was not the most articulate but his dedication to training was superior. I later shared my concerns with Chief Truth (to include the reporting of husband to wife), and she immediately had me reorganize the training program to eliminate these concerns. We were working on an electronic version of recording field training when I left the agency.

Chief Truth asked me to bring back the department's honor guard, and she gave me Sergeant Vincent Carter to lead the effort. Sergeant Carter was a former military man and was perfect for the job. His pride and esprit de corps made him the ideal candidate. Getting him to create a budget for the honor guard was a completely different story. While administrative work was not one of his strong points, we managed to get his paperwork in order and bring this unit into existence during my tenure at the agency.

Chief Truth had put me in charge of the mobile field force (MFF) and the special weapons and tactics (SWAT) team when I assumed my new position. Both of these units existed only on paper when I arrived. The SWAT team had been disbanded, and we were utilizing memorandums of agreement with surrounding agencies when we needed either service. The most we were able to accomplish during my tenure was to get budgets created for both units that were submitted to city management during budget talks, which were subsequently denied due to lack of funding.

The crime analysis unit was composed of three civilian employees whose lead analyst was Bella Lane. Mrs. Lane was very bright and full of energy, with more ideas for improving than most people had the time to hear. I made sure I listened. Unfortunately, most of them involved spending money, which I have previously explained was difficult to spare. The other two analysts (Katie Shield and Karla Camp) were equally energetic and proficient in their specialties. Mrs. Shield knew every juvenile criminal in the city, and Mrs. Camp could create just about any research document I needed (and I needed quite a few). Together they were quite a team and one of the few units that did not need dire attention.

As with many of the other positions in the department, the department armorer was a part-time position staffed by a patrol officer, Officer Harley Action. One of my mandates from the Chief of Police was to conduct a complete audit of the department's armory. According to Officer Action, this had not been done since he had been armorer and it was overdue. It was another large task that was on my growing list of assignments.

CHAPTER 3

The Tragedy

As I had previously explained, I retired from my first law enforcement agency in May, and in April of that same year, there was a tragic circumstance that occurred at the second law enforcement agency that I would work for. A young Black man, whom we will call David Samuel, was pulled over on a traffic stop by a veteran police officer, whom we will call Than Campbell. As Officer Campbell was attempting to arrest Mr. Samuel for misdemeanor marijuana, Sergeant Benjamin Brown arrived on scene and attempted to help quell the situation. The situation escalated, and ultimately, Mr. Samuel lost his life. The details of how that occurred will be covered in much greater detail later in this book, but part of the issue that made the situation tense in this city was that both of the officers were White.

When I arrived in the city in August of the same year, this case was being investigated by the local sheriff's department jointly with the local state attorney's office at the request of Chief Truth. It is typical for smaller agencies in the state of Florida to have cooperative agreements with surrounding agencies when one of their own officers is involved in a serious situation. The thought is that it helps to remove any allegations of favoritism. A grand jury was impaneled, and in the latter half of September (one month after my arrival), the grand jury returned a "no true bill" for the officers involved in the shooting. In other words, the officers were not going to be charged with a crime.

The State Attorney's Office and the Sheriff's Office held a joint news conference wherein they explained the ruling, and handed out copies of their investigation on CDs. Chief Truth had informed me shortly after my arrival that I would be in charge of the internal affairs investigation of Officer Campbell and Sergeant Brown once the criminal investigation was complete. I had to send a sergeant to the news briefing to obtain a copy of the CD, which was something I found highly unusual. I was later to learn that this was common practice against our agency, which was seen as "subordinate" to the others.

The grand jury issued a stiff rebuke of the police department. For those who are not aware, the state attorney basically authors the letter under the pen of the grand jury. In summation, the grand jury found long-term significant issues with training (or a lack thereof on the in-car camera system), found a lack of supervisory oversight, recommended reviewing the usefulness of the current camera system, suggested the adoption of body-worn cameras, and suggested the agency adopt de-escalation and scenario-based trainings.

Chief Truth held a staff meeting to get organized for what was going to happen next. She had been informed that one of the sitting city commissioners was organizing a march from the city hall down to the police station to protest the grand jury ruling. Again, I was shocked! I later learned that Commissioner Nabal Schiff was up for re-election and was a local attorney of very little prominence (in fact, I believe he has been censured at least twice by the Florida Bar Association). Commissioner Schiff proudly led the march of about twenty citizens holding signs complaining about police brutality, while the commissioner held a bullhorn, shouting, "Hands up!" and the crowd responding, "Don't shoot!" The local media drew the camera shots in tight to make it seem that the demonstration was much larger than it was, and the commissioner concluded his march by standing on a bench dedicated to a fallen officer in the police memorial garden in front of the police station. He loudly proclaimed that this injustice would not be tolerated and he would personally ensure justice was meted out.

I then watched as Commissioner Schiff ushered his crowd over to a waiting county bus to drive them all back to their cars. Taxpayer money used in the form of a bus to fund an election campaign? Would someone call the ethics commission? This was my welcome to the new department for which I had just decided to delay my retirement to try to help. Maybe I had made a mistake.

It took the sheriff's department almost a week to get me a copy of their entire investigation that was unredacted on a CD that also included the state attorney's office investigation (while they ran a joint investigation, they made their own copies of audiotapes and transcripts). Altogether, there were over forty hours of audio/video to listen to/watch, there were 4,712 pictures to review, and there were 6,589 pages to read. While tedious, my habit was to listen to an audio while following along with the accompanying manuscript. It might seem redundant to read and listen to both sets of investigations, but I noted discrepancies in doing so that led to additional, eventual questions. I had learned my lesson from my time on the commission.

The grand jury recommendations led to more work for me too. I was tasked with researching a body-worn camera system that had to be presented to city leaders, who would have to okay the cost. Then I needed to develop a policy and training for the implementation of the system. Prior to implementation, Chief Truth wanted to educate the public, so that involved multiple community meetings to answer questions after the demonstration on how they worked. Since training was in my bailiwick, I was tasked with researching and recommending training that met with the grand jury's suggestions. Once it was okayed, we then had to design and implement said approved training across the entire agency. I also had my everyday work to complete too. It was going to be a process to get it all done in a timely manner.

Chief Truth asked for my best guesstimate for how long the internal, administrative investigation would last. I told her I believed I could get all the materials provided to me reviewed by the end of the year, which would be necessary prior to starting my own interviews/investigation. I hoped that I could complete the entire thing by the spring of the following year. Chief Truth then had to explain to her bosses the process and the projected time frame. The civilians would have to be patient while the investigation progressed.

CHAPTER 4

Felicia Direct

There is a natural competition in the upper management of any police agency, and while members are attempting to do their best for the department, they sometimes selfishly protect the stars who work for them from helping the greater good if it means they will lose them to another manager. Being the only major on the senior staff and outranked by the other three senior staff members, I had to be politically astute in making personnel moves that would benefit my area and the department as a whole (at least from my perspective). As a twenty-eight-year veteran of my previous agency, and having sat at their staff table on multiple occasions, I was not intimidated by those who outranked me, and my once-retired, loose tongue seldom held when I had an opinion to share. This led to many spirited debates at the staff table, and I preferred humor (albeit sometimes sarcastic humor) as my choice of verbal weapon.

Besides my having established an excellent working relationship with Chief Truth at our previous agency, Deputy Chief Alex King, too, was a friend from our previous agency, and he was probably one of the main reasons I kept my sanity at our new agency. We tried to have lunch together at least once a week and would laugh about similar or shared experiences from our past. It was a retreat from the then-current situation we found ourselves in. We shared a mutual disbelief about how the city operated in funding (or lack thereof) their police department. For example, Chief Truth had me complete an audit of our police vehicle fleet, and I discovered that we still had a 1995 Ford Taurus in our fleet. I jokingly told the chiefs that I had discovered one way we could save money, which would be to apply for a collectible tag for that vehicle.

As the head of the Internal Affairs Bureau, I was obliged to review each complaint as it arrived. One of Chief Truth's pet peeves was wasting money, and one of the largest unpredictable items in any police department budget was fuel for the fleet (due to the ever-changing prices). Citizens who saw waste, such as a police vehicle left running and unattended, would sometimes complain about it to the department. In looking into the complaint, the guilty officer's supervisor explained that the reason the officer had left the vehicle running was that if he did not, it would need to be jump-started each time it was shut off! Such was the condition of the dilapidated police vehicle fleet that Chief Truth had inherited. How did it get this way? In preparing the budget for the department, I discovered that there was no capital budget for the police department. When I asked how we got new cars (a capital item), Chief Truth explained that she begged the city manager, Mr. Heath Claus. Mr. Claus was a very large man (and not fat) whom I learned I could trust about as far as I could pick him up and toss him.

Lunchtime discussions between Alex and me revolved around such topics to include who we could trust and whom we needed to watch out for. At one particular lunchtime discussion, Alex made the mistake of bragging about one of the detectives that worked in his district (Felicia Direct). As I explained earlier, the detectives worked in my chain of command, but there were two squads and each deputy chief had a district that had a detective squad assigned to it. This was how Deputy Chief Trust could have such influence in moving Detective Sergeant Simpson out of the detective division, because Sergeant Simpson was the detective sergeant in Trust's district. When Deputy Chief Trust brought the recommended move up at the staff table, I did not defend Sergeant Simpson based on the lack of performance I had described previously. Early on in my career, I decided I would never use whatever position I had earned for my own personal advantage (or for grudge avenging). I also decided that while

I would not personally go after somebody, I would not defend him/ her if he/she had not earned my loyalty (i.e., by failing to work as I instructed). The ironic thing about Sergeant Simpson's being moved back to patrol was that Sergeant Simpson would not speak to me thereafter even though it was his friend Deputy Chief Trust who had been responsible. Quite frankly, it was the right move for the department, and Deputy Chief Trust did what needed to be done to improve his detective squad.

Sergeant Felix Frank was in charge of one of the department's special operations plainclothes squads. They dealt with narcotics, gang violence (which was big), and prostitution. They worked closely with the detective division and patrol to help solve flare-up issues all over the city. Sergeant Frank was innovative and meticulous in solving crime. He was dedicated, and his people loved to work for him. He was a union representative and was leery of management (typical for most police agencies). I liked him immediately, and after a while, he seemed to warm up to me. He would share occasional snippets from his agency's past that helped me understand the agency culture that I was working in. Deputy Chief King was in charge of both of the special operations squads, and when Deputy Chief Truth suggested Sergeant Frank to replace Sergeant Simpson at a staff meeting, the fight was on. Deputy Chief King argued vehemently that his specialty squads needed to be staffed with the best supervisors, and Sergeant Frank was one of the best, if not the best (born out by his promotion to lieutenant just before I left the department). Ultimately, Deputy Chief King relented when Chief Truth granted him some concessions to help with the transition. It really was the best move for the department at that time.

Through my years of knowing Deputy Chief King, I had discovered that he really was an excellent judge of character and talent. I heard Alex when he told me about Detective Felicia Direct, but I needed to find out myself to be sure about the position that I needed filled. I pulled reports that the detective had authored, and I spoke to the detective's peers and supervisor without tipping my hand. I spoke to Chief Truth and to Deputy Chief Trust. Deputy Chief Trust was not really keen on Detective Direct because of some of her past history that he was aware of. I did not care about troubles in the past, because I believed that once the agency reprimanded you for whatever the perceived offense had been and you served out that punishment, the case was closed and your reputation now depended upon how you resumed your employment. From everything I had seen of Detective Direct's current work, she had left her checkered past behind her.

I would not ambush my friend, so I brought up the potential move of Detective Felicia Direct from the detective division to the open internal affairs bureau investigative slot. Of course, Deputy Chief King was initially against it, and to be fair, he had a solid argument. Deputy Chief King had come to this agency one year prior to my arrival and had been through quite a lot in that year. One of the things he had done was find the talent (Felicia Direct) and move her from patrol into the detective division, where she shone as an investigator. The old saying "If something ain't broke, why fix it?" bore consideration in this discussion. Deputy Chief King knew that this internal affairs position was *hugely* important for the department, and a solid investigator with department credibility was needed to fill the vacancy. When one considered the magnitude of the upcoming internal affairs investigation into the officer-involved shooting of Mr. David Samuel, the focus of the pick sharpened. I won my friend's support by asking him the following question: "If not Felicia Direct, then who?" At the next staff meeting, Felicia Direct became my internal affairs investigator.

Prior to getting permission to move Detective Direct (but after speaking with Alex), I asked Felicia to come speak with me. My office had a smaller office in front of it (where my secretary initially sat), and I could close the door to my office for privacy (though the walls were pretty thin). I broached the idea of moving Felicia into the internal affairs investigator's position as a possibility and inquired if she would be interested. She assured me she would, and I told her that it would have to remain quiet for now until I secured permission at staff.

After the staff meeting, where I gained permission for the move, I called Felicia into my office to give her the news. At that same staff meeting, I requested permission to move Molly Mad's work area to the detective area (which was on the opposite side of the building). This would free up that smaller office for Detective Direct and would make our confidential work more secure. Chief Truth immediately granted my request without discussion (you should have seen the look on Deputy Chief Trust's face).

Felicia knew detective work, but transitioning her into the internal affairs arena was a task that was solely mine, and it is not an easy transition for even the brightest of stars. Felicia was an eternally happy individual who felt the need to confess her past transgressions immediately to me. It sounded to me as if she had been "headhunted" by a supervisor (Sergeant Ethan Powers), and the violations she was found guilty of were purely administrative in nature. Black marks on your record can stymie promotional chances, and it appeared as though Felicia had settled in her mind that she would be a career patrol officer. Then she worked her butt off to be one of the best, which was what made her shine in Deputy Chief King's eyes. A lot of good police officers get bad raps, and the character of the individual can be seen in what they do with the end result. Do they let it create a disgruntled employee who just answers calls for service, or do they put it behind them, attacking the job they still have with enthusiasm? Felicia was the latter.

CHAPTER 5

Welcome to Internal Affairs

For the remainder of the year after I arrived, the Internal Affairs Bureau was relatively quiet, with only three formal (serious) cases arising, and two of them were the cases against the aforementioned officers involved in the shooting. There were twenty-three informal cases (minor) that required internal affairs to act as an intake and distribution center. The informal cases were investigated by the supervisor of the officer being complained upon. Once formal cases were completed, a summary with all supporting documentation was turned over to the Chief of Police for distribution to the affected deputy chief. The affected deputy chief reviewed the material and made a recommendation to the Chief of Police for the final disposition. The two deputy chiefs and the Chief were the three votes in determining an outcome, and the Chief of Police had the final say regarding discipline (at most agencies).

I discovered early on that this was not the case at the new agency I now served. There had been a complaint against Chief Truth, and there were several open cases against Officer Alea France. Certain formal cases had time limits that had to be met per Florida state statute, and I was up against the clock inheriting the cases against Officer France. Lieutenant Powers had been the investigator, and she had clearly taken a stance that Officer France should be found guilty in all three cases.

In speaking with Chief Truth, I learned that in the most serious case, it was alleged that Officer France's then live-in boyfriend was a local gang member and she had been present when he was smoking marijuana with another gang member but did nothing about it. The internal affairs investigation had supporting documentation that the responsible deputy chief concurred with, and Chief Truth recommended Officer France's termination. The employee's union did not want to fight the Chief's recommendation to terminate Officer France, and Chief Truth discussed her recommendation with Mr. Heath Claus, who agreed with the Chief's decision. Once one was terminated, the Internal Affairs Bureau had the responsibility of notifying the commission via a state-mandated form.

The one peculiar thing about how this termination was done was that since Officer France was a probationary employee at that time, she did not have the right to dispute her termination for cause. In fact, by the city's personnel manual and settled Florida law, probationary employees serve at the pleasure of the department head and can be terminated without cause anytime during the employee's probationary first year. Had I been at the city during this case, I would have pointed this out to Chief Truth, but she was without my advice or the advice of an attorney since the city would not provide her a police legal adviser (but that is a whole other chapter).

Chief Truth was being complained upon by one of the local antipolice activists (Hugh Iris) for having "falsely" reported Officer France's termination. The letter by Mr. Iris was written anonymously but was under the pen of a group that he had been known to associate with / lead (so duh). Chief Truth explained to me that Mr. Claus had changed his mind after initially agreeing with the termination of Officer France and Officer France was brought back to work at Mr. Claus's direction. Chief Truth did not remember having sent the required form to the commission, and I could not find a copy of it in the file. The internal affairs case was still open in our system, and I needed to know how to clear it.

Thoroughly confused, I contacted one of the intake managers (Frank Clean) at FDLE. It should be noted that the commission oversees the certification of a little more than eighty thousand police and corrections officers in the state of Florida. Several thousand of the required forms are submitted every year for consideration on whether additional action needs to be taken against an officer's certification. Once I had explained the situation, Mr. Clean started to say he would look into it for me, then paused, asking for the officer's name because the circumstances of the case sounded familiar. When I shared Officer France's name, Mr. Clean exclaimed, "Oh, I know that case!" Mr. Clean said that in the state of Florida, the Sheriff is the head of the organization and all his/her decisions regarding discipline are final (meaning, the power to terminate is his/hers alone). Mr. Clean said that was also the case in most police department's throughout the state with a strong mayoral executive. However, in the city I now served, the city manager has the final power and the mayor's position rotates among the city commissioners. Mr. Clean distinctly remembered Mr. Claus calling him to request that the required form that had been received by the commission regarding Officer France be rescinded. In essence, it was as if all the allegations against Officer France had been pardoned and no longer existed.

With Chief Truth's concurrence, I cleared this case as "not sustained," which means "the investigation failed to produce a preponderance of evidence to either prove or disprove the allegation." I also added a note to the file that read, "Per the city manager, Mr. Claus, this case is to be cleared with no discipline." As an interesting aside, the required form that was sent regarding Officer France was authored and signed by Lieutenant Powers. Also, the union representative of Officer France was then-officer Felicia Direct, who later told me that the union had unanimously decided not to defend Officer France once they saw the city's evidence against her. When Detective Direct came to work for me, she was no longer a union representative but still a union member. It was December of my first year at my new department, and Officer France got an early Christmas present (though I doubt she ever knew how lucky she was).

CHAPTER

The Investigation Begins

My first full year at the new job (and my calendar year there) saw a marked increase in internal affairs cases. The number of formal cases rose from eight to thirteen, the number of informal cases rose from forty-seven to fifty-six, and civil lawsuits rose from two to seven. Of course, we carried over unfinished cases from the preceding year, so our workload was tremendous for just two of us (one of whom was not yet ready to solo).

I had completed the review of the voluminous material supplied by the Sheriff's Department and the State Attorney's Office within the projected time frame and was ready to begin interviews to help answer some of my own questions generated from this review. Each agency has its own policies, procedures, rules, and regulations. To be clear, these officers had been cleared of any criminal wrongdoing, and it was not my job as an internal affairs investigator to look at any possible criminal aspects of the case. My job was to review the officers' actions regarding possible violations of agency, city, and accepted state training guidelines (the basis for officer certification).

The witness interviews began in December of my initial year, and the first witness I spoke to was Mrs. Bright Action. Normally, the order of interviews could be important during an investigation, and I decided to start with our civilian information technology manager, who had testified in the sheriff's department and state attorney's cases. Her expertise involved the department's in-car video cameras and how some of them worked one way while others worked a totally different way. The preceding investigations had required Mrs. Action to physically download Officer Than Campbell's in-car camera (something I learned was missing from the initially supplied investigative materials). My reasoning for starting with her was that I believed her to be trustworthy and I would know if rumors started before I could get further into my interviews who the possible source was. I interviewed her husband, Officer Harley Action, immediately after her interview, for obvious reasons.

The pertinent parts of Mrs. Bright Action's interview were that she had inspected Officer Campbell's in-car video after the death of Mr. Samuel and found it to be in working condition. The in-car video is triggered when an officer activates his overhead lights (position number 2, with everything on standby in position number 1) on some of the department's cars, while on others you had to advance to position number 3 (lights and siren) to get the camera to activate. Officer Campbell's in-car camera was set to go off when he placed it in position number 3. Mrs. Action also shared that Officer Campbell did not submit an IT ticket to her to have his in-car camera fixed. Officer Campbell never asked Mrs. Action to instruct him on the use of the in-car camera either.

Officer Harley Action was a veteran officer who was dependable and still energetic despite his numerous years on the job. He appeared very friendly but somewhat standoffish when dealing with me (due likely to my being new and the general distrust associated with the brass among the rank and file). Officer Action was asked to look at two pictures of long guns found in the vehicles of Sergeant Benjamin Brown and Officer Than Campbell. Officer Action identified the AR-15 as being a department-owned and department-issued long gun that was assigned to Sergeant Brown. Officer Action said the long gun in Officer Campbell's trunk was definitely not department issued and would not have been approved to be carried on duty. There was no authorization on file for Officer Campbell to carry the long rifle in his trunk on duty, which was a violation of department policy.

I had seen several local news stories on the death of David Samuel, and I started paying close attention to them when I began to suspect someone at the police department was leaking information to the press. It is a misdemeanor in the state of Florida to release any information regarding an ongoing police investigation being conducted by Internal Affairs. Too many specific, factual information was showing up on the nightly news and in newspapers, and I suspected that Officer Campbell might be attempting to try his case in the court of public opinion. The following interview with my training sergeant further strengthened my suspicion.

> ME: This interview is being conducted at the police department's Internal Affairs Bureau. I'm conducting an interview with Sergeant Ethan Quick. As a point of reference, this interview is regarding an administrative investigation ordered by the Chief of Police as a result of Officer Than Campbell and Sergeant Benjamin Brown's officer-involved shooting of a gentleman by the name of David Samuel. If you recall, the grand jury released its findings on September 20, correct?
>
> QUICK: Yes.
>
> ME: On that particular day, I have an email that was forwarded to me from the department's public information officer, Mr. Ward Innocent. Please look at the email and read it aloud for me. Jenny Graham is the first author.
>
> QUICK: Jenny Graham, "Can you answer if the department has body-worn cameras in its possession and why they're not being used? How many body-worn cameras do you have?"
>
> ME: What was the date and time of that email?

QUICK: That was September 20, at 10:31 a.m.

ME: Do you happen to remember when they released the grand jury findings?

QUICK: I think it was in the afternoon.

ME: It was. Please continue to read aloud.

QUICK: Ward says, "We don't have any body-worn cameras."

ME: At what time did he say that?

QUICK: **Uh,** 10:37 a.m.

ME: The same day?

QUICK: September 20, yes.

QUICK: Jenny Graham, "I was told you have them in storage."

ME: Again, what time?

QUICK: September 20, at 10:40 a.m.

ME: And Ward's response?

QUICK: "No, we are looking for grants to get them."

ME: What time?

QUICK: Uh, that was at 10:43.

ME: Okay, and next?

QUICK: Jenny Graham, at 10:44, "There are ten in SWAT storage." And then Ward wrote back at 11:34 a.m., "You are right. We have eight in storage but are not using them because we don't have a program in place to cover the ongoing costs."

ME: Okay, stop right there. So between 10:30 and 11:30 a.m. that same morning was when you and I were talking about these cameras.

QUICK: Yes.

ME: We had just realized that they existed. *We* being the upper staff. I have another article that was written here by Ms. Graham that's dated September 26. Can you read just the part that's in highlighting right here?

QUICK: All right. "Officers tell us that at the time David Samuel was shot and killed, in the trunk of the car of the officer that fired the fatal shot, Sergeant Benjamin Brown, was a body camera, but the cop was ordered not to use the camera."

ME: Sergeant based on this last article and this email string that I showed you and your knowledge of when the grand jury findings were released, can you give me a characterization of how you believe the media obtained this confidential information?

QUICK: Someone must have told them.

ME: Specifically, ten cameras? Okay, we discovered there were fewer. So that number was incorrect. "SWAT locker," "Locked up in Sergeant Brown's trunk," and all these are things that are...

QUICK: Someone would have to have knowledge of that.

ME: Somebody in the police department?

QUICK: That would be my inclination.

ME: Do you, Sergeant, remember making a comment to me at one point in time when we were preparing for a civilian protest march to the police station that you thought you knew who had provided information to Ms. Graham on at least one of these items?

QUICK: I was guessing that it was somebody that was involved in this situation that was upset. In this case, it would have to be someone that had knowledge of SWAT, had knowledge of what was in the lockers and had knowledge that we even had those cameras.

ME: But I'm going to remind you, Sarge, it was one particular thing you said because at that time, again, it was not in the news about the *ten* cameras. You made a phone call. You spoke to an individual, and that person said to you that same number, 10, that made you suspect that that person was the person leaking information.

QUICK: I had to call Campbell. I had to call Detective Walter O'Reilly. I even called Lieutenant Drake Smoke because Deputy Chief Trust was asking based upon a request from the Chief. They provided me different numbers. Campbell said 10, O'Reilly said 8, and I hadn't heard back from the lieutenant.

ME: Okay. Again, I have a permanent recollection of—

QUICK: Campbell told me 10.

ME: Which is when we were looking for 10 based on what Jenny Graham told us.

QUICK: You asked me to go check the SWAT locker with O'Reilly, and that was when we found 4.

ME: You guys went and pulled them out of the SWAT locker?

QUICK: Yes, and I believe there was still the one that was in the trunk of Sergeant Brown.

ME: Ah, 6 was what we ended up with. Again, we were looking for 10. And at that time, when you called Officer Campbell to find out where they might be, he was the one who told you 10.

QUICK: He told me, "You should have 10."

ME: Right.

QUICK: Yes.

ME: My recollection was, you got angry and said you thought, "Dammit, if he's the one giving this information, that would upset me."

QUICK: Yes, if he was the one, I would be very upset. Because it would jeopardize the lives of officers if that was the case.

ME: Please explain.

QUICK: Well, if somebody from our department specifically was releasing information to rile people up and to cause hysteria, that could have a direct impact or a direct threat to officers because it's creating a rough environment in the community. If the community believes there was some type of a cover-up, it could create a dangerous atmosphere for our officers on patrol or at the upcoming march.

ME: Do you know who Geoffrey P. Alpert is?

QUICK: He's the civilian-use-of-force expert that the State Attorney's Office used for the grand jury hearing.

ME: Specifically, he questions the officers, allowing Mr. Samuel to have his vehicle keep running when they decided that they were going to try to take him into custody. Do you train to take people into custody while vehicles are running and potentially in gear?

QUICK: Specifically, as a result of this, we are conducting training now to make every opportunity to have the vehicle turned off if you are going to try to make a vehicle extraction, to avoid a situation where you would have to do an extraction and then deal with the possibility of a person putting it into drive.

ME: So prior to that, the department didn't train on this topic, or you don't ever recall having any training on this topic?

QUICK: There was no specific training to turn the car off that I am aware of when doing a vehicle extraction. Would that be a good tactic? Absolutely. Was there specific training to say, "Turn the car off if you're going to do a vehicle extraction"? I don't remember any training.

ME: Would you say, then, that the reason it wasn't covered in the past was, it would seem like common sense?

QUICK: It would either be common sense or it would be that, unfortunately, people make mistakes.

ME: Entering a vehicle that's running, especially of someone that you intend to arrest, is that not dangerous as far as officer safety goes?

QUICK: That…that's a tactical mistake.

ME: From not just Officer Campbell's perspective but also from Sergeant Brown's perspective?

QUICK: It's a tactical mistake.

ME: If you're teaching this, the question becomes as well, how serious of a crime are we talking about that the person we want to arrest has committed? Based on the totality of the circumstances at that time those two officers were facing, what they knew they had, for which they testified under oath, were two misdemeanors.

QUICK: They had two arrestable misdemeanors, correct.

ME: And one of two officers possessed the driver's license of the individual.

QUICK: Correct.

ME: So if the guy drove off, they could have found him later?

QUICK: Yes, but we're playing hindsight, twenty-twenty.

ME: Hindsight is beautiful. It's one of those things that should be done after every police incident: hot-wash. It's not necessarily meant to indict what occurred as much as to talk about what training needs to occur. I'm glad to hear, as the department's training supervisor, that you're making sure officers look at all their alternatives. I certainly hope we preach heavily against reaching into a car on a misdemeanor on a known subject. Because reaching into a running car places our officers' lives in danger. Of course, we're concerned about the general public too. But specifically, our officer's actions that night of entering a running automobile to make an arrest—

QUICK: I think it was a tactical mistake.

ME: There's a term that you had used once before, and I think it's widely out there. It's called "officer created jeopardy." That is something that in law enforcement these days is preached at the executive level throughout the nation. There were times when we chased automobiles without any other thing than the failure to stop, and we've modified that behavior at most agencies. This concept is growing strength around the country, and given the current state of policing, we have to remember we need to keep up with the times as well.

QUICK: Absolutely. And we have an obligation to also arrest bad guys.

ME: Yes, but in the safest way possible. Given the set of the circumstances, and that's all we can go with, that "tactical error," as you described it, was an officer safety mistake that two senior, tenured officers should have probably known better?

QUICK: It was a mistake.

ME: The issue in this particular case is whether those two guys made a mistake.

QUICK: They made a tactical mistake.

ME: And it was simply a tactical error that unfortunately ballooned into something larger as a result of those earlier mistakes.

QUICK: Exactly. I agree with you.

The next interview needed to be conducted very gingerly. For an investigator to be interviewing a superior officer requires skill and courage. When I first met Deputy Chief Wily Trust, I could tell he was a polished member of the "brass." He had a very likable personality, but you knew you needed to be leery of giving him your complete trust, because in the world of the "brass," information is power. Power that can be used to your own detriment. As the FNG at the department, I was still learning all the relationships of the past. Chief Trust had applied for the vacant Chief of Police position and he was the odds on favorite to take the job. He had worked his way up through the ranks in this department and knew where all the skeletons were hidden, plus the locations of the closets. I am sure there was disappointment when he did not get the job, but there was also likely distrust of all the people Chief Truth was bringing in from the outside, which might have caused a little job insecurity worries for Deputy Chief Trust. His demeanor with me was that of someone who was not sure he could trust me either. The following interview with Chief Trust should be read with that background in mind:

ME: This interview is being conducted at the police department. I am the major of the

Support Services Bureau and currently the lead investigator of the Internal Affairs Bureau. In the latter capacity, I am conducting an interview with Deputy Chief Wily Trust. As a point of reference, this interview is regarding an administrative investigation ordered by the Chief of Police as a result of Officer Than Campbell and Sergeant Benjamin Brown's officer-involved shooting of a gentleman by the name of David Samuel. Chief, I want to draw your attention to your deposition that was conducted with the State Attorney's Office in preparation for the grand jury. Do you recall a specific reference to policy and procedures of our department regarding body-worn cameras?

TRUST: Yes, I do.

ME: Can you tell what was asked about the body-worn cameras and our department?

TRUST: The state attorney asked if the police department had a body-worn camera program, and I believe I explained to him that we did not have an official body-worn camera program. However, at some point in time, the police department had demoed a couple of body-worn cameras. He asked me if the police department was in the near future going to have a body-worn camera program, and I said undoubtedly that is coming at some point in time, because it is technology that is going around many communities, and our community has spoken and wants such a program, so I expect to have that program in the near future. That was what I explained to him on that day.

ME: Chief, you authored a memo to Chief Truth on September 28 regarding your further recollection after having gone back through some notes regarding the body-worn cameras that the agency had acquired. Can you please explain, again in your own words, your recollection after having authored that memo of the body-worn cameras and that discussion now?

TRUST: Certainly. I was the interim chief for eight months while the city conducted a selection process to replace our previous chief. When Chief Truth was hired, she had asked me at one point in time whether or not the department had body-worn cameras. In my recollection, at that time I said no. I said I did not recall us having purchased body-worn cameras. However, we had demoed a couple of those cameras. I think that over the next couple of months she had asked me a second or third time, because it had come up during interviews with the media. I had always explained to her that, no, we did not have any body-worn cameras, because that was the best of my recollection at the time when she asked me. It was not until we had the unfortunate incident with David Samuel that that issue came to light again, so I did a little back-checking. I went to our civilian budget manager, Edwina Rich, and pulled our previous purchase orders. I did not recall the dates when we had officially purchased body-worn cameras, but I then certainly uncovered the fact that we did purchase body-worn cameras. We purchased a total of six cameras. Initially, five for the

SWAT team. My signature is on the purchase order request. I was not the one that was making the request. I was the administrative services bureau captain in charge of the budget at that time, so my signature is on there, attesting that our purchasing procedures were done correctly. The request was through Lieutenant Drake Smoke and our former deputy chief, and I just did not recall. I processed hundreds of pieces of paper a day, thousands of purchase order requests, during those years I was in charge of the administrative services bureau, so I just did not recall. The other camera, the sixth camera, was purchased for, I believe, our invest detective for domestic violence cases, and that purchase order also had my signature on it as well. So I wrote my memo explaining to the Chief that I just did not recall when she asked me on those several occasions, and that is the gist of it.

ME: Chief, while you were interim chief, you attended a conference on body-worn cameras. Can you tell us what you learned from that?

TRUST: Yes, as the interim chief, I went to a future chiefs of police conference held by the Florida Chief of Police Association, and one of the topics of discussion during that conference was on body-worn cameras and how to implement a body-worn camera program. It is not as simple as buying a camera and developing a policy. There is a lot more that goes into it because we have criminal justice partners—i.e., the state attorney's office, the public defender's

office, the court system, and the community. Everyone needs to be informed so that
we understand what their expectations are
and they understand what our expectations
are. We need to cover all the legal pitfalls
of body cameras and public record requests,
i.e., filming children or stuff that is protected by the Florida State Public Records
Law. So we had an in-depth conversation
with that, and one of the things that the
instructor had mentioned is, if you do have
body cameras out there, if you are demoing
them, or if officers are buying them personally, and you do not have a policy, then you
need to take corrective action and either
pull them off the street until a policy and
a program are developed, because there is
some liability issues attached to having officers have that technology without such policy and program in place.

ME: So following that conference, Chief, when
you got back to the department, did you
give an instruction or issue an email to one
of your subordinates to remove cameras
from the street?

TRUST: Yes. Again, I recall that we had demoed
or the SWAT team was demoing body cameras. I met with Lieutenant Smoke, who
was in internal affairs at that time and our
acting deputy chief and our commander of
the SWAT team, and I said, "Please pull the
body-worn cameras back until we develop a
policy or program that governs body-worn
cameras."

ME: Chief, will you please look at this copy of
this memo dated January 15 and read for

the record what the lieutenant wrote in the email to Sergeant Brown?

TRUST: The email is from Lieutenant Drake Smoke. It was sent January 15 to Sergeant Benjamin Brown, copied Officer Than Campbell, with a subject of body-worn cameras, and it reads, "Sergeant Brown, please collect all issued body-worn cameras and place them into the SWAT locker. We cannot use them for training or operation purposes until we get a policy or directive. Officer Campbell, please do not use your personally owned body-worn camera for training/operational purposes until we get direction from Chief Trust referencing a policy or procedure governing the use of body-worn cameras." And it is signed "Drake Smoke."

ME: Now, to your recollection, Chief, is that basically the instruction you gave to Lieutenant Smoke?

TRUST: That is.

ME: Okay. Chief was there any leeway in there for a decision other than exactly what this has said?

TRUST: No, that was my directive to Lieutenant Smoke, to pull them all back until we developed a policy, procedure, and program for them.

ME: So there is no choice here?

TRUST: No.

ME: This is an order from you to a subordinate officer, Smoke, that is now being relayed to a subordinate of his.

TRUST: That is correct.

ME: Okay. So when you found out in September of this year, shortly after the release of the grand jury verdict, that Sergeant Brown actually had one of these cameras in his car, can you think of a reason he might have one of those in his car?

TRUST: No, it is in violation of the directive that I issued and that Lieutenant Smoke had issued.

ME: If you gave an order to remove a previously authorized camera from the street, is it considered authorized anymore, or would you say under that policy, it is no longer authorized since, as the chief of police, you had it removed from service?

TRUST: It would not be authorized.

ME: Okay. Let me ask you to look at the department policy regarding insubordination and read it aloud.

TRUST: "Insubordination. Employees will promptly obey any lawful order or direction of a supervisor. This includes any lawful order or direction relayed from the supervisor by an employee of the same or lesser rank." So I gave Lieutenant Smoke an order. He then relayed that order to Sergeant Benjamin Brown.

ME: So you were very surprised to find out one of those cameras was not in the SWAT storage but was actually in a police vehicle?

TRUST: That is correct.

Sergeant Buck Young was a law enforcement veteran with quite a bit of book learning. He had his master's degree to prove it. However, many people will tell you that there can be quite a bit of difference between book learning and street smarts (commonly referred to as common sense). Sergeant Young lacked quite a bit of common sense. In fact, at one point he was facing demotion and a friendly lieutenant "saved him" from that fate. Sergeant Young knew his time on the department going forward was likely grim, and he was actively looking for a career in law enforcement elsewhere. The problem was that his personnel jacket was littered with red flags that prevented his being hired elsewhere when the imminent background check was completed. Our interview could have been more compelling had the sergeant been more highly respected in the department. The following is the pertinent portion:

> ME: This interview is being conducted at the police department. I am conducting an interview with Sergeant Buck Young. As a point of reference, this interview is regarding an administrative investigation ordered by the Chief of Police as a result of Officer Than Campbell and Sergeant Benjamin Brown's officer-involved shooting of a gentleman by the name of David Samuel. Were you Officer Than Campbell's supervisor during the time the officer got involved in the shooting of Mr. Samuel?
>
> YOUNG: Yes, sir.
>
> ME: From January to April, is that correct?
>
> YOUNG: Yes, sir.
>
> ME: Looking at the transcript of your deposition with the sheriff's department and the state attorney and some files that were provided by them to me, one says at the top of the page, "Police Department Vehicle Inspections," and then it says, "Inspected by Sergeant Buck Young in March." On the second page it has again your name with nine officers, to include Than Campbell. March and then April with Campbell's name on it

as well. Can you take a look at those for a moment and verify their veracity? It did not say in the case file where they came from. Do you recognize those inspection reports?

YOUNG: Yes, I do.

ME: Are they yours?

YOUNG: Yes.

ME: How do you inspect an in-car camera to make sure that it is operational, as you have marked there?

YOUNG: I go in and actually have them fire up the camera, fire up their computer and listen for the audio while it is in the vehicle, and I listen to make sure the mikes are working.

ME: Okay.

YOUNG: If they do not have anything on there, if it has all been uploaded before, then I go ahead and ask them to record something while I am there.

ME: Okay, because in your prior testimony you said at one point that it was brought to your attention that Officer Campbell's vehicle camera was not working.

YOUNG: Correct.

ME: But on both of these inspection reports, you marked all of them as working.

YOUNG: Right, and I either did not correct the boxes because I copy these month to month and I make adjustments accordingly, or I marked them incorrectly.

ME: Okay, so these records, while they are yours, you are saying it is incorrect in the records that his camera was working?

YOUNG: Right.

ME: Please tell me what you told Officer Campbell regarding his camera not working.

YOUNG: The first month I asked him when he was new to the shift. I asked Than in February if his video was working. He said it was not.

ME: Okay.

YOUNG: And I said, "What is the problem?" and he said there was a problem with it interfacing with the car. He said he was not trained on the in-car camera and did not know how to use it.

ME: Okay.

YOUNG: So I said, "You need to get with IT [Bright Action], and you need to get with the trainer, Officer Jack Dens, who was on my squad, and get this taken care of." The second month was the exact same thing. I asked, "Did you get that fixed yet?" Than replied, "No." I asked, "Why not?" Than responded, "Because I didn't." I repeated, "Get with Bright, get it done." Than argued, "Well, I wasn't trained on it." I told him again, "I told you to get with Dens, get it done. You need to know how to run this. This needs to be operational in your vehicle."

ME: It is your testimony that you told Officer Campbell not once but twice, at least?

YOUNG: That is correct.

ME: To have his camera repaired if it was not functioning?

YOUNG: Correct.

ME: And to get with Jack Dens, to teach him how to use it if he did not know how?

YOUNG: That is correct.

Officer Jack Dens was a veteran patrol officer who worked as one of the department's training officers. He was also one of the traffic specialists on the department and was adept at both jobs. He was not a ball of fire, but he was not lazy either. He had something of a slow-but-steady approach to police work that would get him to the end of his career. He was suspicious of the brass and likely because he had professional reasons to be so. His attitude was something akin to that of a cynic, and he appeared to be a loaner. I suspected he was friends with Officer Campbell, as they had similar attitudes about the department and the current administration. The following is the pertinent portion of our interview:

> ME: This interview is being conducted at the police department. I am conducting an interview with Officer Jack Dens. As a point of reference, this interview is regarding an administrative investigation ordered by the Chief of Police as a result of Officer Than Campbell and Sergeant Benjamin Brown's officer-involved shooting of a gentleman by the name of David Samuel. Were you on Sergeant Young's squad earlier this year?
>
> DENS: Yes.
>
> ME: Between January and April, when the shooting occurred, you would have been on that squad at that point in time?
>
> DENS: Yes.
>
> ME: And Officer Than Campbell, it is my understanding, came to that squad sometime in January?
>
> DENS: Yes.
>
> ME: You are a field training officer for the police department, correct?
>
> DENS: Yes.
>
> ME: Part of your job as a field training officer is to make sure that probationary officers understand how to use the in-car camera system in your car, is that correct?

DENS: Yes.

ME: Okay. If somebody came from somewhere else, like, for instance, Officer Campbell, who had been on a specialized assignment for a while, who would be the likely person to teach him the in-car camera system if he did not know it? Would that be you? Or you do not know? You have never done that before?

DENS: Yeah, I have never taught anybody that had come up from a different unit.

ME: Okay.

DENS: Unless they assign him to me, that would be the only way I would do it, if he was assigned to me or if he came to me and said he did not know it.

ME: Did Officer Campbell come to you and say, "Hey, can you show me? I do not know how to use this."

DENS: Not that I recall. I know I showed him how to use the computer system.

ME: Okay.

DENS: The department's report writing system, I kind of helped him refresh that, and I helped him with paperwork here and there when he did not know.

ME: But not the in-car camera system?

DENS: Not that I recall, no.

ME: Do you ever remember your sergeant, Sergeant Young, asking you to help Campbell with the in-car camera system?

DENS: No, I do not.

ME: Or saying to you, not necessarily in front of him, "Hey, when you get a chance, will you help him with the in-car camera system?"

Dens: I do not recall.

Sergeant Tristan Ulixes was the other street crimes sergeant on the department, and he had some personal issues with his wife's failing health. It was very difficult for the sergeant, and it made me wonder if some of that homelife stress did not bleed over into the job. After a short period of getting to know Sergeant Ulixes, I nicknamed him the Angry Sergeant. The first time I said it, I was talking to Deputy Chief King and I could not think of the sergeant's name, so I said, "You know, the angry sergeant." Deputy Chief King just about busted a seam in his pants laughing over my characterization of Sergeant Ulixes, and the moniker stuck. To be sure, Sergeant Ulixes was a dedicated and passionate supervisor who would argue vehemently (and loudly) about any subject he was discussing with an opposing point of view. He was the kind of sergeant that everyone wanted to work for and no one wanted to disappoint. The following are excerpts from our interview:

> ME: This interview is being conducted at the police department with Sergeant Tristan Ulixes. As a point of reference, this interview is regarding an administrative investigation ordered by the Chief of Police as a result of Officer Than Campbell and Sergeant Benjamin Brown's officer-involved shooting of a gentleman by the name of David Samuel.
>
> ME: I would like to draw your attention to September 20, which was the date that the grand jury released its verdict. Do you recall that day?
>
> ULIXES: Yes, sir.
>
> ME: Okay. I believe you said you were at the courthouse on that day?
>
> ULIXES: Yes, sir, I was.
>
> ME: Later on that same day at the police station, you became aware of the staff looking for body-worn cameras that the media had

reported that we had in storage somewhere, correct?

ULIXES: Yes, sir.

ME: Can you please tell me about the camera that you located for me? It is my recollection that you told me that there was one in Sergeant Brown's car. Can you tell me how you knew that?

ULIXES: I was helping Sergeant Ethan Quick and Detective Walter O'Reilly check the SWAT locker for cameras. We found a couple of cameras in there and were trying to locate the rest of them. O'Reilly said that Sergeant Brown may have had one. I actually called Brown, and he told me there was one in the trunk of his car, which was parked at the station, and I went to retrieve it.

ME: When you got it out of the car, whom did you bring and give it to?

ULIXES: To you.

ME: Okay. How many of us do you think were present during that conversation?

ULIXES: There was only a handful. Both deputy chiefs, I believe, were there, the Chief, you, Sergeant Fred Skinner, Sergeant Quick, Detective O'Reilly, and myself.

ME: Can you take a look at this article, please? It is an article out of the newspaper. Please read the highlighted section.

ULIXES: It says, "Officers tell us the night David Samuel was shot and killed in the trunk of the officer who fired the fatal shot, Sergeant Benjamin Brown, had a body camera, but the cop was ordered not to use the camera."

ME: Okay, Sergeant, that article was dated the twenty-sixth of September, and only a

handful of us were aware at that time that
the camera was in the trunk of the car. Do
you have any knowledge of who might have
tipped the media off about the existence of
that camera in the trunk of the sergeant's
car?

Ulixes: No, I do not know who did that, but I
would like to know.

Lieutenant Drake Smoke was a very bright man and an obvious up-and-comer within the agency prior to Chief Truth's arrival.
He was a protégé of Deputy Chief Trust's, and he had quite a bit of
inner-agency trust among his subordinates. He had been the department's internal affairs commander prior to Lieutenant Powers. He
had also been the agency's SWAT commander prior to my arrival,
which is a position that is highly regarded among many police agencies throughout the nation. Most SWAT officers will tell you that
there is a bond among SWAT team members that is thicker than the
thin blue line that exists among police officers. Lieutenant Smoke was
the acting deputy chief, while Deputy Chief Trust was the interim
chief during the search for a police chief, and I did not doubt that he
had aspirations of filling that position permanently one day. In fact,
he frankly admitted his ambitions to me long after this investigation
was complete, but that was not a bad thing. A drive to succeed can
be very good for an up-and-coming professional. The following is an
abbreviated version of our interview:

Me: This interview is being conducted at
the police department's Internal Affairs
Bureau. I am conducting an interview
with Lieutenant Drake Smoke. As a point
of reference, this interview is regarding an
administrative investigation ordered by the
Chief of Police as a result of Officer Than
Campbell and Sergeant Benjamin Brown's
officer-involved shooting of a gentleman

by the name of David Samuel. Lieutenant, I want you to look at a copy of an email that was authored by you, and I would like you to give me the date and time that you authored that email.

SMOKE: Yes, sir. I recognize this as being an email that I authored in January while I was acting deputy chief of police during the department's search for a new chief.

ME: Whom was the email directed to?

SMOKE: To Sergeant Benjamin Brown, and it was carbon-copied to Officer Than Campbell.

ME: Please read the email aloud that you wrote.

SMOKE: Yes. The subject was body-worn cameras. The narrative states, "Sergeant Brown, please collect all issued body-worn cameras and place them into the SWAT locker. We cannot use them for training or operational purposes until we get a policy/directive. Officer Campbell, please do not use your personally owned body-worn camera for training / operational purposes until we get direction from the chief of police on a policy or procedure."

ME: Okay, do you have an independent recollection of that email?

SMOKE: I do.

ME: Okay, and the role you were in with the police department at that particular time?

SMOKE: I was the acting deputy chief at that time.

ME: Who gave you that direction to remove those body-worn cameras?

SMOKE: It was the interim chief, Wily Trust.

ME: This is a copy of Deputy Chief Trust's testimony in IAB, and his testimony is, in fact, that he had instructed you, and that is your recollection as well?

SMOKE: It is.

ME: Okay. In that email, is there fudge room for using the body-worn cameras on the side when you want to?

SMOKE: No, I do not believe so. That was not my intent.

ME: Okay...so you would say that was an order you issued to Sergeant Brown?

SMOKE: Yes.

ME: Okay. Now, I am also going to provide you a copy of the police department's policy and procedure, which was in effect at the time of the shooting. I would like you to read the highlighted portion that may be applicable.

SMOKE: Okay, it says, "Employees will promptly obey any lawful order or direction of a supervisor."

ME: That is under "Insubordination"?

SMOKE: Yes, sir.

ME: Please continue.

SMOKE: It says, "This includes any lawful order or direction relayed from a supervisor by an employee of the same or lesser rank."

ME: So, Lieutenant, would you be surprised to learn that there was, in fact, a body-worn camera, one of the ones from this directive, in the trunk of Sergeant Brown's car on the night of the shooting involving Mr. Samuel?

SMOKE: I would be, yes.

ME: Because that would be what?

SMOKE: That would be contrary to my instructions.

ME: Or—and therefore—a violation of this policy?

SMOKE: Correct.

ME: Please direct your attention to this news article written by Ms. Jenny Graham on September 26, right after the grand jury verdict was released. Specifically, please read the highlighted part.

SMOKE: Okay, it says, "Officers tell us the night David Samuel was shot and killed, in the trunk of the officer who fired the fatal shot, Sergeant Benjamin Brown, was a body camera, but the cop was ordered not to use the camera."

ME: Okay. I'm going to tell you some things that you do not know. There was in fact a camera in the sergeant's trunk that we recovered. It was actually recovered by Sergeant Ulixes the day of the grand jury presentation release, which would have been September 20. The fact that the camera was locked in a SWAT locker, was in a box in storage in that locker, was brought to our attention via email that same day by Ms. Jenny Graham at around ten o'clock in the morning, before the grand jury details were released. Do you find any of that troubling as an internal affairs investigation is going on?

SMOKE: Sure. I would wonder who or what her source was.

ME: Using an educated guess, would you think it was some general citizen out there?

SMOKE: I would say no. It would have to be information passed on from either within our agency or the sheriff's office. Was Sergeant Brown's car in their possession?

ME: No, his was in our possession. Just Officer Campbell's car was in their possession.

SMOKE: Okay. All right. If no other agency had access to the sergeant's vehicle, then it probably came from within our agency. Yeah.

ME: How many people were on SWAT at the time you asked that the cameras be collected?

SMOKE: I would say eight to ten.

ME: Eight to ten people?

SMOKE: Yeah.

ME: Do you have an independent recollection of how many cameras were actually in SWAT's possession when you ordered them not to be used?

SMOKE: Yeah. I want to say it was five, because I know we ordered them as a half-test and evaluation. The intent when we got them was to evaluate them for implementation in the agency primarily for documentation of training and operational settings, to record search warrants or critical incidents for either training purposes, to review or for critical incident debriefing.

ME: Okay. We were only able to find six total. There were four in the SWAT locker, one in the sergeant's trunk, and one in the invest detective's possession, which I believe was specifically ordered for that. I was just curious if you knew of any additional ones, because your email mentions Officer Campbell having some type of personal one?

SMOKE: Yes. So I was aware that Officer Campbell worked with the company that supplied us the cameras. Campbell told me, and I saw it, that the company either gave him or he bought one to help in his training. But I was aware that he had a personally owned one.

ME: Okay. And did you ever see any of those in use after the order that you had given?

SMOKE: No.

ME: By any of those people?

SMOKE: No.

ME: Okay. Do you have any knowledge of anybody who may have said something to the media?

SMOKE: No, and no one has told me that they have contacted the media. And no one has said that so-and-so contacted the media.

ME: You have not heard anything like that?

SMOKE: No, sir.

Detective George Williams was relatively new on the department, but he was a natural at his job. He had an affable personality and was clearly energetic in trying to do the right thing. His approach to our interview was that he was very serious and forthright. He did not try to be guarded, as some of the other people had been. His attitude appeared to be that the truth was the truth and whatever happened as a result of it would be the right thing. The following is a synopsis of our interview:

ME: This interview is being conducted at the police department's Internal Affairs Bureau. I am conducting an interview with Detective George Williams. As a point of reference, this interview is regarding an administrative investigation ordered by the Chief of Police as a result of Officer Than Campbell and Sergeant Benjamin Brown's officer-involved shooting of a gentleman by the name of David Samuel. Your interview with the state attorney's office was four days after the shooting, correct?

WILLIAMS: Yes.

ME: I have not had the opportunity to listen to the traffic stop tapes yet because I am waiting on the state attorney's office to provide me a copy, but in your interview with them, you said that you were leaving the police station on your way to another call when you heard the traffic stop by Officer Campbell go out and you said, and I quote, "Because of how the traffic stop started to evolve, I decided to hold off on the noise complaint and start heading toward the traffic stop." Please explain to me what that means.

WILLIAMS: I heard, "is he stopping," so I assumed that the traffic stop was now possibly going to turn into a foot chase or car chase or something like that.

ME: Okay.

WILLIAMS: So based on my perception, I decided to go ahead and start heading that direction. As I had worked the area of the traffic stop for some time it was not uncommon for people to tend to want to bail out of the car and run or something similar so I started heading toward Officer Campbell so that he would have enough units in the area if my suspicion was true.

ME: Okay. Obviously, that was a correct call. Further on in your interview, you said, and I quote, "So as I am approaching northbound, I can see all three vehicles." Then you said, "Campbell's vehicle was facing southbound, and I can see a vehicle directly in front of his vehicle, which would have been Mr. Samuel's vehicle."

WILLIAMS: Yes.

ME: Then you also said that you saw the sergeant's vehicle on the side of the roadway.

WILLIAMS: Yes.

ME: Which direction was the sergeant's vehicle facing?

WILLIAMS: Northbound.

ME: You are the only other eyewitness other than the two officers. You also stated, "The moment that I pulled up, and as I was getting ready to position myself to pull around to get on the back side of Officer Campbell's car." Your intention was to go past and get behind Officer Campbell's car?

WILLIAMS: Yes.

ME: What was the purpose of doing that? Have you had training in traffic stops?

WILLIAMS: Yes. I have had training in traffic stops, and that is something you just do not want to do. You do not want to put yourself in a position where now you are looking at the driver of the vehicle being stopped.

ME: With you as a secondary unit on a traffic stop, your training has told you that you should approach from behind?

WILLIAMS: If I can. Yes. Drive past it and pull up behind.

ME: You said in your interview your intention was to "approach from the passenger side because you are the cover officer."

WILLIAMS: Right.

ME: You are the officer safety guy, more or less?

WILLIAMS: Yes.

ME: Your role was backup?

WILLIAMS: Sure.

ME: He is dealing with the driver trying to get the ticket or whatever he is going to do.

Your role is to make sure he stays safe, right? That is your point of being there. Why you went. But I do not want to put those words in your mouth.

WILLIAMS: No, you are absolutely correct.

ME: That was how I learned. I was just asking, Is that your experience as well?

WILLIAMS: Yes.

ME: Okay, you said after what your intention was, "I noticed Officer Campbell standing in the middle of the road with his firearm drawn, and he proceeded to fire approximately three shots at the vehicle." Now, I am going to stop here. The words you used were "the middle of the road." I have been out there to look at it. That is a wide, wide road.

WILLIAMS: Yes.

ME: You could probably put three and half cars side by side there. So was it the middle of the road, or can you further describe?

WILLIAMS: It is going to be more approximate. This was something that rapidly happened. As I am pulling up, Mr. Samuel's vehicle began speeding past me, which I originally concluded was as a result of Mr. Samuel being pissed off because he just got a citation.

ME: Okay.

WILLIAMS: So as I am approaching, I am headed northbound, so Campbell is going to be somewhere close to the middle of the road, but possibly more to the west side of the road. Where exactly, I am not 100 percent sure, because once those shots were fired, I checked on Campbell and he told me that

Sergeant Brown was in Mr. Samuel's vehicle. At that point, I turned around and started heading toward Mr. Samuel's vehicle. So it would be more fair to say Campbell was in the middle of the southbound lane, approximately.

ME: Okay. You said, "Once Campbell's fired his last shot, as I stop, I see him begin to go down."

WILLIAMS: Yes.

ME: So he was standing the entire time he was shooting?

WILLIAMS: Yes.

ME: You distinctly recall him firing three shots?

WILLIAMS: He was standing when he took his shots.

ME: All three times?

WILLIAMS: All three times.

ME: Not maybe falling on the third time?

WILLIAMS: No.

ME: Okay. Did you ever see him on the ground before that?

WILLIAMS: No. When I pulled up, he was standing.

ME: Okay.

WILLIAMS: Once he hit the ground was when I got out of my car because I thought Officer Campbell had just gotten shot.

ME: Okay.

WILLIAMS: I was assuming he got shot or he was seriously injured of some sort, so I checked on him. It did not even dawn on me that Sergeant Brown was not there. I mean, I know I just saw his car when I pulled up, but it was something that just rapidly happened, and my initial thought was to check on Campbell. As I was checking on him, he said, "I am fine, I am fine. Brown's in that car."

ME: Okay, so you are now with the sergeant. The second shooting is over. You are trying to help him gain his composure and to help him fill in blanks. At one point, I guess you told him that Campbell had actually shot at the car, so he knew where the gunshots that he thought were coming from Mr. Samuel actually came from. You explained Brown's reaction as saying something along the lines of he was going to have to "check his sack." What did you take that to mean?

WILLIAMS: Sergeant Brown was completely unaware that Officer Campbell was the one that actually fired into the vehicle. The sergeant was upset, but it was more of a startling. His reaction was really shocked that Officer Campbell would be firing, knowing that he was in the car. That was his reaction.

As I completed what I believed would be the last of the witness interviews prior to Christmas, I believed I had the information I needed to begin interviewing the two subject officers (Sergeant Brown and Officer Campbell). As you could see from my last interview with Detective Williams, there were still some items that were missing from the original investigations by the Sheriff's Office and the State Attorney's Office that I wanted prior to speaking with either of them. I could not understand how I could have been provided an incomplete file in a case of such magnitude, but I chalked it up to the lack of respect those offices had for the police department. Detective Felicia Direct had been sent to formal classroom training for the IA detective slot, and I was anxious to get her back so that I could begin her "field" training in the actual conducting of an internal investigation. I also thought I might get her to begin to trust me and share some of the informal communication pathways that were elusive to a newcomer.

CHAPTER 7

Other Stuff Happens

Chief Truth and I talked often about the progress of cases in internal affairs, and one of her rules were that there would be no surprises for her because of my lack of keeping her updated. I knew and understood that directive based upon my experiences at my previous department. When asked if there was anything she could do to help me with my cases, I mentioned to her that while my internal affairs budget included a line item for paying a transcriptionist to type my interviews, there was not any money in the budget to cover the cost of having it done. Chief Truth asked if Detective Felicia Direct could type them, because she was concerned about having someone else seeing the interviews, but I had investigated the transcriptionist, discovering that she was held in very high regard concerning her case confidentiality. I further assured the Chief that we would have her sign a confidentiality agreement and that she had no relationship with anyone in our department. Chief Truth directed me to have the fiscal bureau manager divert some funds into my line item to pay for the transcriptionist. This took a load off my otherwise very busy schedule.

Detective Felicia Direct returned from her formal classroom training ready to tackle her new position. We had several conversations about how we would conduct her field training with me as her mentor. She was obviously eager to learn, but I could sense she was not ready to completely trust me. She would ask me questions regarding my conversations with Chief Truth about cases that were active, and I would share certain aspects of our discussions because she needed to be able to speak with Chief Truth directly herself. Felicia confided in me that Chief Truth intimidated her, and I assured her that Chief Truth would need the detective's candor when it came to internal cases. I reminded Felicia that any of our conversations needed to remain confidential, which could be challenging, given that her husband, Detective Chuck Direct, worked on the street crimes unit for the department. She assured me that would not be problematic.

One of the first formal cases of the new year involved Sergeant Ethan Powers. I worked Monday through Friday and had weekends off but was always subject to recall. Early on one Saturday morning after the first of my second year, I was awakened by a call from Chief Truth. She informed me that there was a citizen that was claiming that Sergeant Ethan Powers had broken his jaw during a traffic stop and we needed to respond to the local jail to obtain an interview. This was going to be a formal case. I contacted Felicia, and she rearranged her day without hesitation while agreeing to meet me at the police station prior to our trip out to the local jail.

The jail was run by the local sheriff's department, and Felicia was very familiar with the protocols in place for gaining an interview with an inmate. There had been some friction recently when the major of the jail declared that the police department would no longer be allowed to interview inmates without a court order, but this unnecessary impediment was worked out with the local state attorney's office. I was not even sure where the jail was located, so having Felicia there to guide me almost felt like I was the one in training. On our way to jail, I gave Felicia the details that Chief Truth had provided me. Felicia got very quiet.

After a few minutes, Felicia told me that Sergeant Ethan Powers was the individual that had come after her, which resulted in her receiving discipline in the past. Felicia said that she was working out at a gym that was outside of her zone prior to the beginning of her shift. Her habit was to shower and put on her uniform prior to reporting to work. One particular day, as she was finishing getting ready, she heard a call go out near where she was. She instinctively picked up her radio, telling the dispatcher that she would handle the call as she exited the gym. Sergeant Ethan Powers was waiting outside the gym and commented to her that she did not appear to be at the location she said she was. She told him it was one block away and proceeded to the call. To her shock and amazement, Sergeant Powers wrote her up and Captain Rod Jerk made sure the complaint resulted in formal discipline.

Felicia told me that prior to this incident, she had a circle of friends that she associated with both inside and outside her police employment, which included Sabrina Powers, Ethan Powers, Kayley Wright, and Than Campbell. I will explain a little more about Kayley Wright in a later chapter, but suffice it to say that there could be a book on just her alone. Felicia never told me why Captain Jerk disliked her, but I have seen plenty of brass headhunt those below them for some perceived wrong. However, Felicia was extremely surprised and hurt when Sergeant Powers became Captain Jerk's henchman. Needless to say, that ended the friendship that had existed prior to her discipline.

Felicia wanted me to know in advance about her past negative involvement with Sergeant Ethan Powers, and I assured her that it would have no bearing in the outcome of this investigation. I explained myself, saying that I had absolutely no regard for the sergeant in either a negative or positive light and I would be the one conducting the investigation. Her role would merely be to learn from my guidance while helping to provide any agency insight that I might not have. I was able to assuage Felicia's concern with this investigation while learning a possible tidbit concerning Felicia's feelings regarding the Samuel shooting investigation.

Upon our arrival at the jail, we were led to a room where the inmate wishing to complain would be brought. I told Felicia which documents needed to be provided to the inmate (Mr. Billy Bad) and what I expected the basic format of the interview would be. I told Felicia that I would allow her to begin the interview and I would jump in if I thought she needed help or had missed something. The following is a synopsis of our interview:

DETECTIVE DIRECT: I am Detective Direct with the police department, and with me is my major, and we represent the department's Internal Affairs Bureau. This interview is being conducted at the jail, and I am conducting this interview with Mr. Billy Bad. I have to explain to you the definition of perjury. It is making any false statements, making any contradictory statements, or providing any false reports to law enforcement in an official proceeding or after having been put under oath. Under Florida state statute, law enforcement officers and/or correctional officers have a right to bring civil suits against any person or groups or organizations for damages from making a false statement. I also have to explain to you your Miranda Rights [which she read].

BILLY BAD: I understand.

DETECTIVE DIRECT: We got the information that you may have a complaint from a third party and that you may want to talk to us regarding your arrest from that same party. It is our understanding that you were arrested three days ago. Can you tell us what happened?

BILLY BAD: Will this mess up my criminal case?

ME: Well, you do not have to make a statement. I mean, that is totally up to you. But our understanding is, through this third party, there may have been something done wrong by one of our officers.

BILLY BAD: Yeah.

ME: We are obligated to look into that. We are the part of the police department that looks into that, okay?

BILLY BAD: Okay.

ME: So that is what is called internal affairs. I do not know if you have ever heard of internal affairs.

BILLY BAD: Yeah, I have heard of internal affairs.

ME: Okay.

BILLY BAD: Lots of times.

ME: That is us.

BILLY BAD: Okay.

ME: So it is up to you. It is completely up to you if you want to tell us about what happened, if you felt there was something done wrong by the police, please help us look into that. If you do not think so, then you can say that, or if you just simply wish to not talk then, just say that.

BILLY BAD: No, there was definitely something done wrong. I have never, ever been treated like that ever in my life, ever.

ME: Okay, so tell us what happened.

BILLY BAD: Well, when the sergeant came to the window, we had stopped at the park near the bridge by the museum. We were right there by the little beach area. So that was where we pulled over at. There were a lot of people out there. So I was heading over there so I could eat my lunch. I got my lunch in the passenger seat, and I got my drinks in the console. So he came to the back of the window on the passenger side. He was by himself. He knocked on the window. He came around. He said, "Roll the window down." I rolled the window down. He said, "Let me see your license and registration." I told him my name. I gave him my birth date, my social. I gave him everything. I was complying. I told him my license was suspended. So he said, "Your license is suspended? All right, hold still." So I knew my license was suspended, and I knew what was about to happen, but my food was right there, so I was going to eat while he checked my license on the computer. He came back to the driver's side and knocked on the window. I rolled down the window, and I unlocked the door, and he said, "Get out." I asked if I could get a drink of my drink because I was about to choke on my food, because there were little bones in the fish. So the sarge said, "No, get out." I said, "All right, I'm gonna get out. I at least just need a drink, just a sip. I do not want to choke on this food." Again, he said no, and he opened the door. I was wearing my hair in a big bun that day, and he reached in, grabbing me by the hair, yanking me out the car by my hair. I said, "Dude, this is not even called for, like, I did not do anything for you to just snatch me out the car." If anything, I would have thought he would have grabbed me by my arm to pull me out, but not by my hair. After he had me out of the car, I was standing in the doorway of the car, and he said, "Put your hands behind your back. Put your hands behind your back." But the way he was holding me, I could not do it, and I was screaming, "Bro, you are going to break my arm!" He was saying, "Stop resisting, stop resisting," and I was saying, "Man, I am not resisting." So he started saying, "Stop resisting, I am going to break it, I am going to break it." Then he took me and he slammed me into the ground. Then my body was contorted into, like, four different directions. My legs this way, my torso this way, which was the reason my ribs right here hurt, and it was twisted this way. My neck was twisted this way. And then my head was, like, pulled back this way. So I was screaming, my face, my whole face, was covered in nothing but sand. He was, like, mushing my face down in the sand. So I said, "Bro, I cannot breathe, I cannot breathe, I cannot breathe!" and he was still on me. I do not know who came over there and grabbed my legs. Somebody grabbed my legs. I do not know who grabbed the legs. I am assuming it was the dude that was in red shorts. So I was telling him, "Bro, get up off me. You are hurting me. Please, get up off me! Somebody, please help me!" I got my girl on the phone, and I was screaming. After that happened, and he cuffed me, snatched me up by my arms, and threw me on the car so that I slammed my head on the car. So I was saying, "Bro, I know my… I know my rights, bro. I did not do nothing to warrant this. I am a human just like you, man." I knew it was nothing serious. I got a driving charge. It was nothing for me to fight with the officer for and catch another charge. No, I was going to be compliant because I had something that was simple. I got kids to get to. I was not trying to get messed up. I was not trying to get paralyzed. I was not trying to, like, not come home and see my kids ever again. I was not trying to do none of that there. I was trying to come home to my kids every night, so you know what I am saying? When all this was going on, he was talking to people that were videotaping. I do not know who they are, and they were videoing.

DETECTIVE DIRECT: When you mentioned *he*, whom were you referring to?

BILLY BAD: The sergeant.

DETECTIVE DIRECT: How do you know it was a sergeant?

BILLY BAD: Oh, because he had stripes.

DETECTIVE DIRECT: Okay, so one, two, three?

BILLY BAD: He had three stripes.

DETECTIVE DIRECT: Was he a White male, Black male, Hispanic male?

BILLY BAD: He looked Hispanic to me.

DETECTIVE DIRECT: Can you describe him for us?

BILLY BAD: Have you ever seen the television show *Everybody Loves Raymond*?

DETECTIVE DIRECT: Yes.

BILLY BAD: Not Raymond, but his brother. The one that talks in a lower voice.

ME: The big, tall guy?

BILLY BAD: Yeah, the big, tall slow-talking guy.

ME: Is the sergeant tall too?

BILLY BAD: He is bigger than me.

ME: How tall are you?

BILLY BAD: I am six feet. I am talking about body size.

ME: Oh, big. Is he taller than you?

BILLY BAD: I really could not tell you. If I see him, I can point him out, because me and him crossed paths before. He has always been a nasty dude.

ME: His name is on the arrest paperwork, you said?

BILLY BAD: Yeah, it's Pow or Powsi or something, something with a *P*.

ME: Now, the guy in the red shorts, was he an officer too?

BILLY BAD: No, he was just somebody from the beach.

ME: Okay. A White guy, Black guy?

BILLY BAD: Yeah, I was the only Black person there.

ME: What about the people that were filming?

BILLY BAD: They were White. That was how we got the video.

ME: I think we got that, too, did we? I have not seen it yet.

DETECTIVE DIRECT: Yes.

BILLY BAD: I have not seen it. I starred in it, but I have not seen it.

DETECTIVE DIRECT: When you say "We got the video," whom are you referring to?

BILLY BAD: As in my people, my people.

DETECTIVE DIRECT: And—

ME: Your family?

BILLY BAD: Yeah.

DETECTIVE DIRECT: Your family.

BILLY BAD: My family, because my girlfriend came to the scene.

ME: Oh, she was there?

BILLY BAD: Yeah, she came after it was over. By the time she got there, the paramedics were there. After the whole scuffle, we were walking to his car cuffed up, and he was on my right-hand side. He was, like, dragging me. He had snatched me by the hair at least two times already. He pulled me off the ground by my hair, for one. And when we were walking off, he was dragging me while walking. I did not go to booking. I went straight to the hospital. I did not come to jail until yesterday.

ME: Who took you to the hospital?

BILLY BAD: A White officer with a buzz cut. He's about five foot nine or five foot ten.

ME: So he took you to the hospital?

BILLY BAD: No. He yelled at me when he arrived and asked me what my problem was. He was very rude.

ME: How did you get to the hospital?

BILLY BAD: The final officer. The last cop car that came up. I really cannot remember what he looked like. I think he had a buzz cut. I was explaining to my girlfriend from in the back of the police car what was going on, and I was telling her no matter how many times I had ever been locked up and arrested by the nastiest officers, I had never in my life been treated like a dog before, and never had I ever felt like an animal a day in my life, until now. I was telling her that, and the officer said, "Roll the window up, roll the window up." So they rolled the window up, and then I said, "Man, listen, I got labored breathing. I cannot breathe. I need an ambulance." So they finally called the ambulance. The ambulance came over and asked if I was okay. I said, "No, man, I am not okay, man." My jaw was messed up, my ribs hurt, I needed to go to the hospital. The EMT gave me the green light to go to jail. He said, "Oh, you are good, you can go to jail. You are clear." So they took me under the bridge for a good little while while they talked and typed up their reports and stuff.

During this time, the sergeant was laughing and explaining how he beat my ass. He was bragging. So I yelled out the window, "Yeah, that is real nice. You are back there bragging about how you whooped my ass, huh? Please believe I am going to get you back. I need your name. I never, ever, ever been treated like that ever in my life. And I've been locked up a lot of times, and I have never, ever… I never hit an officer. I never resisted with violence. The only time I ever resisted arrest was when I took off running, and that was because I had some serious charges, where I was facing prison time. But I am not about to hit an officer and pick up extra time because I know it is eight years that is mandatory prison time. And I am not trying to go back to prison." So the officer that was transporting me said, "Sarge, I got to take him to the hospital because he is complaining about his ribs." The sergeant said, "Good. I hope he broke some ribs." I went from there to the hospital. They x-rayed and saw that I had a fractured jaw. They operated and fixed it, but it still hurts. That is basically it in a nutshell.

DETECTIVE DIRECT: You stated that your girlfriend showed up.

BILLY BAD: Yes.

DETECTIVE DIRECT: How did she know to show up?

BILLY BAD: Because I had called her. I was on the phone with her during the whole thing. I got audio because it was on voice mail, me screaming, the officer, it is all on voice mail.

DETECTIVE DIRECT: Okay. Can I have your girlfriend's name and contact information?

BILLY BAD: I do not know her number off the top
of my head, but my sister knows it.

DETECTIVE DIRECT: I am interested in getting
the voice mail.

ME: We need your permission, if you would give
it to us, for your medical records. We cannot get them otherwise. It is protected.

BILLY BAD: Okay.

ME: Going back to when the sergeant picked you
up off the ground. You had said at one point
that he had both of your arms back like this.

BILLY BAD: Yeah.

ME: But then you also said he grabbed you up
by your hair. So was he holding your arms
back with one hand and then using his
other hand to hold you by the hair? Or how
did that happen? Because you told us the
sergeant snatched your hair at least twice.

BILLY BAD: Yeah. All right, he snatched the hair
first when I was sitting in the car.

ME: Pulling you out of the car.

BILLY BAD: Yeah. He got the bun.

ME: And the second time?

BILLY BAD: I was on the ground. He pulled me
up by my hair and my arms. That is wrong,
for anyone to pick me up by my hair. You
do not pick a person up by their hair, and
that is when I am saying I was on the car.

ME: And all this should be on your girlfriend's
voice mail?

BILLY BAD: I think all that is on there.

For her first internal affairs interview, Detective Felicia Direct
did a pretty good job. It is hard to tell when reading something ver-

sus listening to it on tape, because voice inflections and pregnant pauses are not noticeable (among other personal attributes). One of the things that is noticeable when reading the preceding transcript of our interview is that I seemed to jump in early on in the interview. That was because Felicia gave me the "Help me, I'm lost" look, so I took over until she felt comfortable again. Once she got rolling, I only joined back in when she would look at me as if to say, "Can you think of anything else?" In witness or complainant interviews, the team tactic can work to internal affairs advantage to ensure a comprehensive interview. According to Florida state statute, unless a subject officer agrees to it, there can only be one interviewing internal affairs investigator. We spoke for quite some time on the way back to the station about how the interview went, because I like to "hot-wash" every performance (even my own). I am looking for ways to improve (yes, even after twenty-nine years on the job). We talked about what needed to be done next, and we believed we had the first formal case of the year well under way. I explained to Felicia that the last thing I had to do was brief Chief Truth on our interview. The ensuing conversation was something of a shocker.

Sergeant Ethan Powers Squared

Remembering that I had visited the jail on Saturday, the following Monday morning, I went in to see Chief Truth to start my day, as was my habit. One of the Chief's strong points was establishing strong ties within the community she served. She had done it as the major in charge of one of the districts at our old department, and she had done so here in this community. She told me that I needed to make time that morning to see a woman, Beth, who wished to remain anonymous, but Beth had information to include a videotape involving Sergeant Powers's use of force last week. Thinking that this was the video from the beach incident involving Mr. Bad, I contacted Beth and made arrangements for her to respond to my office under the guise of seeking guidance on a separate project.

Beth provided the video to me in a format I was unfamiliar with, and Felicia could not help. I had brought Felicia into the fold, explaining that Beth's identity was to remain confidential. I had a sergeant who worked for me, and he had been an internal affairs investigator under one of the previous administrations. Sergeant Reynoldo Late was extremely bright and very efficient with technology. In fact, I had chosen him to assist with the introduction of the body-worn camera system in our department, and that was just one of the multiple tasks I had assigned him. This particular morning, after swearing him to secrecy, I asked him to please help us get the video/audio file off Beth's phone and into a file on my computer where we could view it. Sergeant Late and I had only recently begun working together, but there was something about his personality and mannerisms that suggested I could trust him. Within minutes, the sergeant had the video working for us, and we were all surprised to learn that this was an entirely different case involving Sergeant Ethan Powers.

The video was taken from Mr. Jose Masters's cell phone during a traffic stop conducted by Sergeant Ethan Powers on the very same day of the traffic stop involving Mr. Billy Bad. This traffic stop occurred earlier in the day, and Lieutenant Chance Bennett had responded to the scene before Mr. Masters was physically extracted from the car. The video did not capture all that occurred at the scene, but the initial viewing brought some questions to mind that would need to be answered. I contacted Chief Truth and requested her presence in my office.

Even though I was a senior member of staff and in charge of Internal Affairs, my position could not authorize the initiation of an internal affairs complaint. Either Chief Truth or one of the deputy chiefs could instruct me to start an internal affairs complaint, especially a formal one. Of course, city hall could instruct that Internal Affairs look into a complaint, and there were certain situations where policy dictated a case be opened, i.e., officer-involved shootings, but for the most part, Chief Truth's direction was required. Chief Truth had instructed that a formal case be opened in the Billy Bad traffic stop, and now she directed that one be opened in the Jose Masters traffic stop. Given that both of these cases originated on the same day and both questioned the appropriate use of force applied to take each of the defendants into custody, Chief Truth contemplated another decision that was hers and hers alone to make. Should she allow Sergeant Powers to remain in his active-duty status or remove him to an alternative kind of duty while the internal affairs investigations were being conducted?

If there had been just one allegation, Chief Truth would have likely left Sergeant Powers in his current assignment; however, the fact that two separate allegations were being made by two unrelated complainants suggested potential liability for the department should a third occur, so Chief Truth opted to relieve the sergeant from active duty. As explained when I first arrived, that there was a shortage of manpower, taking an officer off the street (especially a senior supervisor) was not an easy decision. As a former police officer, I certainly understood the feeling of the department not having your back when you are relieved from active duty prior to the rendering of a formal decision. Chief Truth ordered Deputy Chief King to serve the "administrative duty" notice on Sergeant Powers, and though it clearly stated in it that this action was not to be viewed as punitive or indicative of a future finding, the sergeant refused to sign the order (not really necessary for it to be in effect). Sergeant Powers was put into the detective bureau on desk duty, working cold cases under Lieutenant Whit Singer. In the long run, this would prove to be an unwise choice, but we did not consider what Sergeant Powers might do in that position at that time.

Chief Truth also ordered that an investigation into Lieutenant Chance Bennett be conducted in the Masters case since the lieutenant was at the scene when the force was used. She wanted these cases resolved as quickly as possible. Felicia and I got together to plan out what needed to be done in each of them and how to divide up the work so that she could do some of it without my direct oversight (but I still needed to check it before adding it to the file). Our first task was to interview Mr. Masters to be certain what exactly his complaints were and whom he was complaining about. The following are excerpts from that interview:

> DETECTIVE DIRECT: Here is your acknowledgment of perjury, which explains that making any false statement, whether you believe it to be true or not, under oath in an official proceeding, could result in your criminal prosecution. It includes any contradictory statements or knowingly making a false information to law enforcement. Please read those and then sign them.
>
> JOSE MASTERS: Okay.

DETECTIVE DIRECT: Also, Florida state statute chapter 112 states that if someone is found to be untrue, making false statements against an officer, that officer can bring a civil suit against the person making the false complaint. If you understand that, please sign the paper.

JOSE MASTERS: Okay.

ME: Mr. Masters, as I explained to you outside, you are not required to make a statement today. It is entirely your decision, and we cannot compel a statement from you. You are here because you asked to be here, and we are not conducting a criminal investigation. Also, you are free to leave at any time, to include any time during your statement that you would like. If you want to take a break, please just tell us and we will stop until you are ready to begin again. This investigation is purely administrative. However, if something criminal arises from this interview, we will pursue it through our criminal investigative division or turn over anything you might say that implicates you in criminal activity to the State Attorney's Office. Do you understand?

JOSE MASTERS: Absolutely. I want to file a complaint against that sergeant. What he did was completely wrong.

DETECTIVE DIRECT: I am Detective Felicia Direct with the police department's Internal Affairs Bureau, conducting an interview with Mr. Jose Masters. Also present is my major of the Internal Affairs Bureau. Mr. Masters, can you please tell me why you asked to speak to us?

JOSE MASTERS: I just dropped my girl off at her work. I was heading to court. I had to be there at 9:00 a.m. So I was about twenty minutes early when I got pulled at 8:40 a.m., and the sergeant, I noticed him coming to the car looking angry. Immediately I turned to get my phone to record the encounter. He came to my window and he asked me for my license, and I looked at him and then I started recording. I asked him for his name and badge number, but he did not give that to me. He asked me again for my license. I showed that I grabbed my license on my recorder, and I handed it to him. Then he asked for my vehicle registration. So I said, "Give me a moment while I look for that." He went to his vehicle, and I guess he ran my license, and when he came back again, he appeared angrier, asking for my registration with a loud voice. The phone was still on recording. I got the recording, if you want to see it.

DETECTIVE DIRECT: Okay.

JOSE MASTERS: Long story short, more officers came. I asked for the lieutenant. Then the sergeant tried to put the tint meter in. First, he put it in my front window. It was 15 percent. Then he put it in my back window. Then he said I tried to break the tint meter, which I did not. That was what he put in the affidavit, that I tried to break the tint meter. I did not want to let the windows down, but I did. I let the front window down, I let the back window down, this back window down, so he could check the tint meter. I also had my driver window down the whole time. That was where Lieutenant Chance Bennett was standing at the whole entire time. So an officer, whose name I cannot remember, went and got the mini ax from his car, bringing it over to Sergeant Ethan Powers, and he was the one that broke my rear window. I think the same officer who gave him the ax was the one that went through the front window to yank me out of the car. There were, like, six officers that yanked me out of the car. They grabbed my neck, my shoulder, and my arm, and I was still in my seat belt. So they were just tugging me out for a good ten seconds before they finally noticed I was in my seat belt, and they said, "Could you please unlock or detach your seat belt?" So I used my left hand to detach the seat belt, and I was still in my work clothes, and then they just yanked me out of the car, dragged me through the ground, all into the dirt. People were at the gas station near the air pumps, and they were recording. So I would assume other people have that part. As they were putting me down, I was not resisting. They had both my arms, and I was trying to put them behind my back. There were about six officers, and I swear I could feel everybody's knee from my neck to my ankles, all the officers on my back putting heavy pressure. It was not like they were just keeping light pressure. They were just kneeling real hard on my back, and then the officer who had this arm—it was Officer Mike Stroller—he put my arm almost like in a chicken wing, trying to break my arm. So I said, "I am not resisting." So then I put my other arm back so they did not hurt it. The first arm was still in a chicken wing when they told me to lie over to my side. They then put a knee to my chest, and then somebody had their knee to my back while I was on my side, which did not make sense, because they were trying to help me up. That was when they lifted me up and they took me to the car. I asked Sergeant Powers, "What am I being pulled over for?" He did not give me a reason. He continued to raise his voice and tell me, "Oh, you are not obeying a law enforcement officer." I said, "You are not a peace officer, because you are not trying to give me any help, you are not telling me why you pulled me over, you are not even considering that I have to go to court in the next twenty minutes." I was recording up until they broke the window.

DETECTIVE DIRECT: What paperwork did Sergeant Powers originally ask you for?

JOSE MASTERS: Just my license, registration, and insurance card. I gave him my license, and I was scrambling through the papers in my car to find the registration. He asked about two or three times, "You got the papers yet?" I responded, "Not yet, sir, I am looking for it still." That was when Lieutenant Bennett came up to my window and I was speaking to him. He was the ultimate reason my window ended up being broken, because he said, "Oh, I'm tired, I'm tired of this." Immediately after that was said, Powers was so happy he said, "Yeah, you ready?" Then the sergeant proceeded to break my window. I did not understand why he broke the back window. They went through the front window to pull me out, not through the back window. They unlocked the front door through the open front window. One officer opened the door, reached in, turned off the key in the ignition or took the key out, because the car was off and it was in park. He took the key out, and they yanked me out from there.

Detective Direct: Okay, and how far would you say that you had the windows down?

Jose Masters: About two and a half inches. The back window was low enough so they could stick the meter in to see how dark the tint was. I am not sure if that was the reason he pulled me over. Like I said, he never told me why. The passenger window was halfway down, so the one officer could put almost his whole arm in to unlock the door. That window remained down for the better part of the whole traffic stop. My window stayed down two and a half inches the whole time the sergeant and the lieutenant were there because I did not want anybody to try to reach in and grab me for no reason if they were not going to tell me why they pulled me over. All I needed was them to tell me why he pulled me over, so I could go to court. Then I would go to work. I will deal with the ticket later, but that was it. But they took it to the extreme and officers got on my back and hurt my chest during the incident, my whole back. I went to the hospital after that, but they had me in the car for two hours before they finally took me, and I requested it because my adrenaline was running down and I could start feeling pains running through my back and my shoulder blades from that kicking, and my ankles because they yanked me. I have big feet, and I have boots, so coming through the steering wheel, my right and my left ankle got tangled up in the holes in the steering wheel and they were just yanking, yanking, yanking until they finally got me out.

DETECTIVE DIRECT: You said that Sergeant Powers said something about not obeying a peace officer? What was he telling you to do?

JOSE MASTERS: Put the window down. And I had the window down.

DETECTIVE DIRECT: Okay, and was that before, after, or while he was trying to put the tint meter on? Or how did that happen?

JOSE MASTERS: When he told me to put the window down was when he initially pulled me over, and then I put the window down. Then he was trying to put the tint meter for the other windows, but when he was saying, "Put the window down," it was, like, for my window. He even tried to unlock the door and force it down. I was saying to myself, "Brother, that is illegal. I know you're not supposed to do that as an officer because I am in this car. I am going to court and work. I am not breaking any laws. There are no drugs, no guns in this car. Why are you trying to force this window down and try to unlock the door?" I know that is some type of violation. I had the window down low enough for him to put the tint meter in and take it out, and then he could do that on the other side.

ME: You said the lieutenant said, "I'm tired of this." What do you think he was tired of?

JOSE MASTERS: When he told me to put the window down, which the window was already down, I guess it was not down low enough, I am not sure, but that was when he said he was tired of this. Then he gave the order to break the window.

ME: So you do not know what *this* is?

JOSE MASTERS: No, I do not know what he meant. Would you like to hear the recording?

ME: Okay.

(TRANSCRIBER'S NOTE: Phone call recording is playing during interview. *Phone call recording will be in italics.*)

SERGEANT: Roll the window down, sir.

JOSE MASTERS: I am going to get you my ID. I am going to court, sir.

SERGEANT: You are about ready to go to jail. Roll the window down.

DETECTIVE DIRECT: Was this the first or second time he approached you?

JOSE MASTERS: That was the first time.

SERGEANT: Sir, your license, and roll the window down.

JOSE MASTERS: I am going to give you my driving license.

SERGEANT: You are not understanding my commands.

ME: Had he already tested the window?

JOSE MASTERS: No.

SERGEANT: Roll the window down.

JOSE MASTERS: I am going to give you my—

SERGEANT: *Now, sir.*

JOSE MASTERS: *You trying to lock me up for no reason, and this is for my lawyer. This is the case. The man trying to tell me to roll the window down more than what it already is. This is legal?*

ME: Was that you talking to yourself?

JOSE MASTERS: Yeah, that was me speaking.

JOSE MASTERS: *I am staying safe. I am not going to play with these police. Right now I am looking for the registration.*

SERGEANT: *Roll your window down so I can put the tint meter on, please.*

JOSE MASTERS: *Excuse me?*

SERGEANT: *Roll your window down so the tint meter can…*

JOSE MASTERS: *Sir…*

SERGEANT: *Go on your window.*

JOSE MASTERS: *Listen, I am…*

SERGEANT: *Roll the window.*

JOSE MASTERS: *Sir, sir, sir…*

SERGEANT: *Roll your window down, sir.*

JOSE MASTERS: *Sir, there you go, that is good enough. That is legal.*

SERGEANT: *Have you found your registration?*

JOSE MASTERS: *That is legal. See, yes, I am good. I am looking for the registration as we speak.*

SERGEANT: *Roll the window down.*

JOSE MASTERS: *No, sir, no, sir. Please, two inches…*

SERGEANT: *Sir…*

JOSE MASTERS: *Is good enough. That is perfectly legal.*

SERGEANT: *Sir…*

JOSE MASTERS: *I am in my right…*

SERGEANT: *I am asking you to roll your window down.*

Jose Masters: That is perfectly legal, watch me. I am not stupid. I am not slow.

Sergeant: Are you not complying, sir?

Jose Masters: And this is...

Sergeant: Are you...

Jose Masters: Still being recorded as we speak.

Sergeant: Are you not complying, sir?

Jose Masters: No, sir, I am compliant. My name is Jose Masters. I live...

Sergeant: And I am asking you to roll your window down...

Jose Masters: [Indiscernible.]

Sergeant: For tint meter purposes.

Jose Masters: I am going to court, so you are making me late for court.

Sergeant: The window is coming out because he is not compliant.

Jose Masters: You guys bust my windows? Noncompliant? Officer, I am complying, Officer. Do not break my windows. Do not break my windows, Officer. Do not break my windows. Officer, I am being compliant. Do not break my windows. Please, do not shatter my windows! I am being compliant.

Sergeant: I am asking you to...

Jose Masters: No, this...this...

Sergeant: Roll your window down and you are not—

Jose Masters: This is...this is for...this is for recording purposes...

Sergeant: And I am going to eject you from the car.

Jose Masters: This is for recording purposes.

Sergeant: And you are going to go to jail for refusing to obey a lawful command from a peace officer.

Jose Masters: Okay.

SERGEANT: *It is pretty simple. What you need to do now is open...*

JOSE MASTERS: *When I sue the—*

SERGEANT: *The window so that I can do what I need to do.*

JOSE MASTERS: *When I sue the state, when I sue the state, you are not going to break my windows, Officer. I am perfectly safe. Yes, I am recording this, if you want to break my windows. I gave my license and registration. I am on my way to court. I got to go to work and you want to break my windows. I am suing the county. I promise you. You are going to make me late for work and court. [Pause.] Not fixin' to make me late. [Pause.] I want to talk to your lieutenant. I want to talk to your lieutenant. [Pause.] If this is a traffic violation, write my ticket and let me go about my business. If it is not a traffic violation, hey, listen, I am on my way to court. Send me your lieutenant, please. And let me talk about breaking my windows. Hey, listen, the man talking about breaking my windows. I need a lieutenant, please. A lieutenant, somebody who is in charge. You are not going to break my window. I am on my way to court. My window is 15 percent tinted, which is legal. And if it is not, just write me my ticket so I can go to court, all right? I am not fixing to play with you all. My license is good. My registration is good. I am just Black. Look at him, he is trying to break my window. Look at him. All right, if that window gets broken, I am suing the county. I am suing the city. There are no drugs, no guns in this car. If it is a traffic violation, write me my ticket, please. If it is a traffic violation, write on my ticket that there are no guns, no drugs in this car. So I am suing this county and city. No, I am suing the county and the city! [Pause.] You all not fixing to get me like no dumb—in the name of God, let these devils go! [Pause.] There it is. This is the posse. Look how deep they are, one, two, three, four, five, six. I am going to court. I am going to tell the judge I got pulled over by you wolves today. They came and tried to eat me. Look at this one leaving because he does not want to be part of this. Yeah. Officer, driving 369, you do not want to be part of this, huh? Oh, getting out of that pothole. Yeah. You all are going to be in for it. Please, in the name of Jesus, you all are going to be in for it. You all are going to be in for it. I gave them my name, my address, my date of birth. Is this the lieutenant?*

LIEUTENANT: *Do you have your documents, sir?*

JOSE MASTERS: *Excuse me?*

LIEUTENANT: *Do you have your documents?*

JOSE MASTERS: *I am still looking for it, sir.*

LIEUTENANT: *You still are?*

JOSE MASTERS: *Yeah, you have my license, which is good.*

LIEUTENANT: *Okay. Hang on.*

JOSE MASTERS: *Do not worry about it. Give me a Black officer who can relate or talk to me, or a captain. Give me somebody. [Pause.] Where the hell can it be? [Pause.] They are not fixing to get me today. Wake up on the wrong side of the bed, want a ticket out of me. That is not the captain, is it? That is just somebody else. They're having a field day today. [Pause.] I do not consent to search, none of that. [Pause.] They try and have me here forever. They are*

going to make sure I miss court so that I get a
warrant because they made me miss court. I
am not fixing to miss court. If I miss court, you
all are not fixing to take me to jail for pulling
me over. You all made me miss court.

LIEUTENANT: *Do you understand me?*

JOSE MASTERS: *Lieutenant, yes. There you go, I need*
somebody.

LIEUTENANT: *This is what I need...*

JOSE MASTERS: *I am looking...*

LIEUTENANT: *You to do.*

JOSE MASTERS: *For the registration as we speak.*

LIEUTENANT: *I need you to roll your window down*
so we can put the tint meter on there.

JOSE MASTERS: *He did. It was 15. He did.*

LIEUTENANT: *Okay. We are going to measure the tint.*

JOSE MASTERS: *He just did. That is what I am tell-*
ing you, Officer. It is recorded. So whenever we
go to court, we can review the video and you
will see where he put the thing there and he
tried to push it down with his hand.

LIEUTENANT: *And I want you to roll down your*
window.

JOSE MASTERS: *Well, listen, listen. I let him do it.*
I let him do it. It was fifteen. So there is no
reason for you to tell me you got to do it again.
I understand you are a lieutenant and you are
the person I need to talk to. The guy—

LIEUTENANT: *Okay, hold on.*

JOSE MASTERS: *Okay, okay. You see, I am not stupid.*
I am not slow. There is nothing in this car you
have to glove up. I am not... I am not... I
am not worried about it. I am supposed to be
on my way to work. This is not the reason I
pay taxes. Not for you all to surround me like
wolves.

LIEUTENANT: *Well, sir, if you will just cooperate so that we can check the tint on the other window.*

JOSE MASTERS: *On the other window? Which one?*

LIEUTENANT: *This one right here.*

JOSE MASTERS: *The back window.*

LIEUTENANT: *Yes.*

JOSE MASTERS: *So I am going to lower that just about two inches and...*

LIEUTENANT: *You can lower it.*

JOSE MASTERS: *A half.*

LIEUTENANT: *We can measure it in the back.*

JOSE MASTERS: *Listen, I am going to talk to you like no one talked to me, as civilians, okay? You have the power. I am going to give that to you over your dogs. Please. I am going to let it down about two inches so you can stick it in and then you measure it how you are supposed to. Okay? I pay taxes. Look, I am dirty. I am going to court.*

LIEUTENANT: *Roll down your window, please.*

JOSE MASTERS: *All right, thank you. I will lower the window.*

LIEUTENANT: *Sergeant Powers. [Pause.] Lower it more.*

JOSE MASTERS: *I will, I am waiting for the tint meter to come. I do not want—*

SERGEANT: *It is not low enough so that I can put the tint meter on there.*

JOSE MASTERS: *Measure it, please.*

LIEUTENANT: *Drop the window.*

JOSE MASTERS: *I mean, this is being recorded, man. This is how you want to play, okay? So be a good officer and—*

SERGEANT: *Okay, thank you. [Pause.] That is right, just crush the meter by putting up your window.*

JOSE MASTERS: *I am not going to crush it! Look. I am not going to crush it.*

SERGEANT: *Do not damage my meter.*

JOSE MASTERS: *Ah, 2 percent? It's all the same thing. Wha...2 percent? I know exactly what the window is. Turn it around so I can see you, so I can put it on the recorder when you measure it. But I do not got time for this. Put it in here, please.*

LIEUTENANT: *What is he doing?*

JOSE MASTERS: *Put it in there, please.*

LIEUTENANT: *Hey...*

JOSE MASTERS: *Sir...*

LIEUTENANT: *Roll down the window or you are going to be arrested.*

JOSE MASTERS: *For what?*

LIEUTENANT: *I am done.*

SERGEANT: *You are done? Thank you. Pop it. Pop it.*

JOSE MASTERS: *Oh my God.*

SERGEANT: *It does not matter, pop it. Either come out—hey! Either come out, sir...*

JOSE MASTERS: *Sir, I am just recording.*

SERGEANT: *Or we are going to take you out.*

JOSE MASTERS: *I am bracing for this. I am recording it. [Pause.] Oh my God, they done broke my window, man! Well—*

(TRANSCRIBER'S NOTE:
Recording is stopped.)

ME: Can Detective Direct take and download that video?

JOSE MASTERS: Sure. I also put it on the internet with no descriptions so people cannot find it. I can send you a link.

ME: I think she can download it if you consent to allowing her to do that, and we will do that real quick. Also, we will need a medical release, because you said you went to the hospital. We will need that so that we can get whatever injuries you said you received from your medical records on that date. Will you sign a medical release?

JOSE MASTERS: Yes, sir. I need to unlock the phone for the detective. There is a code, because right after the incident happened, I saw the lieutenant try to delete the recording.

(TRANSCRIBER'S NOTE:
Detective Direct leaves.)

JOSE MASTERS: Powers wrote me seven tickets. He wrote me a ticket for speeding. He wrote me a ticket for improper lane change. He wrote me two tickets for each tint, and then he wrote me one other ticket, but I am not sure what it was for. The reason I went to jail was for not obeying a police officer, and I had to bond out on that.

(TRANSCRIBER'S NOTE:
Detective Direct returns.)

ME: So while you were gone, Mr. Masters was saying he got a bunch of tickets, and one includes speeding and an improper change of lane. You said you were just going with the flow of traffic?

JOSE MASTERS: Going with the flow of traffic.

ME: Do you know how fast the traffic was going?

JOSE MASTERS: Like, fifty-five. I knew the other traffic was going a little bit fast, but he wrote me for going sixty-four.

ME: What was the speed limit there?

JOSE MASTERS: Either forty or forty-five, something like that.

ME: So you were going faster than the speed limit?

JOSE MASTERS: I know I was going fast, but just write me the ticket—that was what I was trying to tell him.

ME: When the sergeant said, "Come out of the car or we're going to pop the window," why did you not just come out of the car?

JOSE MASTERS: Because I did not do anything wrong. So if I had come out of the car, they would have arrested me and I would have missed court anyways. So what did I do wrong in the beginning? What was the criminal reason, the suspicion for me to come out the car so he could arrest me? Because that was what he was going to do anyways. I already felt that was what was going to happen.

ME: But up until that point, did you feel like you had been cooperative with him?

JOSE MASTERS: Yes, sir.

ME: You do not think you interfered with him trying to do his job at all?

JOSE MASTERS: No, sir, I do not think I did anything wrong other than record, which I know kind of got him angry, that I was recording.

ME: Okay.

JOSE MASTERS: Cops do not like being on film, because if they want to do something illegal, they are going to do it, you know, with all due respect, sir.

ME: Have you had problems with the police in the past?

JOSE MASTERS: Yes, very, oh my God. I think the same sergeant, if he used to be a supervisor back in the day, threw me on top of his hood and called me the N-word. If he was a supervisor back, like, ten years ago, then that is the same guy. But other than that, I have had numerous occasions with them.

ME: So you have been arrested before?

JOSE MASTERS: Yeah, I have been arrested before.

ME: By that sergeant, you think?

JOSE MASTERS: Not by Powers, no.

ME: Okay.

JOSE MASTERS: That was my first time encountering him. But the other guys on the scene, I have seen them multiple times when I was younger.

ME: Okay.

JOSE MASTERS: When I was younger, it was tougher out here, man. Even if you were not doing anything wrong, just for being out late, because, you know, kids like to be out late. I was a child, so I liked to be out eleven o'clock at night, ten o'clock at night, midnight. So they would just rope you up or take you to DJJ for being out too late.

ME: But as an adult, have you been arrested?

JOSE MASTERS: Yes, I have been arrested maybe three times.

ME: For?

JOSE MASTERS: First time was for possession of a firearm, which was not for me but I just so happened to be in the location. The second time was for domestic violence. The third time was for driving with a suspended license, which was what I was going to court for.

DETECTIVE DIRECT: During the incident, you said that you heard that there were about ten other officers there, ten other cars. Whom did you hear that from?

JOSE MASTERS: My cousin's baby's mother. She told me she had seen a bunch of units and it was about ten of them. Also, my little cousin rode by. If you need these people, I can have them get in touch with you.

ME: That's where she's going.

JOSE MASTERS: Okay. My little cousin told me he passed by and he had seen the same number, so that was how I knew it was about ten.

ME: Did either, any of them stop to talk to you or see what was going on?

JOSE MASTERS: No, they kept going.

DETECTIVE DIRECT: You were on your way to court for a DWLS hearing?

JOSE MASTERS: Yes. I had my license.

DETECTIVE DIRECT: When did you get that reinstated?

JOSE MASTERS: Over a month before this traffic stop.

DETECTIVE DIRECT: Okay, and the vehicle, is it registered to you?

JOSE MASTERS: It is in my girl's name. It is our car, but it is in her name.

ME: All the damages that you showed us today, those are from the incident?

JOSE MASTERS: Yes. From the police search after my arrest.

ME: I know you told me that outside. We are on the recorder now. I am making sure I get your sworn statement.

JOSE MASTERS: No problem, no problem. Yeah.

DETECTIVE DIRECT: Okay. Uh, so other than your body hurting from being pulled and tugged, were you injured in any other way?

JOSE MASTERS: After they put so much pressure on my back, I still have back pains after sitting down for long periods or standing up for a long time. When I go to work, I use a back brace. I bought a back brace. It flares up from time to time because I am an active person, and so I like to play basketball, but I cannot play like I used to. Since that incident, I do not know if it scarred me mentally or physically, but I feel the sharp pains shooting up on this left side, the right side here behind my kidney.

ME: Did the doctor tell you there was any kind of damage or injury?

JOSE MASTERS: No. I mean, I do not know, because the doctor did not really talk to me. They gave the police officer the report. They never gave me the report. When I went to jail and got out, the only thing I had was the affidavit. All I know is, the doctor tried to give me eight hundred milligrams of Motrin. I refused that because I do not usually take pills.

DETECTIVE DIRECT: You said that after they yanked you out of the car, your phone fell? Did the phone go with you to jail?

JOSE MASTERS: It went with me in my property. When I was in the back of Stroller's car, I was looking back to make sure because

I did not have it in my possession, and I saw Lieutenant Bennett trying to delete the video from my phone. This phone here. When he figured out he could not get in, he gave it to somebody. I think he gave it to Stroller, who put it in my property bag.

ME: The police took you to the hospital after that?

JOSE MASTERS: Yeah. I asked Stroller to take me. Stroller then asked Powers if it was okay to take me, and then Powers said, "I guess if he is hurt, take him."

DETECTIVE DIRECT: So the phone went with you. When did you get out?

JOSE MASTERS: The same day. I bonded out.

DETECTIVE DIRECT: Okay. So basically, you got pulled over. You were asking the officer what you got pulled for.

JOSE MASTERS: Uh-huh.

DETECTIVE DIRECT: He never told you. He asked for a driver's license, insurance, registration.

JOSE MASTERS: Uh-huh.

DETECTIVE DIRECT: You gave him your driver's license. You were looking for your insurance and registration.

JOSE MASTERS: Uh-huh.

DETECTIVE DIRECT: Then came the tint meter, which he tried to put in the windows. Then continued the bickering between you and the sergeant and you and the lieutenant about lowering down the windows.

JOSE MASTERS: I would not necessarily call it bickering.

ME: Well, how would you characterize it, then?

JOSE MASTERS: Well, I mean, I was trying to get to the bottom of the stop. So with him tell-

ing me to roll down the window, I was following orders. When I asked him...when I
asked him what I was going to jail for was
when he gave up and said, "I am done."
So—

ME: No, but I mean, you said you would not call
it bickering. What would you call it when
you both were going back and forth? And
nobody really seemed to be listening to anybody because... I am just a person who just
saw the video.

JOSE MASTERS: You are right.

ME: What would you call that? She said *bickering*. You said, "I would not call it that."

JOSE MASTERS: Yeah.

ME: What would you call that?

JOSE MASTERS: She is probably right, because
there is not a better word I can use than
bickering. I will use that word, then. I am
sorry.

As part of her training, I hot-washed the interview with Felicia
after Mr. Masters had left the building. We normally would have
conducted the interview in our office, but we decided to conduct
it in the detective division's interview room. One reason was that
the detective interview room is both audio- and video-recorded. The
other (and more important) reason was that if things got into the
criminal arena, it would be easy to turn over the investigation to the
detective division. I felt pretty good about Felicia's progress in her
training, and we made plans for the next steps in the investigation. In
the meantime, I was about to get a lesson in how small towns work.

CHAPTER 9

Welcome to Small-Town Policing

Coming from an agency of almost one thousand sworn officers for a city with a population of 350,000 people that swelled to over 1 million Monday through Friday during business hours, I found it tough to understand just how many people knew one another or were related in some way in this small town of 45,000 people. If you lived there any length of time, you developed a reputation. Everyone seemed to know everyone else, and a lot of them were either married to each other or had some type of relationship in the past. My secretary, Molly Mad, had been married to the State Attorney's son, and I hoped that Molly's prior relationship might help me get a new program (which I planned on putting Molly in charge of) instituted in this new city that would save everyone in the police department and the state attorney's office some time. I had called over to the state attorney's office, requesting a meeting with Bob Mad, but had been put off for several months. About a week after the Sergeant Powers complaints came in, I got an invitation to meet with Mr. Mad's right-hand man and heir to the SAO throne, Mr. Todd Mason.

I decided to take Sergeant Reynoldo Late with me to the meeting for a few reasons. Perhaps the primary one was that there were more than one issue we needed to discuss, and one of them was the implementation of body-worn cameras. We needed to understand the SAO's input so we could accommodate any of their concerns and create a policy in line with their expectations. Another reason I asked the sergeant along was that he was married to Mrs. Wendy Late. Mrs. Late was the misdemeanor division chief, and with her as a member of the SAO team, having her husband along might get me further with my requests. Sometimes you just cannot help but be wrong.

Mr. Todd Mason was a very bright man and would not suffer a fool. He felt very confident in his positions and obviously did not feel like he had time for the likes of me. It was obvious from the outset that he merely granted this meeting to avoid the appearance of dodging my requests. I had not gotten three words out regarding my proposal for improving the misdemeanor assaults program before he cut me off, telling me that we would not be adopting that type of program here. It was almost like, "I do not care how you big-city folks did it. We do not do that here." Having other topics to cover, I immediately relented and continued with the other topics we wanted to cover. I had learned a long time ago that the *chief* law enforcement officer in any city/county was the state attorney, and once he spoke, it was the law. Let it go.

As we were getting ready to leave the building, Reynoldo reminded me that he would like to introduce me to his wife, Wendy. As we arrived at her office, I noticed she had a young attorney in her office discussing a case. Right after Reynoldo introduced us, Wendy said, "Major, I'm glad you are here. I was just discussing a case involving Sergeant Powers with this young attorney, and it is our understanding that you have a video that might help us?" I immediately turned to look at Reynoldo, who got this shocked look on his face that resembled that of a pet dog getting caught with his master's favorite slipper in his mouth. Wendy could not miss the obviously pregnant pause in our conversation or the grief-stricken look on her husband's face because she had just allowed some pillow talk to creep into a business conversation, so she quickly attempted to cover for him by saying something to this effect: "Oh, we learned of the video from the police report." Of course, I had already read the police report, and there was no mention of it in there, but I deflected by agreeing with her that we had something that could be useful for an eventual prosecution. I told Wendy I had some legal questions I wanted answered, but if her young attorney would get with Detective Felicia Direct, then we could work out the transfer of the information.

I was walking through an uncharted minefield at this new city and finding that if I were not careful, I could end up with a knife in my back. My former chief at my first agency used to joke about wearing her trauma plate in the back when she entered the office. I was beginning to understand just how she felt. I had become friends with several attorneys through the years, and one of them was a former commission administrative specialist, Mark Gable. I would run some of my adventures by him in the evening time and seek his sage advice. On this particular issue, I sought his counsel.

As I explained to Mark, I knew I had a strict obligation to turn over any and all evidence to the state attorney's office involving criminal cases. Since both of Sergeant Powers's cases were active criminal investigations, this would include anything we derived during the course of an administrative investigation. It is for this reason that internal affairs cases are typically conducted after the completion of any criminal investigation (like in the Samuel shooting). However, life is not always so neat, and this was not the direction provided by Chief Truth in the Powers cases. I also had to walk gingerly around the previously discussed land mines and did not want to be accused of conducting a police-biased internal affairs investigation. Mark asked if Wendy Late was a reasonable person. I told him that she appeared to be but I had only met her once and knew her husband better than her. Mark suggested that I ask Wendy if she would not mind issuing me a subpoena for the Powers cases, which would take the onus off me for having released the otherwise-confidential material during an administrative investigation. Without giving her my reasoning, I told Wendy that I had an attorney friend who made the suggestion that I ask for a subpoena and asked her what she thought. She said she did not think it would be a problem and would get back to me. The following is the email she sent as her response:

> From: Wendy Late
> To: Me
> Cc: Wendy's boss
> Subject: Additional Material Request / Discovery Obligation
> Date: 2 days after our last discussion
>
> Major,
>
> I hope this correspondence finds you well. I am writing to you in reference to the case of Jose Masters. When we first met last week, I inquired of you whether your agency was in possession of a videotape made by the defendant. You confirmed that there is a video, and after consulting with attorneys, you believe it is best practice for the state attorney's office to issue a subpoena to request a copy of this video.
>
> During our last discussion, we covered the mandatory disclosure of these statements and the possible exculpatory nature, Brady material, of these statements and the need to provide them in discovery, and you stated as well that you think the state attorney's office should issue a subpoena because you are treating these materials as part of an internal affairs investigation pursuant to Florida statute 112.
>
> Florida statute § 112.533 (c) provides, "Notwithstanding other provisions of this section, the complaint and information shall be available to law enforcement agencies, correctional agencies, and state attorneys in the conduct of a lawful criminal investigation." Furthermore, regard-

less of whether your agency institutes an internal affairs investigation, it does not change the fact that these individuals provided your agency with evidence concerning a criminal case that we must disclose pursuant to our discovery obligation.

Florida Rule of Criminal Procedure 3.220 clearly defines the prosecutor's discovery obligation. I have included the three sections relevant to this discussion:

a) A list of the names and addresses of all persons known to the prosecutor to have information that may be relevant to any offense charged or any defense thereto, or to any similar fact evidence to be presented at trial under section 90.404(2), Florida Statutes. The names and addresses of persons listed shall be clearly designated in the following categories:...

b) The statement of any person whose name is furnished in compliance with the preceding subdivision. The term "statement" as used herein includes a written statement made by the person and signed or otherwise adopted or approved by the person and also includes any statement of any kind or manner made by the person and written or recorded or summarized in any writing or recording. The term "statement" is specifically intended to include all police and investigative reports of any kind prepared for or in connection with the case, but shall not include the notes from which those reports are compiled.

c) Any written or recorded statements and the substance of any oral statements made by the defendant, including a copy of any statements contained in police reports or report summaries, together with the name and address of each witness to the statements.

The obligation under Florida Rule of Criminal Procedure 3.220 is so ingrained in the law that "knowledge of law enforcement officers is imputed to the prosecutor," *Rojas v. State*, 904 So.2d 598, 600 (Fla. 5th DCA 2005); *Smith v. State*, 882 So. 2d 1050, 1053 (Fla. 4th DCA 2004); *Griffin v. State*, 598 So. 2d 254, 256 (Fla. 1st DCA 1992). To be sure, in *Smith v. State*, 882 So. 2d S1050, 1053 (Fla. 4th DCA 2004), the court clarified that "though the rule requires disclosure of persons known to the prosecutor," case law makes clear that the knowledge of law enforcement officers is imputed to the prosecutor for purposes of this rule. See *Griffin v. State*, 598 So.2d 254, 256 (Fla. 1st DCA 1992); *Hutchinson v. State*, 397 So.2d 1001 (Fla. 1st DCA 1981). Thus, we agree with the defendant that the trial court abused its discretion in finding no discovery violation based on the prosecutor's intention not to call the witness and her lack of knowledge of the witness's name. Presumably, the officer knew the name, and that was enough to trigger a full *Richardson* inquiry into the discovery violation.

In *Tarrant v. State*, 668 So. 2d 223, 225 (Fla. 4th DCA 1996), the court held thus: "As an initial matter, we reject the state's contention that there had been no discovery violation because the prosecutor had disclosed the existence of the tape to Tarrant's counsel as soon as possible after it had been found." It is well settled that the state is charged with constructive knowledge and possession of evidence withheld by state agents, including law enforcement officers. *Gorham v. State*, 597 So.2d 782 (Fla.1992); *Hasty v. State*, 599 So.2d 186 (Fla. 5th DCA 1992). The mere fact that the prosecutor had no actual knowledge of the existence of the tape does not relieve the state of its obligation to properly respond to Tarrant's discovery request.

The Florida Supreme Court summarized the state's obligations pursuant to *Brady v. Maryland* in *Way v. State*, 760 So. 2d 903, 910 (Fla. 2000). In *Brady v. Maryland*, 373 U.S. 83, 87, 83 S.Ct. 1194, 10 L.Ed.2d 215 (1963), the United States Supreme Court held that "the suppression by the prosecution of evidence favorable to an accused...violates due process where the evidence is material either to guilt or to punishment, irrespective of the good faith or bad faith of the prosecution."

The prosecutor's obligation under *Brady* extends to the disclosure of evidence that could be used for impeachment as well as exculpatory evidence. See *United States v. Bagley*, 473 U.S. 667, 676, 105 S.Ct. 3375, 87 L.Ed.2d 481 (1985). "In order to comply with *Brady*...'the individual prosecutor has a duty to learn of any favorable evidence known to the others acting on the government's behalf in [the] case, including the police.'" *Strickler v. Greene*, 527 U.S. 263, 119 S.Ct. 1936, 1948, 144 L.Ed.2d 286 (1999) (quoting *Kyles v. Whitley*, 514 U.S. 419, 437, 115 S.Ct. 1555, 131 L.Ed.2d 490 [1995]). Whether the prosecutor succeeds or fails in meeting this obligation to learn of any favorable evidence known to others acting on the state's behalf in the case, "the prosecution's responsibility for failing to disclose known, favorable evidence rising to a material level of importance is inescapable." *Kyles*, 514 US at 438, 115 S.Ct. 1555.

By definition, the above-referenced materials in the Masters case is a mandatory disclosure of the state attorney in fulfilling its discovery obligation. It remains the investigative agency's duty to present all relevant evidence to the state attorney's office for consideration. There is no need for this office to issue a subpoena for materials that we are charged with knowing and possessing and are mandated to disclose to the defense. As such, please provide the above-referenced materials, along with any other discoverable material, in the Masters case so that we can fulfill our discovery obligations. I will be out of the office next week but will be glad to discuss this with you when I return.

Thank you for your assistance in this matter.

Wendy Late
Assistant State Attorney, Supervisor
Misdemeanor and Juvenile Divisions

Obviously, Wendy did not like my request. If she had listened carefully, she would have understood that I was looking for cover and not a lesson in what I clearly knew was my obligation. When I spoke to my friend Mark later that evening, he exclaimed, "Boy, that's better than a subpoena." Sometimes you just cannot see the forest because the doggone trees get in the way. Mark was absolutely correct. All I needed to do was add the email to the file and quite clearly there would be a reason for my releasing the information prior to the completion of the case. The SAO made me do it! I sent a reply email the following day, thanking Wendy for supplying me the email and assuring her that her young attorney could have whatever he needed from our files. All he had to do was contact Detective Felicia Direct, like I had told her the very first day. Coincidentally, this was not the only IA case that had gone over to the SAO. We had several others that were getting similar attention. This was just the one involving a sergeant under multiple internal affairs investigations who was married to a lieutenant at the same department, both of whom had ties throughout the community.

10

Let the Sparring Begin

As I have said, I was used to working for a department where once the internal affairs unit notified the officer under investigation that the investigator was ready for the officer's statement, it occurred within days (if not hours). That was not how it worked at this department. Sergeant Benjamin Brown and Officer Than Campbell had been placed on administrative leave with pay by Chief Truth, which meant that both officers were to communicate daily with a designated person in Internal Affairs and be available to report for duty within one hour as directed by command staff. They were allowed to keep their equipment but not allowed to engage in any law enforcement activity or exercise any authority as a police officer during the leave. Their access to department facilities and computer databases was restricted during this time, and they were informed that none of these actions were to be considered punitive or indicative of a finding in the administrative case.

This meant that these officers had been off from work for eight months leading up to the new year. They were required to request leave if they wanted to leave their home for any destination that would prevent them from reporting to the department within one hour. That request had to be approved by the City Manager. One would think that given all these restrictions, both of them would be ready to finish up the administrative investigation. I had decided to interview Officer Than Campbell first, but to my amazement, he dodged the attempt by claiming his chosen union representative was not available during the month of January. I then contacted Sergeant Brown, who was eagerly available to come in for the mandatory review of all case materials prior to my taking his statement. The case materials were voluminous, but the sergeant went through them fairly quickly because, as I had previously explained, both the Sheriff's Office and State Attorney's Office had put their investigations out into the public after the grand jury announcement. The following is a synopsis of the sergeant's interview:

> ME: I am the major in charge of the Internal Affairs Bureau and the lead investigator for the police department's administrative review of the officer-involved shooting case involving Mr. David Samuel. Also present with me, representing the department's IAB, is Detective Felicia Direct. The interview we will be conducting is with Sergeant Benjamin Brown. And for the record, sir, you are?
>
> BACAND: Craig Bacand, Benjamin Brown's PBA attorney.
>
> ME: Can you spell the last name?
>
> BACAND: B-A-C-A-N-D.
>
> ME: Thank you, sir. Sergeant, according to the Police Officer's Bill of Rights, only one interviewer is allowed to ask questions during the interview. Do you waive this right so that Detective Direct may also ask questions?
>
> BROWN: I just want one person asking questions.
>
> ME: Okay. The complainant in this case is the Chief of Police. You are the subject officer of this investigation, and the allegations are as follows: There are no specific allegations made against you. This is an administrative review that is required by policy due to your

use of deadly force. This interview is part of an official proceeding per Florida state statute. This is an administrative investigation, not a criminal one. You have been given and have signed copies of the Officer's Bill of Rights, Garrity statement, and perjury form. Do you understand your rights?

BROWN: Yes, I do.

ME: Okay. Do you have any questions concerning these forms?

BROWN: Not with the forms, no.

ME: Okay. You have been given an opportunity to review all the evidence and interviews to date. Have you had sufficient time to review the evidence and interviews?

BROWN: Yes, I have.

ME: Please initial here, indicating that you have been afforded sufficient time to review the evidence and interviews.

BROWN: Correct. Just one question.

ME: Sure.

BROWN: I reviewed them last week and quickly with my attorney this week. Since last Wednesday, when I came to review, has anything been added to the files?

ME: No, sir. You have had the complete file.

BROWN: Great. Thank you.

ME: Okay. Please raise your right hand. Thank you. Do you swear or affirm that the statement you are about to give will be the truth, the whole truth, and nothing but the truth, so help you God?

BROWN: Yes, I do.

ME: Okay. At the end of the investigation, Mr. Bacand, I will give you an opportunity to ask any questions or clarify anything, okay?

If at any time, Sergeant, during the interview, anything that I ask confuses you or
you think you need legal advice, you may
ask me to stop and consult with Mr. Bacand.

BROWN: Okay.

ME: Okay. Mr. Bacand, this is not a hearing. This
is simply an administrative interview. So he
is not going to act as an "I object" type of
attorney during this interview, all right?
[Laughter.]

BACAND: Okay.

ME: I just wanted to clarify the ground rules in
advance. I know you are an experienced
attorney, so I do not want to seem offensive.

BACAND: That is fine.

ME: Sergeant, I would like to cover some of your
background to lay the basis of your knowledge in law enforcement. I believe I have
your complete training record, but if you
would, take a few minutes and look at this.
Is that your training record?

BROWN: It has my name on it, yes. It appears to
have my training on it with the department,
yes.

ME: So you have almost two thousand hours of
training?

BROWN: Yes.

ME: Okay, and you were the department's lead
training officer at one point in time?

BROWN: For a short period.

ME: And you were a field training officer?

BROWN: Never an FTO.

ME: Just went through the class?

BROWN: Went through the class, yes.

ME: Okay. How long were you in patrol as a
sergeant?

Brown: Four years before I was placed in the internal affairs bureau as an investigator, and then one year after coming out of IAB.

Me: Okay. Is part of your job as a sergeant the training of new officers when they come onto your squad after they have gotten through the FTO program during that first probationary year?

Brown: I oversee the officers on the shift and assist them if I see that they are lacking in certain performances.

Me: So if you see a performance deficiency, you would either correct it through training or send the officer back to training?

Brown Correct.

Me: Can you tell me what your experience has been as far as traffic stops and what you have learned through your career? What is the training you have had on how to conduct them? Please just walk me through a simple traffic stop.

Brown: As a primary officer?

Me: Yeah, sure.

Brown: You see a traffic infraction, call it out over the radio, give the dispatcher the pertinent information, the description of the vehicle, location, tag information, and then where your final stop is.

Me: Okay.

Brown: Position your vehicle behind the suspect's vehicle, slightly to the left to protect yourself from traffic in the same direction, proceed up to the driver after you get information back from the dispatcher, if it is available—sometimes it takes a little longer to get information back from the dispatcher, the system may be down—approach the vehicle...depending on the terrain and environment, it could be the driver's side, it could be the passenger side. If for some reason you feel that it is not safe to approach the vehicle, you could always call the person back to your location, where you are parked. Once you do that, introduce yourself, inform the person why they are being stopped, gather the information needed for the traffic stop—i.e., driver's license, insurance, registration—and then proceed with making sure the driver's license is valid, issue a citation if need be, or warning, verbal warning, written warning, and finish it up.

ME: Okay, Sarge, if you are a backup on the traffic stop, what is your typical approach when you do that?

BROWN: Typically, the secondary officer approaching can park behind the lead officer stopping the vehicle. However, there are other ways to stop if you are not pulling up behind the vehicle. For instance, like what I did on the side of the road. Could be there are other traffic, other cop cars there. One way in the academy they teach you is to pull up behind the first vehicle. However, you learn over time and through experience there are different approaches to different traffic stops, domestics, other aspects of the job that they do not teach you in the academy.

ME: Let us go to the traffic stop that night. On that particular night, you parked, basically beside the two vehicles. Right? Campbell and Samuel were parked facing southbound, and you parked across the street, basically parallel with them, correct?

BROWN: No. I was parked across the street, on the east side of the street. The back of the bumper of my patrol car was in the center of, roughly in the center of, where Officer Campbell's vehicle was, so I was still well behind the suspect vehicle and halfway behind Officer Campbell's vehicle.

ME: Okay. Officer Campbell testified in his deposition with the sheriff's department and state attorney's office that when he first saw Mr. Samuel's car—and I know you…you testified that you did not realize that there was anything wrong with the stop—that Mr. Samuel did not stop right away, and so when Mr. Samuel ultimately did stop after making a funky movement with the car, Campbell said as a result he felt like the guy was getting ready to bail. As a result of that suspicion, when Samuel stopped, Campbell stopped less than a foot off the bumper of Mr. Samuel's car. In fact, Campbell said he was so close you, Sarge, had to walk around the back of your car to get to the passenger side of Samuel's car. Now, in your deposition testimony, not once, but twice, you said you walked between the two cars. You said there was ten to twenty feet between them. Obviously, we have a different sort of recollection there. Is it possible that he was that close and you are wrong or you are certain he was ten to twenty feet off that car?

BROWN: It could be possible that I was incorrect on the distance, but my deposition was taken three days after the shooting and I was still a little upset about what had happened. That was my perception of what happened at that time, but after seeing the pictures from this investigation you're conducting of where my vehicle was compared to where I may have initially thought it was, I definitely would say that I went around the back of the vehicle, after reviewing the evidence that you showed me.

ME: Now, this drawing is not to scale at all. It was just to try to get in my head what was going on.

BROWN: I am referring to the pictures that the sheriff's office took. They showed my vehicle and Officer Campbell's vehicle side by side. So at that time, I thought that maybe I had passed in between Campbell's car and Samuel's car, which would not have been a good idea. After looking at the pictures in reference to where my vehicle actually was, then I feel very comfortable that I went around the rear of Campbell's vehicle and approached Samuel's passenger side, instead of going in between. Especially if Officer Campbell said he was a foot off Samuel's car, then no, there definitely would not be a chance that I walked between them.

ME: Which leads to my next question, Sergeant, because I know. I was a field training officer, I went through the academy and learned traffic stops, and I have taught them throughout my career as well, and there is an area of danger that we try to keep the officers out of and we preach to them, and that is between the two cars, right?

BROWN: Right.

ME: Because you know that at any given time, that driver could throw that car in reverse and we would have a squashed cop, so...

BROWN: Right.

ME: That was a question I had, but you answered it just then. So you went around to the passenger side of Mr. Samuel's car?

BROWN: Yes.

ME: And you had heard Officer Campbell say that Mr. Samuel needed to come out of the car, roughly at that point?

BROWN: He was saying multiple times, "I smell marijuana, I see marijuana, you need to step out of the car," at least two times, and maybe three or four times by the time it took me to get from my car to the passenger side of Mr. Samuel's car. And that was all I heard. There was no arguing between Campbell and the driver...it just seemed, like, "Okay, I smell it, I see it, come on, step out of the car."

ME: So why did you open the passenger door and put your head in Mr. Samuel's car?

BROWN: Because it was close to midnight, it was dark out, the windows were tinted, and I could not see inside the car. After I heard Officer Campbell asking the guy to step out and there was no response and Mr. Samuel was not getting out, my first concern was to peek inside and take a quick look and try to get the driver to comply. I found that it has helped me many times, where I have been able to communicate with the driver. Sometimes an officer comes out and is maybe a little abrupt or the driver might not appreciate the way the officer is talking to him. I try to come in with an approach of "Hey." I try to be Mr. Friendly, try to introduce myself to the driver, and I also try to get them to comply with the officer without any further force.

ME: But a quick peek turned into a conversation?

BROWN: Quick peek and an introduction of myself and that he needed to step out of the car. It was not a conversation.

ME: Okay. Where did you learn to open a door and put yourself into a position of danger?

BROWN: Well, I did not feel it was a position of danger at that time.

ME: Okay. A running automobile, with a guy arguing with your officer?

BROWN: He was not. I did not hear him arguing. Like I said, I did not hear him say anything. I heard Officer Campbell tell him to step out of the vehicle. I never heard Mr. Samuel arguing, yelling, or anything like that toward Officer Campbell.

ME: Okay. But as a sergeant in charge of a squad, if you saw one of your officers go inside a running automobile, would you not correct that action?

BROWN: Well, I did not go inside. I opened the door to look inside and talk to the driver.

ME: It is an inherently dangerous move, would you not agree, Sarge?

BROWN: There are a lot of inherently dangerous moves that we do throughout the day. That is part of the job. We try to minimize it the best we can, but my main concerns were the dark-tinted windows, nighttime, I cannot see. I was not going to try and say, "Hey, Officer Campbell, can you tell this guy to roll down his window, open the door?" and get his attention away from the driver while I was trying to do a quick peek inside.

ME: Would that not have been safer?

BROWN: Why would you say that? I do not want to take his attention off the driver. He starts looking at me, we start having a conversation over the roof of the car, and the guy goes down and grabs a gun. Campbell was communicating with the driver. If the window was down, they were not tinted, no problem. I had no ability to see inside. I opened the door. It was unlocked. I opened it up. I took a peek inside.

ME: We can all agree that twenty-twenty is perfect hindsight, right?

BROWN: Yes.

ME: Given the experience of this lesson, would you suggest in the future that people take a quick peek inside a running automobile?

BROWN: Well, now that we are discussing possibly having training with asking people to shut off their vehicles, yeah, I might. If I had the opportunity to do so and felt that it would work, it is possible I could have done that. But if this guy is not coming out, not, you know, following commands, am I going to? I guess I could try. But I did not have the opportunity to ask the driver to shut off the car.

ME: In a recent interview with Detective George Williams involving this case, I asked him about pulling up behind the car and why he did not stop beside the car. His response to my inquiry of whether not stopping beside the car was training or experience was, "No, it seems more like common sense."

BROWN: If I remember correctly, I think you asked him if it was more common sense.

ME: No, I can tell you exactly what he said. This page here. The bottom is where he says *common sense*.

BACAND: May I take a brief moment with him?

ME: Sure.

BACAND: Outside?

(Brown and Bacand leave the room. The audio remains on. Inaudible whispering.)

ME: So again, Sergeant, I do not think I have to tell you every night that you need to put bullets in your gun prior to reporting to work. I am not certain that the police department has to tell you in every policy that they write that it is dangerous to put yourself or any part of your body inside a running automobile. That is my point with Detective Williams's statement about common sense.

BROWN: Right.

ME: He said, "I would not pull up beside a traffic stop, because it is dangerous." It would be common sense to pull behind it. The state of Florida trains officers, both as primary and secondary, to pull behind. You ever heard of that wall of light?

BROWN: Yes.

ME: The night helps protect officers? That is the whole officer safety concept here. I am asking you, in hindsight, now that you have seen what happens when we put ourselves inside moving cars, would you not agree that that is an inherently dangerous thing to do?

BROWN: Well, I am not going to say that it is
dangerous. Like I told you, our job is dangerous. I have to look out for myself, to find
out what the best safety for me is. Tinted
windows, open up the door, look inside,
park on the side...parking on the side of
the street, to me? I could have passed him
and turned around, done a three-point turn
in that residential area, lost track of Officer
Campbell while he was on the side of the car.
To me, it is faster to pull up, and Detective
Williams was saying, "Yes, I would not pull
up next to a vehicle so we are door-to-door.
I agree with that. I did not do that. So I
agree with Detective Williams that I am
not going to pull right next to, side by side,
where I can turn and look at the driver of
the vehicle being stopped, because it is a
dangerous situation. Officer Campbell was
slightly behind the driver's window, where
you are supposed to be positioned. I was far-
ther down the road. I had Officer Campbell
between the driver and me. I pulled off on
the side. I felt comfortable doing it. If I were
coming the other direction, southbound, I
would have pulled up right behind the suspect vehicle and Officer Campbell's vehicle. However, I was traveling northbound,
three-point turn, losing sight of Officer
Campbell, backing into something. I have
already been written up once or twice for
getting into some fender benders. I felt safe
doing it. Now there is a way that...one way
that the department or the academy says
you are going to do a traffic stop this way.
There are a hundred other ways to do traffic

stops. I try to conduct them to the best of my ability, which I feel is the safest for me and the other officer.

ME: Okay, let us move forward from that point.

BROWN: Sure.

ME: I still did not get an answer on sticking your head inside a running car. I asked, with hindsight being twenty-twenty, Would you not agree that it is a dangerous thing to do?

BROWN: I did not stick my head... I looked in the car from in between the door and the threshold.

ME: Okay. So you do not want to admit that that is a dangerous thing to do. That is fine. We will move forward. You initially stated that the reason you jumped into that now-moving car was that you did not know if it was going backward or forward.

BROWN: Correct.

ME: Yet in Officer Campbell's statement, and now your corrected recollection, that car was too close to have done much backward moving at all. So why did you jump in the car?

BROWN: Well, like I said in my original testimony, like you told me, I thought the car was ten to twenty feet away. That is plenty of distance to back up and injure someone. A foot or two is enough damage to get caught up underneath a door that is open. So whether it is one or two feet or ten, twenty feet, I still felt there was a possibility of serious bodily harm or death just from that little bit of space.

ME: Especially in the position that you put yourself into?

BROWN: Doing my job, trying to get the vehicle…

ME: Your job is to safely, you said, as safely as possible…

BROWN: Uh-hmm, uh-hmm [in the affirmative].

ME: But that was not the safe move, moving into that danger zone. Which you just created. Which you just told me about.

BROWN: At that moment, I could not…when I saw his hand going to the shifter, I did not feel I could have adequate time to get out of the way. So if you are saying that it was dangerous and that it was not policy or proper training…would I do it again? I do not think so. I mean, there are a lot of things I might not do again. We learn as we go on. We learn from experience. We learn with our mistakes and training.

ME: That is a good answer. You made a mistake that night by putting yourself in danger, unnecessarily. Now, what you did not know, and that I had the advantage of seeing in my review, was that Campbell had possession of the gentleman's driver's license, is that true?

BROWN: I did not know it at that time.

ME: Okay. Let us fast-forward to when you were in the car and you heard shots. Are you certain you were not above the car, still hanging on? I read your statement, and you said you jumped aboard and then thought, "Oh crap, I am going to get hit," and slid into the seat immediately. Was it instantaneous that you went into that seat?

BROWN: I do not know how long it actually was. It felt awfully quick. I did not want to stand on the side of the car for forever, so…the whole incident took twenty-five seconds…

ME: That is from stop to stop. I know we are talking split seconds here, but how long would you say your head was above, hanging on, when you first planted your feet inside?

BROWN: Very short period. I could not tell you how long.

ME: A second?

BROWN: It was within seconds.

ME: Okay. Two seconds, at max?

BROWN: One, two, three seconds. As soon as I realized that we were going and I was on the outside.

ME: After you were in the car, how long after that before you heard the gunshots?

BROWN: I would say a few seconds.

ME: Okay, so maybe three to five seconds total time?

BROWN: I would say that would be accurate.

ME: But you are definitely positive you were in the car when the shots were fired.

BROWN: I was in the car, yes. No doubt about it. I was inside the car when the shots were being fired.

ME: Okay, there is no possibility your head was still out?

BROWN: No.

ME: Okay. Do you remember making a comment to Detective Williams when he was trying to help you put this whole picture together after the second shooting, in the backyard, and he told you that Campbell was the one doing the shooting? I believe that your comments were that you did not know that at that time.

BROWN: Correct.

ME: So do you remember making a comment about checking a sack or hitting Campbell in the nuts or...?

BROWN: I do not remember any of that.

ME: According to Detective Williams, you did not know who was shooting at you. Initially, you thought it was Mr. Samuel. When you found out it was Officer Campbell shooting at the car, you said, "Are you kidding me?" basically, and then something like, "I am gonna have to check his sack." And then you said, "Oh, wow. I trust his shooting, but I trust his shooting." Something like that?

BROWN: I do not remember that.

ME: Okay. Were you surprised to learn that Officer Campbell was the one shooting at the car?

BROWN: I was.

ME: Why?

BROWN: Because I was inside of it.

ME: And again, an inherently dangerous thing to do?

BROWN: Yes.

ME: Does this help support that conclusion? This is a picture of the back of the car with the rods entered to show you where the bullets entered. Where were you?

BROWN: I was in the front passenger seat.

ME: Where were those rods?

BROWN: In the back of the trunk, on the passenger side of the vehicle.

ME: Two of them on your side of the car, right?

BROWN: Yes.

ME: You are a lucky man, yes?

BROWN: Very lucky.

ME: He was firing. Three shots. Two at you. One at Mr. Samuel. Were you happy when you found out about it, or were you displeased when you found out?

BROWN: I was displeased.

ME: As a supervisor—again, you are a supervisor—you are expected to correct officer safety issues when you see them. Had you seen somebody do that, you would have corrected that immediately, would you not?

BROWN: After I found out the circumstances of what took place, I am not just going to automatically jump to conclusions. I do not know if Campbell saw me there, thought I was outside the vehicle, inside the vehicle... I do not know.

ME: His testimony was, your head was above the top portion of the car. He said that he stopped shooting as soon as he saw your head disappear and heard the door close.

BROWN: Okay.

ME: Your testimony is that you were inside the car when you heard the shots fired.

BROWN: Yes.

ME: Are you familiar with an email sent to you by Lieutenant Smoke regarding body-worn cameras?

BROWN: Yes.

ME: Okay, and what does it tell you to do with the body-worn cameras that the SWAT team had?

BROWN: Collect the body cameras and place them in the SWAT locker.

ME: There was a body-worn camera in your car. What was it doing there?

BROWN: After receiving the email, I collected all the body-worn cameras and placed them in the SWAT locker, as indicated by

Lieutenant Smoke. I am one of the SWAT members that like to participate in a lot of these community events with SWAT displays, SWAT demonstrations, so we would go out and bring a lot of the equipment and tools that we have to show the public. I had participated in several recently before this incident, so I had taken it out to use as demos when I went to these events.

ME: Whose permission did you seek to take those cameras out of the locker for that purpose?

BROWN: I was a SWAT team leader, and having access to the locker…and as the email indicated that it was not to be used for training or operational purposes—and they were neither for training for the SWAT team or any type of operations—I believed that it was okay. Operating in the capacity where I was interacting with the public, we bought them and I would like to show them off to the public. So I made a decision that, since we were not using them for training or ops, it would be okay if I took them out and used them and brought them back. However, I had it in my trunk. For whatever reason, I forgot to take it from my trunk and put it back in the SWAT locker after the last demo we had. If I felt that it was going to be an issue and that it was strictly "Put it in a locker and you can never take it out again," then I would have asked Lieutenant Smoke if it was okay if I used it for a SWAT demo, which, there is no doubt in my mind, he or Deputy Chief Trust would have allowed.

ME: You did not seek either of those person's permission, and both have testified that they told you to lock those up. And yet it was still—

BROWN: That we were not allowed to use them for training or operational purposes. This was not, so I did not feel it would be inappropriate for me to take them out of the locker and use them and then bring them back and lock them up.

ME: Okay, Sarge, the lieutenant and the deputy chief have both testified under oath that they did not give permission to have the camera out of the SWAT locker, and if it was in your possession for any reason, it would be insubordination. You do not believe that was insubordination after your superiors told you to do something and you did something contrary?

BROWN: I do not believe that was insubordination, because there was no intent for me to directly defy their orders. I was using the body-worn cameras in an official capacity as a police officer on a SWAT demonstration that I had done plenty of times before.

ME: So you were SWAT leader?

BROWN: I was one of the SWAT team leaders, yes.

ME: Mr. Bacand, do you have any questions? Or any points of clarification you would like to make?

BACAND: Sure. Sergeant Brown, when you said you used the body-worn cameras for a demo, did you ever actually turn them on and videotape anything?

BROWN: No, they were never turned on. I just had one there.

BACAND: Just to show the equipment?

BROWN: Yeah. If people had questions, like what they were used for, I could explain to them what it was, why we had it, and that we were not using it as of right now because we had to get a policy together. I just had one for show-and-tell with the community, because that was something they wanted the police department to have. We have some, and I thought it was a good community-relationship type of item to discuss.

BACAND: Was it your understanding of the order to take them and lock them in the locker that the order was to make sure that they were not to be used? To be turned on and used to videotape stuff?

BROWN: For training and operational purposes, as indicated in the email, yes.

BACAND: Okay, so do you believe, as you sit here today, that what you did follows the intent of the order?

BROWN: Yes.

BACAND: Okay, going back to traffic stops, would you agree that it is a good idea to routinely have people stop and turn off their vehicles when you make a traffic stop on them?

BROWN: Yes.

BACAND: Are there times when you would not have people turn off their vehicle during traffic stops? For example, if it was ninety-eight degrees and you had a woman with three small infants in the car and it was a hot, sunny day, 90 percent humidity, would you ask them to turn off the vehicle?

BROWN: No.

BACAND: Why not?

BROWN: Because it is hot, and there are kids in the car. Especially in Florida, you have a matter of minutes before the interior of the vehicle can exceed a temperature that is unsafe for children.

BACAND: So it is a good practice to turn off the vehicle routinely, but there are times when you would not ask someone to turn off the vehicle?

BROWN: Yes.

BACAND: The night of the shooting, that traffic stop in particular, did you ever have an opportunity to tell the driver directly to turn off the vehicle?

BROWN: No.

BACAND: Would you have if you had had that opportunity?

BROWN: Yes.

BACAND: The major was trying to make a very valid point that, in general, officer safety–wise, it is a terrible idea to open up a vehicle that is running with a subject inside behind the driver's wheel. It is, is it not?

BROWN: Yes.

BACAND: Was it just your safety you were concerned about that night?

BROWN: No, it was Officer Campbell's safety also.

BACAND: Do you ever approach a vehicle from the passenger side when you are making the traffic stop and there are no other officers there?

BROWN: I have done that before, yes.

BACAND: Why? Why sometimes that and not going up to the driver's window?

BROWN: It depends on the traffic. If the vehicle is not pulled over or unable to pull over enough or I do not feel safe on that side, I

will sometimes go to the passenger side of
the vehicle.

BACAND: The night in question, you said you
could not see through the tinted window.

BROWN: Correct.

BACAND: If you could not see through the tinted
window, then is it fair to say you would not
have been able to tell if that driver had a
gun next to his right hip that would have
been within reach but out of view of Officer
Campbell?

BROWN: Correct.

BACAND: Was that one of the reasons you opened
up the door?

BROWN: Yes, to look inside the vehicle to make
sure there were no other occupants, no
weapons, from my vantage point, and to
explain to the driver who I am and try to
get him to comply.

BACAND: When you parked your vehicle, you
parked on the opposite side of the road,
facing the opposite direction of the subject
vehicle and the first officer's vehicle, correct?

BROWN: Correct.

BACAND: At that time, was Officer Campbell
already at the driver's window?

BROWN: Yes, he was.

BACAND: So is that a different situation, then, if
the officer is already back, protected by his
car, and the subject's window is open, with a
clean sight of view to your vehicle?

BROWN: Yes, that would have been a different
scenario.

BACAND: If that had been the scenario, would
you have stopped where you did and gotten
out of your vehicle?

BROWN: No.

BACAND: Because Officer Campbell is already at the window, your priority is to get with Officer Campbell as soon as you can…

BROWN: Yes.

BACAND: Or to park your vehicle in a safer location for you?

BROWN: To get out and assist Officer Campbell.

BACAND: Thank you. I'm finished for now.

ME: This was a normal traffic stop, as far as you were concerned?

BROWN: Until I got out of the car, yes.

ME: Okay. So you would not have known, prior to getting out of the car, that it was not a better idea to pull up, as training and practice have taught you, to be the second vehicle behind the car, giving you additional cover and allowing you to approach from a position that the driver would not have seen you?

BROWN: I felt that I was safe in that position to.

ME: I know you have testified that you felt, but your attorney just tried to make a point that your goal was to get to help Officer Campbell.

BROWN: Yes.

ME: But this was a normal traffic stop, so there was no immediacy to your getting out of your car, parking where you parked, ignoring what officer safety teaches you, which is to put your car behind the other police car. If you are telling me, "I am trying to get there in a hurry, I knew there was a problem," I certainly would understand why that part of officer safety would be set aside, because you are trying to get somewhere in

141

a hurry. But your testimony was that this
was a normal stop. Campbell was at the
window, dealing with somebody. You had
no clue there was a problem. So why not
put the car in the most optimal place for
your own officer safety?

BROWN: I pulled up there because Officer
Campbell was already dealing with the
driver, and I was back far enough where
I was fine with my safety. Whether it was
a regular traffic stop, as you are referring
to, or a traffic stop where I needed to get
there immediately, like he was fighting with
someone, my concern was, regardless of the
type of stop, I wanted to get there with the
officer and back him up as soon as possible. As I said, I did not want to try to do
a three-point turn in that residential roadway and get behind the car. It was safe to do
so, Officer Campbell had his car there, the
lights were on...

ME: You did not feel there was any sense of
urgency so parked it just where it was most
convenient for you, got out, walked over
casually?

BROWN: It was not convenient. It was...

ME: Sergeant, I have seen plenty of people who
have gotten comfortable in their career...

BROWN: Uh-hmm [in the affirmative].

ME: And then get lax with their officer safety. Is
it possible maybe you were just a little lax
that night with that decision?

BROWN: No.

ME: The opening of the car door and sticking
your head inside? You certainly could have
opened the car door, stayed out of that area

that would have dragged you, and pointed your flashlight in there and seen just as clearly. That same right hand, you could have seen that just as clearly.

BROWN: If I open up the door, and now you are telling me to position myself in front of the window and look in? I got a tinted window...

ME: In front of the window? No, sir. You got the door opened, and you were standing back with your flashlight, looking in without entering that area where it was inherently dangerous to be. Where if he threw it in gear, you were going for a ride, one way or another. You put yourself in that position, Sergeant. You did. Nobody else, nobody else in this room.

BROWN: I am trying to grasp this concept about—

ME: Officer safety?

BROWN: No, no...backing up and looking inside. Which we are also taught in the academy to stay behind the front...

ME: The B-pillar, yeah.

BROWN: Pillar on the vehicle, which I am not sure how I would be able to see the back seat and next to him with the door open right. I would have to get adjacent to the door and look in, where I am out of a direct line of sight with the—

ME: The rear window was not tinted. You approached from the rear. You could have illuminated the rear and seen the rear seats, as is taught in police training. Then looked safely from the outside into that car in the front seats while keeping yourself behind the B-pillar. Nothing in your training or experience that I know of has taught you to get into that car. That is an inherently dangerous thing to do. And you placed yourself in that position. That is a violation of officer safety for most officers. Maybe you are the exception to the rule. I do not know. It does not sound like common sense to me. I am asking you, and you have already answered me. You think it was a mistake in hindsight and you would not do it again.

BROWN: We all make mistakes.

ME: And you would not do it again, and you would not do it again? I did not say you were perfect, sir. Very few of us are perfect. I am going to take myself out of that category, okay? People make mistakes. You hotwash afterward, right? On a SWAT event? You sit down and you talk about what went right and what went wrong?

BROWN: Yes.

ME: What you could do better for the next time? How about we say, for the next time, do not go inside a moving car if you can help it?

BROWN: [Inaudible.]

ME: That is a bad idea...

BROWN: You are right.

ME: From an officer safety standpoint.

BROWN: Yes.

ME: From an administrative standpoint, we have to look at what went right and what went wrong and if the policy needs to be changed? Or are these things that people were taught and they decided to go outside of what they have been taught?

BROWN: Uh-hmm [in the affirmative].

ME: I am waiting to hear where you were trained to go inside of a running car, and I have not heard you say it. You have not told me what training you have, and I am told that you have over two thousand hours of training that I can see, and you were the department's training officer. What training taught you to go inside of a car that was running?

BROWN: I did not go inside. I looked inside. So you are referring to me going inside the car—

ME: You put your head inside a running car?

BROWN: Uh-hmm [in the affirmative].

ME: With a suspect that you knew Officer Campbell was heading toward arresting. What training taught you to do that?

BROWN: I would not say that there is any specific training that says A-B-C for traffic stops, but I was operating on a split-second decision.

ME: You made a decision, Sergeant. That is fine.

BROWN: It was what I felt was best at that time. I did it. I stand by it. It happened. It was an awful situation, how it ended up. But I did it. In our policies, it says that we can use our experience and we may have different approaches to traffic stops or other calls for service. There is no one way to handle every single call. I used a different approach that did not turn out well. It happened. I cannot take that back.

ME: You say you do not think there is training out there that goes through step by step on how to conduct a traffic stop. I can point you to the Florida Department of Law Enforcement's basic officers training course, which talks a lot about how to conduct a traffic stop, and it talks all about officer safety and not placing oneself in danger. So not once, but twice, from what I can hot-wash from this event, you placed yourself, unnecessarily, in danger, outside of your training. By parking yourself in a poten-tially dangerous position, because you just lined yourself up for someone with really bad intent to take you both out like doves on a power line. You were the SWAT team leader, and you just lined yourselves up for a direct shot, did you not? Now, if Mr. Samuel had a gun, like you said was possible and one of your primary concerns, he would not have to pivot or rotate—he could just go bang-bang. Two of you in a row. Gotcha. You put yourself in a dangerous position by parking where you parked, right?

BROWN: That is your opinion.

ME: No, I am asking you. Did you not just line yourself up for two people being shot in a row? If he had a gun, as you talked about? He would not have had to turn now and try to worry about somebody back over his right shoulder. He could have taken both of you out, because he could see you and him. Right there. Over the peephole, where you put your car.

BROWN: If he were sitting here in the driver's seat, I was over there...so I am not sure...

ME: And where was Campbell?

BROWN: Campbell was right here.

ME: Bang-bang.

BROWN: Okay.

ME: Right? You are in a line, right?

BROWN: If you want to measure it and say that that is right...

ME: Sarge, you put yourself in a dangerous position, all right? Did you put yourself in a dangerous position, outside of the training?

BROWN: Okay.

ME: Mr. Bacand, did you have a follow-up question?

BACAND: Major, I can see you are passionate, and your concern for officer safety and that people learn lessons, and I guess it is just not familiar to do it in the IA interview itself.

ME: These are questions that I have to get answered. Obviously, the sergeant made decisions, and they are his decisions ultimately to make. And the department has to figure out, as I said, in the long run, if there is something that needs to be changed for policies and procedures, or is there adequate training out there? I am trying to make sure we are clear there was no training that taught the sergeant that, or is there some kind of training that I have missed, a class you had that taught you to place yourself into an inherently dangerous position, such as a running vehicle with somebody who is about to be arrested?

BROWN: The only training that supplied me with inherently dangerous position information...but I have not had any...there is no policies or training that I am aware of that I had with the agency that says... I mean, I do not recall ever seeing the FDLE step-by-step traffic stop policy...

ME: For basic recruits?

BROWN: But there may be.

ME: For basic recruits?

BROWN: Yep. I do not remember. I went through the…the consolidated course. I had military experience. I went through a two-week course and took the state exam. It was mostly high-liability issues. But from the agency and training that I have attended here, I do not recall having any training that says, "Turn off the car." The only time I can recall doing that is for the felony traffic stops when we are conducting a high-risk traffic stop. We get on the PA, tell them to turn off the car, throw the key out the door, which I have done before. So there may be training out there. I do not recall. I've had over nineteen hundred hours of training, not all of it traffic stops or SALTS or anything else. It is a wide variety of training.

ME: For the record, SALTS is "Safe and Legal Traffic Stops."

BROWN: Yes.

After we concluded our interview, Mr. Bacand asked if he could speak to me privately, which I agreed to only after Sergeant Brown said it was fine. With my office door close, Mr. Bacand told me he had noticed that I did not bring up the issue of the shooting of Mr. Samuel, and wondered aloud why that might be. I told Mr. Bacand that the issue of the legality of the shooting itself had been settled by the grand jury and I had listened to the audio interview of Sergeant Brown that was taken three days after that shooting. I told him that it was obviously an emotional thing for Sergeant Brown to have to relive, which I could clearly hear on the tape, and so I saw no point in having him relive it in my office. A man was dead, and it was a tragedy. My investigation found no policy, procedural, or officer safety issues with the actual shooting itself, and all the facts supported the sergeant's decision at that time based upon the totality of the circumstances. Had there been questions that arose, I would have asked, but finding none, there was no sense in asking anything about it. Mr. Bacand then thanked me, saying he was grateful, on both his part and the sergeant's, for not having to cover that part of this investigation again. I then asked Mr. Bacand if he would share with me why he had characterized my questioning of the sergeant at one point as "unfamiliar." He laughed and replied that it was just refreshing from his viewpoint to see an internal affairs investigator going at a question from multiple angles to illicit a response. I took it as a compliment, and we departed company.

I called Felicia into my office after they left, to talk about the interview. I wanted to know what she thought of the line of questioning, which we had discussed beforehand, and asked for her general impression of the sergeant's responses. Felicia was her typical happy self. She asked if I believed we had proven any of the possible policy violations, and I told her that a deputy chief or above would have to decide. She questioned the sergeant's response to his seeming violation of the insubordination policy, which appeared to be the most egregious infraction, and again I told her that the chiefs would have to weigh his response in their decision-making. Ultimately, I almost felt that Felicia was trying to get me to commit to how serious all this was and what my impression of an outcome might be. I told her that I honestly did not know what the ultimate decision would be, and I did not. I asked her what she thought of the sergeant's attempts to avoid the obvious answers, and she agreed that he tried to avoid any answer that he believed might make him look bad. I told her that I felt as if I had just sparred with someone in the proverbial boxing ring that was our interview, and she laughed, saying I had not seen anything until I interviewed Officer Campbell.

CHAPTER 11

Liar, Liar

When I first started in law enforcement, I learned a philosophy from veteran officers that went something like this: When you get called into internal affairs, admit nothing and deny everything, unless they have pictures. Then and only then should you demand to see the pictures before answering and go back to the original premise. I thought this was mostly said as a joke, but I was about to learn that there are those who take this to heart. Sergeant Brown had been difficult to interview, but I had not seen anything yet. Today, I would tell you that Officer Than Campbell outfoxed me on the order of the interviews. He wanted to go after Sergeant Brown so that he could see what the questions were going to be in advance of his own interview. At that time, I was not that impressed with the tactic and felt that the truth would surface, even if I laid out all the questions in advance for Officer Campbell to prepare for. Officer Campbell came in and took several days to complete his review of all the materials our investigation had generated. In February of that year, we were able to schedule a date for his formal interview. Officer Campbell's advantage to going second as a subject officer was that he got to see the questions I asked of Sergeant Brown. That is important to remember as you read the following synopsis of our interview:

> ME: I am the major in charge of the Internal
> Affairs Bureau and the lead investigator
> for the police department's administrative

review of the officer-involved shooting case involving Mr. David Samuel. Also present with me, representing the department's IAB, is Detective Felicia Direct. The interview we will be conducting is with Officer Than Campbell. And for the record, ma'am, you are?

LUNA: Attorney Mary Luna, and for the record, we have no objection to the recording.

ME: Okay, good. Can you please spell your name?

LUNA: L-U-N-A.

ME: By contract, you are entitled to have a representative. You have elected to have as your representative Ms. Luna. And you are with IUPA, is that correct?

LUNA: Yes.

ME: Officer Campbell, according to the Police Officer's Bill of Rights, only one interviewer is allowed to ask questions during the interview. Do you waive this right so that Detective Direct may also ask questions?

LUNA: No. [Attorney answers instead of Campbell.]

ME: Okay. The complainant in this case is the Chief of Police. You are the subject officer of this investigation, and the allegations are as follows: There are no specific allegations made against you. This is an administrative review that is required by policy due to your use of deadly force. This interview is part of an official proceeding per Florida state statute. This is an administrative investigation, not a criminal one. You have been given and have signed copies of the Officer's Bill of Rights, Garrity statement, and perjury form. Do you understand your rights?

CAMPBELL: Yes, I do.

ME: Do you have any questions concerning these forms?

CAMPBELL: No, sir.

ME: Okay. You have been given an opportunity to review all evidence and interviews to date. Have you had sufficient time to review the evidence and interviews?

CAMPBELL: Yes, I have, and on that, has there been any new evidence or any new interviews since the date I reviewed?

ME: No, you had the complete record when you reviewed it.

CAMPBELL: Thank you.

ME: Please initial here, indicating that you have been afforded sufficient time to review the evidence and interviews. Okay, please raise your right hand. Do you swear or affirm that the statement you're about to give will be the truth, the whole truth, and nothing but the truth, so help you God?

CAMPBELL: Yes, I do.

ME: Okay, just so we are clear here today, this is not a trial. So we are not going to have an interaction where you, Ms. Luna, interrupt and interject. This is an interview, an administrative interview. At the end of the interview, I am going to give you a chance, Counselor, if you would like to ask some clarifying questions, but as you answered for him earlier, please do not do that. Allow him to answer these questions, okay?

LUNA: Um-hmm [in the affirmative].

ME: Do you understand this, ma'am?

LUNA: I understand it...

ME: Okay.

LUNA: And he also has rights, just so you understand.

ME: Right, and he…

LUNA: But I am not going to abbreviate his rights.

ME: He can stop me at any time and ask to consult with you. At any time he would like a break, he can ask for one. If he would like to talk to you in private, we will stop the interview and you can get up and walk into that other room and have your discussions. This is an interview. The questions are coming from me, to him. He is to answer me, okay?

LUNA: Uh-hmm [in the affirmative].

ME: Okay. Thank you. And also, "Uh-hmm" means *yes*?

LUNA: Oh, I can see we are already going to be contentious.

ME: No, ma'am. I am just trying—

LUNA: Yes.

ME: The recorder does not pick up—

LUNA: I understand his rights. I have been doing this almost exclusively for fourteen years. So I understand the process. I understand the law. I hope we are both on the same page.

ME: I hope we are, too, but, Counselor, what I asked you was if "Uh-hmm" means *yes*, correct?

LUNA: Yes.

ME Okay. The recorder does not pick up "Uh-hmm." "Uh-hmm" doesn't tell us "Yes" or "No" on a recording device that will later be transcribed. "Uh-hmm," as you well know from practicing law for fourteen years, can be debated—

LUNA: Oh, no. I practiced law longer than that.

ME: Okay.

LUNA: I've practiced public employee labor representing law enforcement officers…

ME: Okay, but…

LUNA: For fourteen years.

ME: Your length of time as an attorney…my
point is that you know as well as I do that
the recorder does not pick up "Uh-hmm" as
either "Yes" or "No" and can be the source
of debate at a later time if not clarified at
that time. So when I asked you, I was not
trying to be contentious. I was only trying
to get you to tell me yes, meaning…

LUNA: Okay.

ME: You understood. That is all.

LUNA: Oh my, perhaps I misunderstood.

ME: All right, I promise I am not trying to be
contentious. We all have jobs to do here.

LUNA: Yes.

ME: Officer Campbell, I have reviewed your
training record, and it is quite impressive.
I have a copy of the department-supplied
training record and would like you to look
at it, verifying that it is, in fact, your training
record. Officer Campbell, there is almost
three thousand hours of training there, is
there not?

CAMPBELL: Yes, sir.

ME: Okay, how many types of discipline are you
an instructor for?

CAMPBELL: Driving, ASP, OC, and I am a senior
master with the electronic control device,
maritime, and am a law enforcement
instructor and use of force subject matter
expert.

ME: You have been in law enforcement how
many years?

CAMPBELL: Going on fifteen.

ME: So suffice it to say, you are fairly well educated in law enforcement and the different tactics used to conduct law enforcement exercises or responses, is that true?

CAMPBELL: Yes, sir.

ME: Okay, you are also on the SWAT team as well, is that correct?

CAMPBELL: Yes, sir, I was.

ME: Okay. So you have had a lot of training, in other words. I mean, I can tell you I have been a police officer a long period, and that is quite an impressive training record. Very few people have I seen that have that kind of a training record. You were also the department's lead training officer, is that correct?

CAMPBELL: Yes, sir.

ME: For how many years was that?

CAMPBELL: About seven.

ME: On the night in question, you were assigned to patrol, is that correct?

CAMPBELL: Yes, sir.

ME: Going back to your training and the fact that you do train, how do you typically train someone to conduct a traffic stop? What is your instruction to somebody new or somebody learning how to conduct a traffic stop?

CAMPBELL: What kind of traffic stop are you talking about?

ME: Uh, just give me a basic.

CAMPBELL: Because there are thousands.

ME: Just give me a typical traffic stop. How it is conducted by a police officer.

CAMPBELL: Depending on where it is at, what time of day... I mean, your scope of question is huge. I mean, if you can narrow it down to what you are asking...

ME: Well, for instance, you know, the basic recruit academy provides a basic traffic stop in their training guidelines and tells us how to conduct it. Can you just tell me...okay, you observe an infraction. What comes next?

CAMPBELL: I observe an infraction, I call the tag number of the vehicle out on the radio, then description of the vehicle, the location upon the stopping of the vehicle. I make the approach to the vehicle, glancing inside, to see if I can see anything. I touch the back of the trunk to make sure it is secured also, leaving a DNA print in case it takes off. I stay between the passenger rear door and the driver's side door. I make contact with the driver, making sure that there is no one else in the vehicle. But there are thousands of different vehicles, so narrowing it down would be better for what you're specifically asking.

ME: You have general guidelines that you typically follow, like, for instance, you would not typically be up on a bumper of a vehicle when you stopped it, but this particular night, you were. Can you tell me why the deviation between what you would not do normally and what you did in this particular case?

CAMPBELL: I was close to the vehicle because he abruptly stopped and I was not too far behind him, so I made the stop. I also did not give him an avenue of backing up and getting out of there.

ME: Okay, because you were concerned, for some reason, that he might what? Was there something that Mr. Samuel did prior to that that made you concerned?

CAMPBELL: Yes, sir, and I am sure you read the grand jury testimony, and my grand jury testimony would stipulate that.

ME: Which was?

CAMPBELL: It took him a while to stop, the time of night, the shaking of the vehicle before the stop.

ME: So you were concerned that he was...?

CAMPBELL: Possibly hiding something or reaching for something in the vehicle or getting ready to bail.

ME: Okay. Let us go back to when you first spotted him. That was a few blocks away from the initial traffic stop, is that correct?

CAMPBELL: Yes, sir.

ME: Okay, and your testimony was—and I am not going to try to testify for you, so that is why I am going to ask you to repeat it—was that you got behind him and paced him. Can you tell me how fast he was going?

CAMPBELL: I would have to look at the testimony.

ME: Okay.

CAMPBELL: That was over a year ago. So I would have to look at the testimony in order to answer.

ME: That is fine. We have it.

CAMPBELL: I paced him at forty-five miles an hour.

ME: Okay, forty-five in a twenty-five, is that correct?

CAMPBELL: Yes, sir.

ME: Okay, so when you caught up to him and paced him, what did you do next?

CAMPBELL: I activated my lights.

ME: Yes, sir.

CAMPBELL: After calling out the tag, description of vehicle, direction of travel.

ME: Did he pull over?

CAMPBELL: No, sir.

ME: Did he slow down?

CAMPBELL: No, sir.

ME: What did you do next?

CAMPBELL: I chirped my siren, manually, just to get him to stop.

ME: Did he stop?

CAMPBELL: Just in case he did not notice me, because the windows were very dark and tinted and I could not see into it. He did not.

ME: Okay.

CAMPBELL: Chirped it, I think, again, but I would have to look at my testimony just to make sure.

ME: That was your testimony, but if you want to look again, more than happy to show it to you.

CAMPBELL: Just to make sure. I am not positive.

ME: No, no…that was your testimony. I'm nodding, yes, because, yes, that was your testimony. I am not trying to… Counselor and Officer Campbell, I am not trying to catch you in a lie here. Okay? If you do not remember, please, at any point in time, stop me, let us let you look at the record, let you recount the record. That is not the game here, okay? So let us be clear. All right, so he did not stop when you chirped it. It was your testimony that you believed at that point he knew you were behind him, is that true?

CAMPBELL: Yes, sir.

ME: Okay. And he still was not stopping?

CAMPBELL: No, sir.

ME: What did he do next?

CAMPBELL: I think he made a right turn, and I chirped my siren again, and midway through the block, he finally pulled over.

ME: Okay, so it was clear to you when you were still on the initial street where you observed him that he was not obeying, and you believed he knew that you were behind him. What is the department's policy as far as pursuits of automobiles? What can you chase for?

CAMPBELL: Fleeing violent felonies.

ME: So at this point, all you had was a traffic infraction, is that correct?

CAMPBELL: Correct.

ME: So if you followed him around the corner even though you knew he knew you were there, and not stopping, are you not then pursuing? I mean, what can you do if he continues on?

CAMPBELL: Define a *pursuit*, Major, because if you pull behind a vehicle and you light that person up...if you activate your emergency lights and he does not stop within two seconds, that could be categorized as a pursuit also. So where you are going with that is another scope that is huge.

ME: But you were eastbound on the initial street...

CAMPBELL: Correct.

ME: And you tried to pull him over, correct?

CAMPBELL: Correct.

ME: He, to your belief, knew you were behind him, yet did not stop and acknowledge your authority, correct?

CAMPBELL: Correct.

ME: Then, he made a southbound onto the next street and, it was your testimony, "so fast," because you followed him at that same speed, "that you could hear your stuff flying around in the trunk" of your car…

CAMPBELL: That is correct.

ME: You followed him. Why are you following him if he is not going to stop for your traffic stop?

CAMPBELL: Major, you are getting into an area where…okay, a supervisor would have called it off on the radio…also…but define a *pursuit*.

ME: The word *pursuit* is defined in department policy as—

CAMPBELL: Uh, Major, you are the one asking the questions. I am asking you to define *pursuit* because you are trying to tell me that I violated department policy by pursuing a vehicle when I—

ME: You are trying to tell me you did not pursue him?

CAMPBELL: I tried to initiate a traffic stop.

ME: Okay, but you already knew prior to turning onto Nineteenth Street that he was not stopping and acquiescing to your authority by your own testimony.

CAMPBELL: Okay, Major, you're getting into a scope of things, because there is plenty of testimony by DOJ focus groups that say…

well, we want to turn into a well-lit area…
we want to turn into a parking lot…well,
if I am trying to initiate a traffic stop on
a busy highway and a guy goes two more
blocks trying to get into a well-lit area, is
that also a pursuit?

ME: So will you just answer the question and tell
me, "Oh, I was not sure he was not gonna
stop yet," or was that it or something else?

CAMPBELL: I was not pursuing him.

ME: Okay.

CAMPBELL: I was trying to initiate a traffic stop.

ME: So…had Mr. Samuel continued through
the next stop sign just south of where you
stopped, you would not have followed him,
or would you?

CAMPBELL: Major, I would not have pursued. It
is against department policy.

ME: So why did you follow him? When he turned
southbound without stopping, why did you
follow him?

CAMPBELL: I was trying to initiate a traffic stop.

ME: So you pulled him over and he came to a stop
and you got up close because you believed
he might be ready to bail, and you got up to
the window and you were addressing him.

CAMPBELL: Yes, sir.

ME: At some point, you had asked him for a driver's license, is that correct?

CAMPBELL: Yes, sir. After several noncompliances
of rolling the window down completely and
my asking him for his driver's license, the
only thing he complied with was giving me
his driver's license, after several attempts to.

ME: Okay, so you did actually receive the driver's
license at some point.

CAMPBELL: Yes, sir.

ME: Was that prior to Sergeant Brown's arrival?

CAMPBELL: I do not remember.

ME: Okay. When Sergeant Brown arrived, he walked around the rear of your car to the passenger side of Mr. Samuel's car, is that correct?

CAMPBELL: That is correct.

ME: And during that time, you were talking to Mr. Samuel, explaining that you saw marijuana, is that correct?

CAMPBELL: Yes, sir.

ME: And that should have been indicative in your mind to Sergeant Brown that you were getting ready to make an arrest. Is that something that would be fair to say?

CAMPBELL: Yes, sir.

ME: At some point, you made the decision to reach into the automobile, to try to take Mr. Samuel out of it. Was the automobile running at that time?

CAMPBELL: Yes, sir.

ME: Was it in gear?

CAMPBELL: No, sir.

ME: What training have you had that calls for reaching into a running automobile? Where did you learn to make a vehicle extraction like that?

CAMPBELL: To pull somebody out to effect an arrest? To get him out of the vehicle?

ME: Mr. Samuel was not cooperating, was he?

CAMPBELL: No, sir.

ME: You decided to physically remove him?

CAMPBELL: Yes, sir.

ME: Have you had any specific training on vehicle extractions?

CAMPBELL: We have done training here with Sergeant Powers where he has taught vehicle extractions, especially with sovereign citizens.

ME: Now, in that training, was the vehicle running?

CAMPBELL: Yes, sir.

ME: It was? I looked everywhere for training that taught vehicle extractions, and in every scenario that I saw, it dealt with the vehicle being off, not on. You authored training on vehicle extractions, do you remember that?

CAMPBELL: Yes, sir.

ME: Okay, I pulled it off your computer. I have a copy of your training lesson, right?

CAMPBELL: Yes, sir.

ME: In that, your lesson plan calls for both officers being on the same side of the car when you do that. Why did you not bring Sergeant Brown back over to your side of the car before you tried to extract Mr. Samuel from the car?

CAMPBELL: Because the sergeant was already on the other side of the vehicle.

ME: It was your testimony that you were talking to Mr. Samuel out loud, telling him he had marijuana that you could see, so you were trying to alert the sergeant that you were going to make an arrest. Why did you not call the sergeant to your side before he made it to the other side to help you with the vehicle extraction? Your training calls for two officers pulling the driver from the driver's side of the car, is that not true?

CAMPBELL: That is true.

ME: So why did you not do that?

CAMPBELL: Because we were not dealt that hand of cards that night. We had to work with what we had. That was it.

ME: So you improvised?

CAMPBELL: Yes, sir.

ME: Okay. Is it an inherently dangerous thing to do, to reach inside a running automobile?

CAMPBELL: Sir...we were dealt those cards. We had to deal with what we had to deal with. It is also in our policy that we are not allowed to leave, let anyone leave a traffic stop without attempting to stop them, if we think that they are impaired and with marijuana on the vehicle dash. That was my thought of his impairment. So we had to make an attempt, according to our policy, to stop him.

ME: You had this gentleman's driver's license, right?

CAMPBELL: Yes, sir.

ME: You had your probable cause?

CAMPBELL: Yes, sir.

ME: You could have gone back and made an arrest later if he had driven off.

CAMPBELL: Did you not... I just told you, in our policy, it states that if you think that the driver is impaired, you will make an attempt to stop them. So we had to make an attempt, and that was our attempt.

ME: You are very conscientious when it comes to officer safety, are you not, Officer Campbell?

CAMPBELL: Yes, sir.

ME: Okay. You even talked about in your interview how you looked around and you knew there was nobody else on the street that night, because you constantly were checking, which is officer safety. That is making sure nobody is coming up behind you, correct?

CAMPBELL: That is correct.

ME: Okay. So you placed yourself into a position of possible death or serious bodily injury to try to extract an individual from an automobile by yourself, even though you had a backup there that you could have brought around to help you, and I am trying to understand what your thought process was at that point. Why did you reach into that automobile?

CAMPBELL: Sir, do you know how long that incident took?

ME: It was a very short period.

CAMPBELL: I was given those cards. We had to deal with what we had to deal with. I would not have changed it any other way. There is no way to change it.

ME: Given the same set of facts today, would you do the exact same thing? Is that what you are telling me?

CAMPBELL: Yes, sir. Those were the cards I was dealt. I do not have the luxury of hindsight, and the US Supreme Court says that we do not either.

ME: Hindsight is perfect, is it not?

CAMPBELL: It is great.

ME: You can also learn from things where mistakes are made. Are you trying to tell me there were no mistakes made in this series of events?

CAMPBELL: Sir, I am not admitting to anything. I am just telling you—

ME: No, no. I asked you a question. Are you trying to tell me—

CAMPBELL: That is going to be my answer.

ME: Are you trying to tell me that there were no
mistakes made during this chain of events?

CAMPBELL: You have my answer, Major. That is
the answer that I am giving you. I would
have done the same thing. I do not have the
luxury of hindsight. I cannot go back and
change whatever I did.

ME: But certainly, you can learn from experience,
can you not?

CAMPBELL: Everybody can learn from experience,
but you have my…you have my answer.
You can badger me…it is going to be the
same answer.

ME: I am not badgering you. I asked a question.
When you do not answer the question, I
will ask it again until you do answer the
question.

CAMPBELL: I would do the same thing.

ME: Okay.

LUNA: Maybe we should take a moment?

ME: Okay. Go ahead. And for the record,
Counselor, we are not turning the tape off.
We are going to leave it on.

LUNA: Okay. Thank you.

ME: Yes, ma'am.

(Luna and Campbell leave the room. Tape runs.)

(Luna and Campbell return.)

ME: The question I asked and that you answered
already but for which I will give you another
opportunity to answer now that you have

had the chance to consult with your attorney and think about it was, is there anything that you would have changed from that night that you did differently?

CAMPBELL: I would have done the same thing that night. If I were given different factual circumstances, different stresses, then maybe I would have done something differently. But that night I would have done the same thing, given the circumstances and facts that I was given that evening, I would have done the same thing.

ME: Well, you certainly had the opportunity to call the sergeant over to your side to do the vehicle extraction, in compliance with the training that you not only created and conducted but had also been taught. So I do not understand why that is going to be the same thing. You certainly know that it is better to have two of you on the same side when doing a vehicle extraction, right?

CAMPBELL: Major, it is better to have everything textbook, but nothing is textbook. We go in service every day knowing that we may be putting ourselves in inherent danger.

ME: Okay.

CAMPBELL: It is not a cakewalk here. We are short-staffed. We run at short shifts. We have 90 percent of our road patrol officers with less than two years on the job. So you are losing a lot of experience on the street that we are having to deal with by ourselves. So I know what you are trying to get at, and my answer is going to be the same: I was given the cards I dealt with, and that was what I had to deal with.

ME: I understand your explanation, but you had a senior officer there with you who was a supervisor. You are both SWAT operators and both, certainly, well trained and capable. You would not, in the future, when you are on the side of a vehicle where you know you are going to do a vehicle extraction, when the sergeant arrives, have him come next to you to do the vehicle extraction in the manner that you have taught and trained other people to do?

CAMPBELL: I understand where you are going with it. I answered your question—

ME: Yes, you did. I am clarifying because you added in facts that did not have a bearing at that scene on that night, which are having junior people and being short-staffed. You had somebody on scene with you in ample time to be able to do it the way you taught and trained, correct?

CAMPBELL: That also I am a subordinate of.

ME: Okay. When you teach traffic stops, who runs the traffic stop? The officer that is at the vehicle window or the officer showing up, doing the covering?

CAMPBELL: What works in training does not work the same way out on the road. You, as a major, know that...so...

ME: I know improvisations occur. I know people stray from training. You are the product of your experience, correct?

CAMPBELL: My training and experience, that was what we dealt with that night, and that was what we did effectively.

ME: Obviously, the outcome was a disaster in the long run, right? Decisions that were made caused the ultimate outcome of this?

CAMPBELL: Disaster? You are saying that he made the decision?

ME: He made the decision.

CAMPBELL: I am injured for the rest of my life...

ME: You are injured...

CAMPBELL: Because of his decision.

ME: Right.

CAMPBELL: He made a felonious act...

ME: Yes, he did.

CAMPBELL: With his decision.

ME: Yes, he did.

CAMPBELL: Of which we were cleared by the grand jury...

ME: Right, so we are not talking criminal here.

CAMPBELL: The county, and the state.

ME: We are not talking criminal here.

CAMPBELL: I understand that, but what you are saying is, we made a disastrous mistake.

ME: No, I said the outcome was a disaster.

CAMPBELL: Same thing. You said it was a disaster.

ME: The outcome was a disaster. I have an injured officer...injured for life. And I have a deceased individual. So again, you are telling me, given the same set of circumstances and facts, in the future, you would not do something differently when you have all these other possibilities and options available that, you now have the experience to understand, might create a different outcome? Officer Campbell, again, I do not understand your earlier answer, and that was why I asked it for the record and why I am asking you again to reconsider. Would you do anything differently?

CAMPBELL: And I am stating you are going into hindsight. I did what I did.

ME: For the future, Officer Campbell?

CAMPBELL: You cannot ask that.

ME: I can ask it.

CAMPBELL: You can ask that, but my answer's going to be the same. You are going into hindsight, which is against the Supreme Court rules.

ME: We are not talking about prosecuting you for any kind of crime. That Supreme Court ruling deals with prosecution. I understand the Supreme Court ruling. This is an administrative function, and again, you learn or you do not learn from your experiences. One way or another. So you are telling me, regardless, you would do exactly the same thing again even though you have now had the experience of what happens when you do it the way you did it?

CAMPBELL: Under the exact same facts, under the exact same stresses, under the exact same conditions, I would. Because those were the cards I was dealt with.

ME: Even with the experience that you now have? I think you are misunderstanding the question...maybe...so let me—

CAMPBELL: I understand it completely.

ME: Okay.

CAMPBELL: You are trying to get me to say I would do something different, and I would do the same thing.

ME: Okay.

CAMPBELL: You are asking...you have asked that question three or four times.

ME: All right. Then we will move on. That is fine. It is not a problem. In your time on the SWAT unit, did you hold a specific position? Were you, I think—maybe I was told—a sniper or something like that?

CAMPBELL: Yes, sir, I was a sniper and an MRAP driver...

ME: Okay.

CAMPBELL: And also a SWAT armorer.

ME: And the armorer? Okay.

CAMPBELL: Yes, sir.

ME: So in those positions, you have had extensive training in shoot/do-not-shoot situations, right?

CAMPBELL: Yes, sir.

ME: It was your testimony that you got...and I think the words you used were "rolled up" by the car door. Can you basically explain? I think I understand, but can you basically explain what you mean when you say "rolled up"? What exactly happened?

CAMPBELL: I was pinned up underneath the car door as Mr. Samuel accelerated away, and after that, I do not remember what happened until I rolled over and saw Sergeant Brown getting dragged by the vehicle.

ME: Okay, but I want to make sure I am clear. When you were trying to reach into the car, you reached into the vehicle with which hand?

CAMPBELL: I reached in and grabbed his wrist with my left hand and reached around the doorframe to extract him from the vehicle.

ME: So your left hand is in the door, grabbing his—

CAMPBELL: My left hand had his wrist, and my right arm was reaching in the door to extract him from the vehicle.

ME: So you have the hands around the door-frame and through the window. So I guess part of it is, your arm—

CAMPBELL: Yes, sir.

ME: Is around either side. So when the car pulled you, and your leg was underneath the door…

CAMPBELL: I got pulled up underneath the door.

ME: Okay. You rolled. Basically, you tumbled underneath the door of the car?

CAMPBELL: I got pinned up underneath five inches of steel, in the road.

ME: Okay. Obviously, we are talking seconds here when that happened, and it was Detective Williams's testimony that, as he arrived, he saw you standing in the middle of the street, shooting. Your testimony was, you were lying down, shooting, but you thought you might have been standing for at least one of the shots. Is it possible you were standing for all three shots, like Detective Williams said?

CAMPBELL: No, sir. The adjacent county's sheriff office's forensic testimony stated the line and direction of shots. The first two were from the ground angle, the last one was from standing, and I collapsed immediately after the last shot.

ME: It is one possible theory, but there was also an eyewitness officer who was definitive about what he saw and said that you were standing the entire time. There is another discrepancy in the testimony provided about your discharging your weapon. It is Sergeant Brown's testimony that he was inside the car when you fired. Now it is yours that he was outside, with his head above the vehicle. Was it possible he was in the car?

CAMPBELL: The last thing I saw was his head above the passenger side of the vehicle. And then I stopped firing when I did not see it anymore.

ME: Obviously, those two testimonies do not match. Is it possible you had just gotten rolled up on by a car, that his head was actually inside the car? You saw his head above the car, but by the time you started firing, his head was gone?

CAMPBELL: I am not going on possibilities. I am telling you what my statement was.

ME: I know what your previous statement was.

CAMPBELL: I am not going to answer to a possibility.

ME: Well, the last comment you made was, "I do not know," to the investigator. You said, "I could have been standing for one of the shots. I do not know." I'm trying to clarify. Are you positive? Are you absolutely positive when you were shooting all three times, his head was above that car?

CAMPBELL: Major...

ME: I mean, I am just asking if you are positive.

CAMPBELL: I understand you are going for a review...

ME: Yes.

CAMPBELL: But you have had trained investigators, trained members of the state attorney's office, that have gone through a grand jury with the testimony. You know the answer to that. My answer is going to be the same.

ME: Which was "I do not know"?

CAMPBELL: I do not.

ME: Okay. That is fine. That was all I was asking, "Were you positive?" "Well, no, I am not." You are telling me you are not positive? Your testimony was, "I do not know"?

CAMPBELL: I do not know, and I can tell you I was not standing—

ME: By the way, I was not there for the testimony of the grand jury. I do not have the testimony of the grand jury. Nobody does. I have your—

CAMPBELL: You read—

ME: No, I do not have the grand jury testimony.

CAMPBELL: I am sorry. You read the interviews from…

ME: Leading up to…

CAMPBELL: The grand jury…

ME: Correct, correct.

CAMPBELL: And it is pretty much the same thing.

ME: Okay. Pretty much. That is fine. I am just making sure I understand. So it is possible that his head was inside the car and not… you know, you saw it…your memory is that he was outside the car when you were firing, but you also said, in your testimony, "I could have been standing for one of the shots. I do not know."

LUNA: Let us take a moment, please. He looks confused. Let us take a moment.

(Luna and Campbell step out. Tape runs.)

(Luna and Campbell re-enter.)

ME: Okay, so you had a chance to talk to your attorney again. Did you want to change something you said prior to, or can we move forward?

CAMPBELL: I do not want to change anything, but I also want to clarify what you are asking out of that question.

ME: I was asking if it was possible that you were standing when the shooting was going on and if it was possible that the sergeant's head was actually already inside the car while you were shooting. I thought we clarified that you told the previous investigator you did not know for sure, and that was how we left it.

CAMPBELL: I understand that. I did not know for sure. You said that Detective Williams was adamant that he saw me standing. Well, going back into training, with stress, as you well know, your mind will see something completely different or will tell your eyes completely something that they did not see.

ME: Right. And it takes a few minutes for you to catch up and process.

CAMPBELL: So you have to think of the possibility that Detective Williams might not have seen the whole incident, because if you go off his radio transmissions, Detective Williams said he was on scene for the entire incident. According to his radio transmissions, he was there, but according to his grand jury testimony, he had the wrong location.

ME: He had the wrong location?

CAMPBELL: He did not arrive on time because he had the wrong block. If you look into his testimony and read from the transcripts of when he said he was there from the 911 tapes—his car was also equipped with a camera, which would have shown everything that he just saw. And then he would have been there for the entire incident.

ME: I think it was his testimony that he was basically there for the entire incident…that he saw the car pull away at a high rate of speed, and as he came parallel with you, he saw you firing the shots. So he missed the first part where you were getting "rolled up" and the sergeant was hanging on for dear life on the outside of the car, but he saw the remainder of it. I am not trying to debate, so let us stop with my verbiage and just go back to questions. So it is possible that you were standing and the sergeant's head was already in the car when the shots were fired? Is that a fair statement? Yes or no?

CAMPBELL: I am going with what my testimony for the grand jury said: I do not know.

ME: Okay.

CAMPBELL: My exact shots? Because of my training from stress… I was stressed and I was injured.

ME: Right. Okay.

LUNA: The shots or the head?

ME: Well, he doesn't know. My understanding is now…

CAMPBELL: I stopped firing when I could not see his head anymore.

ME: Okay. That is your recollection.

CAMPBELL: That is my recollection. And that was what I told the investigators.

ME: Why would you shoot at a car where there is an officer inside of it?

CAMPBELL: My officer is getting dragged. My friend is getting dragged by a vehicle. So exigent circumstances are applied to stop that vehicle. From him further getting injured or killed.

ME: Even though your shots could have potentially injured him as well?

CAMPBELL: I tried to stop the vehicle that had just run over me and that was dragging my supervisor down the street. It could cause further injury or death.

ME: Even though you are highly trained with a firearm and are a sniper, you have just testified that you were seriously injured as well. Does that diminish your ability to make that kind of very difficult shot?

CAMPBELL: I did not know I was seriously injured at that point. Until I stood up and had no use of my leg.

ME: Okay. You know two of the shots went to his side of the car, right?

CAMPBELL: Yes, sir. From the grand jury testimony.

ME: And the pictures?

CAMPBELL: Yes, sir.

ME: And only one of the three was toward the driver's side of the car?

CAMPBELL: Yes, sir.

ME: All right. Was that inherently dangerous? You were taking a chance of injuring your friend, your supervisor, when you were firing shots at a car that he was in, right?

CAMPBELL: I am trying to get him, a suspect that made a felonious decision on running me over and, from my knowledge, was dragging and possibly going to kill my supervisor. So I was trying to stop that suspect.

ME: Okay. How long were you on the squad that you had been on at that time?

CAMPBELL: Since the first of February.

ME: So February to April. A couple of months?

CAMPBELL: Yes, sir.

ME: And it was your testimony when they asked you about the in-car camera that you told "them"—and that is your word—that it was not working. I want to know who "them" is that you told it was not working. Do you... do you recall?

CAMPBELL: My supervisor when they did the inspections.

ME: Okay, and that would be Sergeant Buck Young?

CAMPBELL: Yes, sir.

ME: Okay. So prior to the night of the shooting, you told Sergeant Young that your in-car camera system was not working. What did he tell you to do about it?

CAMPBELL: To get it fixed.

ME: How did he tell you to do that?

CAMPBELL: Turn it in for PM, which it was going, and in the sheriff's department evidence logs you will see in the picture my green card to turn the vehicle in. It was going in that night to get serviced.

ME: How many times did he tell you to turn it in?

CAMPBELL: The card would still be there, but the department issued my car out without doing inventory.

ME: How many times did he tell you to turn it in?

CAMPBELL: I do not remember.

ME: His testimony is two. Would that be fair?

CAMPBELL: I do not remember.

ME: Okay, Officer Jack Dens, you know who he is?

CAMPBELL: Yes, sir.

ME: He was on your squad at that time?

CAMPBELL: Yes, sir.

ME: He was the training officer on the squad at that time?

CAMPBELL: Yes, sir.

ME: It was his testimony that you came to him and he helped you with the CAD, the computer, because you had been off the street for a while?

CAMPBELL: Yes, sir. The report writing system.

ME: Okay. Sergeant Young says he told you also to get with Jack Dens to learn how to operate the in-car camera system. Do you recall?

CAMPBELL: That, I do not remember.

ME: Okay. Were you surprised to learn from Mrs. Bright Action's testimony that the in-car camera system would have worked that night if you had turned it on?

CAMPBELL: Yes, sir. And I also read in the testimony that the vehicle was set up wrong.

ME: Correct.

CAMPBELL: That it would not have. It does not work properly.

ME: It does not?

CAMPBELL: It only works in code 3 mode.

ME: Right.

CAMPBELL: Not the way it is supposed to, according to the agency's guidelines and policy.

ME: Right.

CAMPBELL: It also states in the policy that before one is to be issued a vehicle, the department will supply training for the in-car camera system with a vehicle that is equipped with it.

ME: So it is your testimony that you went to Sergeant Young and told him that the in-car camera system was not working? Correct?

CAMPBELL: Yes, sir.

ME: Sergeant Young's testimony is, he told you to get with Jack Dens for him to teach you how to use it, and also to get with IT to have it fixed, not once, but twice, prior to this. Had you done that, you would have known that the in-car camera system was not working correctly and how to activate it, but you did not, and you are a trainer. I am trying to reconcile, a guy with your extensive background in training and knowledge about how a lot of these things work and given the instruction by the sergeant to go to these people to have this done, and yet you delayed it for two months leading up to that?

CAMPBELL: I was turning in my vehicle to get it fixed. The evidence from the sheriff's department and pictures show that. So it was getting fixed. Even if I did turn it in before that night, we have spare cars out there with no camera systems. Also, you are telling me that there is ample amount of time on a shift to train somebody accordingly in the in-car camera system when we are short-staffed?

ME: You had the opportunity to go talk to Jack Dens about the computer report writing system?

CAMPBELL: He helped me do my reports sometimes while I was doing reports. You have to understand, I was off the road for seven years. I was immediately put back on the road because I was disliked by the chief. And that is a known fact because she stated that in front of Deputy Chief Trust when she called me two days later about my knee hurting.

ME: I am trying to understand what that has to do with—

CAMPBELL: I was thrown back on the road. I did not even have my own. I had to go scrounge equipment up in order to get back on the road.

ME: So you were given a car with a camera, but you did not try to—

CAMPBELL: I was not trained on it. And according to agency policy, the department will furnish the training before being issued that equipment, which the department failed to do that. The department knew I was going back on the road.

ME: If the department is the sergeant and the sergeant instructed you to get with Jack Dens to have the training done, then I do not see where you say the department failed to provide you the training when in fact the department did tell you to get trained and you did go to Jack Dens for other training. Did you just chose not to do the in-car camera system training?

CAMPBELL: Major, the policy states—and the policy is signed by the chief of police— that before one is to be issued a car with an in-car camera, the department will furnish the training. They had three weeks to furnish that training before I was put back on the road. The department failed to do that.

ME: You are an officer with over three thousand hours of training, and you know that part of your responsibility to be safe out on the street is to obtain the training necessary in order to make sure your safety is the best that it can be. Yet even though your supervisor told you and you know that you do not know how to operate it, you did not go get it done? You had Officer Dens, who could have shown you, on your squad, and you did not do it?

CAMPBELL: Major—

ME: It certainly does not take that long to learn how to operate the in-car camera system. There are multiple ways to turn it on. One of which would have included pushing a button and it would have come on. Right?

CAMPBELL: You are getting into a realm of possibilities.

ME: No, I am trying to understand why you did not do the training that you were...

CAMPBELL: I was turning in my vehicle...

ME: Instructed by your supervisor to do.

CAMPBELL: To get it fixed. If you are saying it's the safety issue about covering myself, well, I had just given the entire command staff minus Deputy Chief Trust, Deputy Chief King, and Chief Truth an overview of the benefits of the body-worn cameras. I instructed them as instructors. Those people were Director Liam Noit, Investigator Blake Adder, and Lieutenant Sabrina Powers, who were all on the chief's command staff. I was already properly trained on the body-worn cameras that we had plenty of but they chose to take off the street, and Investigator Adder had a copy of a policy that I had created for them.

ME: How many of those body-worn cameras were there?

CAMPBELL: I think around ten, according to my previous testimony.

ME: Okay. I have heard that number a couple of times, but only in conjunction with you, no one else. I have read it only one other place, and that would have been in the newspaper.

CAMPBELL: It is in the grand jury testimony, as well as my interview with the sheriff's office with five other detectives there.

ME: Again, each time associated with you. That number, 10, is associated with you each time I hear it.

CAMPBELL: Right.

ME: The only other time I have heard it was when I read it in the newspaper. Do you know Jenny Graham?

CAMPBELL: Yes, I know several reporters.

ME: Okay. Did you speak to her about these cameras sometime leading up to the grand jury or sometime before the presentment?

CAMPBELL: No, sir, I did not.

ME: So her having that number 10 is just by coincidence? Nobody else mentions that number—

CAMPBELL: I saw the news video with her. So also it came up where they found a camera in the trunk of Sergeant Brown's car.

ME: Yes.

CAMPBELL: I have been out on administrative leave.

ME: Okay.

CAMPBELL: That is number 1. And number 2, we have no access to the building.

ME: Right.

CAMPBELL: You all cut that off completely. So how would I know what is in the trunk of the sergeant's vehicle, which is here at the station?

ME: That is a different topic.

CAMPBELL: It is the same topic. You are asking about the body cameras.

ME: No, I am asking about the number 10 involving body-worn cameras and the SWAT locker.

CAMPBELL: Do you know how many people had access to that testimony?

ME: Okay.

CAMPBELL: No, I did not, and even if I did, I was given permission to speak to *The Washington Post* by PIO Ward Innocent that came from Chief Truth two weeks after the shooting, to discuss the shooting. So if I really wanted to give it to somebody, I would have given it to *The Washington Post* with a lot more bite...

ME: Okay.

CAMPBELL: And I would have also given them the aspects of "Hey, the command staff knew about the whole thing and they had a policy." But I was given specific orders not to speak of the department or to the news media, which I did not, because you all did not even have an idea about how bad I was injured. I was told directly by the state attorney not to speak to anyone about it.

ME: There was a rifle in your trunk?

CAMPBELL: Yes, sir.

ME: Why would you have a rifle in your trunk that is not for use on the police department...?

CAMPBELL: I was bringing it in to actually have Harley Action look at it, but I also wanted to try to bring it in. I bought it from the pawnshop in town. I was going to try to do it before work, but I did not have time. So that was why that rifle was in the vehicle. It is too big to be used on duty. It is a .308 caliber. I know better. So that was why there was no ammunition with it. I would never use something like that on duty.

ME: It just happened to be that night that you brought it in?

CAMPBELL: It was, yes.

ME: Is there anything you would like to ask, Counselor?

LUNA: At one point, Officer Campbell said something to the effect of "ample time" related to the traffic stop. Please express the amount of time that you had to make decisions during the traffic stop?

CAMPBELL: Everything happened within seconds, so there was really no ample time to do anything.

LUNA: Okay. So what you are saying is that your decisions were made under the stress of the moment?

CAMPBELL: Yes, ma'am.

LUNA: I believe, at some point, you said that you recall two shots while sitting, you attempted to stand, shot once more, and then collapsed.

CAMPBELL: Yes, ma'am.

LUNA: Is that correct?

CAMPBELL: That is about as close of a recollection that I have.

LUNA: With each shot you observed Brown?

CAMPBELL: Sergeant Brown.

LUNA: Sergeant Brown's head above the vehicle?

CAMPBELL: Yes, ma'am. Above the...in between the doorjamb on the passenger side of the vehicle and the roof.

LUNA: You ceased firing when you no longer saw his head?

CAMPBELL: Yes, ma'am.

LUNA: That is all I have.

I was mentally exhausted after the interview. Detective Direct and I had a conversation about it later. Detective Direct confided in me that it was a well-established rumor that I had been brought to the department to "get them." After laughing, I asked her if she believed that to be true. She told me that after all the interviews we had done together by this point, she knew the rumor was the furthest thing from the truth. I asked if, from her personal experience, it was common for Officer Campbell to avoid answering questions directly, and she shrugged, saying she believed he had stayed within the character of the person she had known for quite some time.

I believe the expression is "Like pulling hen's teeth" when it comes to having difficulty with any task. I believed that I had been lied to several times by Officer Campbell in his interview, but proving what I believed to be true would be difficult. When Detective Direct asked me how that might be accomplished, I reminded her that our job was simply to gather facts and present them to the senior staff to determine any violations. It was not to go after an officer to prove that he/she was wrong. If Officer Campbell's statements were the truth, we would find supporting facts to back up his version of events. Several months after the case was decided, I would learn from several of Officer Campbell's friends and senior officers who had known him their entire careers that his nickname was Liar, Liar.

CHAPTER 12

Follow-Up

Any good investigator knows that when questions arise during an investigation, following up with answers to those questions is necessary. Why? The simple answer is that it is the right thing to do, but the practical answer is that if you do not, then the reviewing authority is going to ask you to do so. Attempting to make sure your report is complete, with all questions answered, can be challenging because you are attempting to anticipate what will be asked. Some of the questions you believe are answered by materials supplied in the package may not be that obvious to a deputy chief or chief who is reviewing the investigation. Detective Direct and I pored over the interviews we had completed to that point and knew that we had to conduct another round of witness interviews. Following these, we needed to allow the subject officers an opportunity to review that information too and conduct a follow-up interview with the subject officers if they wished an opportunity to address any of the new information prior to wrapping up our investigation.

Mr. Ward Innocent was a former police officer in Miami, Florida, before moving into the realm of being a public information officer (nonsworn civilian). He had been hired by the department prior to my arrival and had been working with the Chief during the Samuel shooting. The following is a synopsis of my interview with Mr. Innocent:

ME: This interview is being conducted at the police department. I am conducting an interview with Mr. Ward Innocent, the department's public information officer. As a point of reference, this interview is regarding an administrative investigation ordered by the Chief of Police as a result of Officer Than Campbell and Sergeant Benjamin Brown's officer-involved shooting of a gentleman by the name of David Samuel. Mr. Innocent, your name came up in an interview with Officer Than Campbell. Officer Campbell was asked if he spoke to Jenny Graham about the department's body-worn cameras sometime leading up to the grand jury or sometime before the presentment. He ultimately answered with, and I quote, "No, I did not, and even if I did, I was given permission to speak to *The Washington Post* by PIO Innocent that came from the Chief two weeks after the shooting, to discuss the shooting. So if I really wanted to give it to somebody, I would have given it to *The Washington Post* with a lot more bite." Mr. Innocent, did you have a conversation with Officer Campbell postshooting in which you told him he had permission from the Chief to speak with *The Washington Post* in reference to the David Samuel shooting?

INNOCENT: No.

ME: Did you have any conversations with Officer Campbell after the shooting that you recall?

INNOCENT: No.

ME: Do you even know Officer Campbell to look at him?

INNOCENT: No.

ME: Did you and the Chief discuss the release of
information regarding the shooting to the
press without consulting the State Attorney's
Office or the Sheriff's Office?

INNOCENT: No.

ME: Is there anything you would like to say or
add to this investigation?

INNOCENT: No.

Sergeant Ethan Powers needed to be interviewed as a witness in
this case, and we called him in for that purpose. The following is a
synopsis of that interview:

ME: This interview is being conducted at the
police department. I am conducting an
interview with Sergeant Ethan Powers.
As a point of reference, this interview is
regarding an administrative investigation
ordered by the Chief of Police as a result
of Officer Than Campbell and Sergeant
Benjamin Brown's officer-involved shooting of a gentleman by the name of David
Samuel. Okay, also present is Detective
Felicia Direct with internal affairs. Sergeant
Powers, I am going to read to you a portion
of an interview from Officer Campbell that
I need some clarification on. I asked Officer
Campbell what training he had had that
taught him to reach into a running automobile to make a vehicle extraction. His
answer was, "We have done training here
with Sergeant Powers where he has taught
vehicle extractions, especially with sovereign
citizens." So, Sergeant Powers, do you recall
having taught any type of training involving
sovereign citizens and vehicle extractions?

POWERS: No.

ME: Can you tell me what you recall of any type of training you had with sovereign citizens?

POWERS: I have attended a few courses regarding sovereign citizens dating back a while. It had to do with legalities, currency, tags, driver's licenses, lawsuits, etc. that they try to confuse the officer with.

ME: Okay, did you bring what you learned back to the department and teach officers about sovereign citizens?

POWERS: I did. My best recollection is that I think it was during roll call. It was not a specific sit-down, three- or four-hour lecture.

ME: Did you do any sort of practical exercises?

POWERS: Verbal. When the individuals became combative, giving legal and constitutional jargon and explaining that they are free men and they have the right to travel upon the road.

ME: Okay. Did you ever have an occasion to do a vehicle extraction of a sovereign citizen?

POWERS: Yes, sir.

ME: How many times in your recollection have you done that?

POWERS: Twice.

ME: During those vehicle extractions, was it done with the vehicle running or off?

POWERS: Running.

ME: Okay, did you ever use those as examples during your training?

POWERS: Training, but not directed toward sovereign citizens. Training as traffic stops, high risk and low risk, and where I was questioned by students.

ME: And you used those examples that you just
   described as examples of how you did that?
POWERS: Yes, sir.

Sergeant Brown was invited into internal affairs to review the two additional interviews that were conducted, and he formally declined to be reinterviewed regarding the information contained within them. Officer Campbell was invited into internal affairs to review the two additional interviews, and after having done so, he immediately requested to be reinterviewed. I told him that was fine and asked if he would like to contact his attorney to arrange a date/time for that reinterview to occur. In the state of Florida, an officer may retract any perjury under oath within ten days of having perjured him- or herself. Officer Campbell appeared panic-stricken and told me that the attorney was not necessary as long as I agreed to stick to just the information in the two interviews. I agreed. Officer Campbell then contacted one of his union representatives (a police officer on the department), who sat in with us on the second interview, which was nine days after his initial interview.

ME: I am the major in charge of the Internal
   Affairs Bureau and the lead investigator
   for the police department's administrative
   review of the officer-involved shooting case
   involving Mr. David Samuel. Also present
   with me, representing the department's
   IAB, is Detective Felicia Direct. The interview we will be conducting is with Officer
   Than Campbell, at his request after having
   read two follow-up interviews. Is this correct, Officer Campbell?
CAMPBELL: Yes, sir.
ME: Okay. By contract you are entitled to a
   representative. You have elected to forego
   counsel for this interview. Is that correct?
CAMPBELL: Yes, sir.

ME: Okay. Also present is Detective Felicia Direct with the Internal Affairs Bureau, who will be participating in this interview. According to the Police Officer's Bill of Rights, only one interviewer is allowed to ask questions during the interview. Do you waive this right so that Detective Direct may ask questions?

CAMPBELL: No.

ME: The complainant in the case is the Chief of Police. You are the subject officer in this investigation, and the allegations are as follows: There are no specific allegations made against you. This is an administrative review that is required by policy due to your use of deadly force. Do you understand that this interview is part of an official proceeding per Florida state statute?

CAMPBELL: Yes.

ME: This is an administrative and not a criminal investigation. You have been given and have signed copies of the Police Officer's Bill of Rights, Garrity statement, and the perjury form. Do you understand your rights?

CAMPBELL: Yes.

ME: Do you have any questions concerning these forms?

CAMPBELL: No, I do not.

ME: You have been given an opportunity to review all evidence and interviews to date. Have you had sufficient time to review the evidence and interviews?

CAMPBELL: Yes, I have.

ME: Okay, raise your right hand. Do you swear or affirm that the statement you are about to give will be the truth, the whole truth, and nothing but the truth?

CAMPBELL: Yes, I do.

ME: Okay, this morning, Officer Campbell, I brought you in to go over additional interviews that were conducted as a result of some of the statements you made in your previous interview. I understand that there is something about that material you covered that you would like to inform me at this point in time.

CAMPBELL: Yes, I do. Our point of contact while we were out on administrative leave was Lieutenant Sabrina Powers, and the information that PIO Innocent said in his interview was incorrect. I request that Lieutenant Sabrina Powers be interviewed about that information that was given.

ME: Because she would have direct information regarding what you were told?

CAMPBELL: Yes.

ME: Okay. Are you telling me those communications were via email?

CAMPBELL: Yes, it was.

ME: Okay. After the shooting?

CAMPBELL: Yes.

The second interview was leading me down a rabbit hole, but it was necessary to prove or disprove Officer Campbell's new version of events. He was so confident in what he told me initially about how things had occurred with such detail, and now he was backtracking while covering his bases. There was no choice but to continue. The next logical step was to have Mrs. Bright Action research department emails for Lieutenant Sabrina Powers and then conduct an interview with Mrs. Action. The following is a synopsis of that interview:

ME: This interview is conducted at the police
department, and I am the major at the
police department in charge of the Internal
Affairs Bureau. I am the lead investigator in
the administrative investigation regarding
the shooting of Mr. David Samuel. I am
conducting an interview with Mrs. Bright
Action, the department's information technology manager. Mrs. Action, in regard
to the department's email system, after a
period, an individual's mailbox can become
full and we are forced to delete it, correct?

ACTION: Yes.

ME: Okay. When that occurs and, for instance, I
ask you to do a search for me for a certain
individual and certain time frame, does that
pull up those deleted emails even though
the individual deleted them or threw them
away?

ACTION: Yes, it does.

ME: So if an email existed during a set period,
there is no way a user could get rid of it so
that you could not get it back?

ACTION: No. There is no way. They could not
have gotten rid of it where I could not get
it back.

ME: I asked you to provide me all the emails from
Lieutenant Sabrina Powers to Officer Than
Campbell and Sergeant Benjamin Brown,
correct?

ACTION: Yes.

ME: Looking at this file, this is a complete record
of those emails?

ACTION: Yes.

There were very few emails between Lieutenant Sabrina Powers and Officer Than Campbell or Sergeant Benjamin Brown during the time the two officers were required to report to the lieutenant. Furthermore, there were no emails regarding Officer Campbell's speaking to the news media. The following is a synopsis of my interview With Lieutenant Sabrina Powers:

> ME: This interview is being conducted at the police department's Internal Affairs Bureau. I am conducting an interview with Lieutenant Sabrina Powers. As a point of reference, this interview is regarding an administrative investigation ordered by the Chief of Police as a result of Officer Than Campbell and Sergeant Benjamin Brown's officer-involved shooting of a gentleman by the name of David Samuel. Your name came up during an interview with Officer Campbell. Officer Campbell was asked about body-worn cameras that had been mentioned in the news media and the number 10. He was asked if he had provided any kind of information to the news media prior to the grand jury presentment, and his response was, and I quote, "No, I did not, and even if I did, I was given permission to speak to *The Washington Post* by PIO Innocent that came from the Chief two weeks after the shooting, to discuss the shooting. So if I really wanted to give it to somebody, I would have given it to *The Washington Post* with a lot more bite." When I interviewed Mr. Innocent, he said he did not give permission from the Chief for Officer Campbell to speak with *The Washington Post* in reference to the shoot-

ing. After Officer Campbell had a chance to review both his statement and the statement of Mr. Innocent, he then referred me to you, Lieutenant. Did you, in fact, provide Officer Campbell with permission to speak to *The Washington Post*?

POWERS: I do not know about permission, but I received an email from Ward Innocent, the PIO, letting me know that some media outlet requested to speak to the two officers involved. I cannot remember if it was *The Washington Post*. I took that request via email and spoke to the Chief. To the best of my recollection, her response was, "Tell them they can talk to them if they want to." I think I forwarded the email to them. I do not remember if I forwarded an email or called them and said, "Hey, these people want to talk to you."

ME: Okay.

Again, I checked with Mrs. Bright, and no such email existed. Lieutenant Powers had been moved to the midnight shift, her husband was under active internal affairs investigation, she had been friends in the past with Officer Campbell, and she announced her plans to retire shortly after our interview. The deputy chiefs and Chief would have to decide whether or not to initiate a formal investigation into Lieutenant Powers's veracity under oath. As far as I was concerned, regarding this portion of my investigation, I had reached a dead end at this point. Both Sergeant Brown and Officer Campbell reviewed these latest interviews, and both of them declined to be reinterviewed. It was time to write my synopsis of the investigation and turn it over to Chief Truth.

CHAPTER

13

Investigative Summary

A best practice in any internal affairs investigation in the state of Florida is including an investigator's acknowledgment affidavit. The affidavit should include the following verbiage:

> I, the undersigned, hereby verify that I have no personal knowledge of the facts relating to the foregoing investigation except as expressly indicated in the report. To the extent to which I have personal knowledge, the contents of the report are true and accurate based upon my personal knowledge, information, and belief.
>
> I, the undersigned, do hereby swear, under penalty of perjury, that, to the best of my knowledge, information, and belief, I have not knowingly or willfully deprived, or allowed another to deprive, the subject of the investigation of any of the rights contained in Florida state statutes 112.532 and 112.533.

Prior to my arrival at this department, their internal affairs investigations lacked this simple but time-tested requirement. It is my understanding of the history of this statement's inclusion that it was to prevent the exact kind of "headhunting" of officers I had been told had gone on in this agency's past. For practical purposes, what it meant for internal affairs investigators was that if any part of that attestation (or the investigation) was proven false, the internal affairs investigator could be charged with a violation of the state statute, which would be a crime and a violation that could include revocation of the investigator's law enforcement certification.

My experience has been that, normally, summaries are two to three pages long, except in intricate cases. This was one of those exceptions. The following is my summary that was turned over to Chief Truth with the entire investigative package:

Investigator's Summary

Officer Than Campbell conducted a traffic stop on a vehicle that he observed speeding in the area. According to Officer Campbell, after he had paced the suspect vehicle at forty-five miles per hour (mph) in a twenty-five-mile-per-hour zone, the suspect vehicle initially and intentionally failed to yield to his overhead lights and "chirped" siren. The suspect vehicle then made a sharp right-hand turn to go southbound, and Officer Campbell followed. While Officer Campbell denied he was in pursuit during his Internal Affairs Bureau (IAB) interview, he noted, "Okay, a supervisor would have called it off on the radio."

The driver of the vehicle, Mr. David Samuel, eventually came to a stop. Officer Campbell parked his patrol vehicle "within a foot" of the suspect vehicle's rear bumper in order to quickly get to the driver's door because he feared the suspect intended to flee on foot. Upon reaching the driver's door, Officer Campbell was confronted with initial verbal resistance when asking Mr. Samuel for his license, registration, and insur-

ance. At some point, Officer Campbell received
Mr. Samuel's driver's license and noticed what he
perceived to be "marijuana shake" on the driver's
"instrument cluster." Officer Campbell did not
request backup for the traffic stop at any point.

On his own accord, Sergeant Benjamin
Brown drove normally (no lights or siren) to
Officer Campbell's traffic stop as a backup officer, approaching the traffic stop from the south.
He opted to park his patrol vehicle on the opposite side of the road, across from the traffic stop,
with his rear bumper "about midway" parallel
with Officer Campbell's vehicle. Sergeant Brown
admits there was no reason to hurry to Officer
Campbell's aid at this point, and he said he "felt
safe" parking in that fashion.

Sergeant Brown initially told the Sheriff's
Department detectives, the State Attorney's
Office (SAO) investigators, and the Assistant
State Attorney (ASA) that to get to the passenger side of Mr. Samuel's vehicle, he walked in
between Officer Campbell's vehicle and Mr.
Samuel's vehicle, which he remembered at that
time were "ten to twenty feet apart." When provided with Officer Campbell's testimony, and
considering the officer safety aspect of walking
between the two cars, Sergeant Brown conceded
it was more likely that he walked around the back
of Officer Campbell's vehicle, thus clearing up
that discrepancy.

As Sergeant Brown was exiting his car
and approaching Mr. Samuel's vehicle, Officer
Campbell began to announce aloud that he
observed marijuana and that Mr. Samuel needed
to step out of his vehicle. Officer Campbell said
this was done to alert Sergeant Brown of the

impending arrest, and Sergeant Brown acknowledges having heard several announcements of this sort from the time he exited his car until he approached Mr. Samuel's front passenger door. Mr. Samuel's car was still running in "park."

Sergeant Brown cannot pinpoint any training he had in the past dealing with vehicle extractions; however, Officer Campbell stated Sergeant Ethan Powers gave training on the subject during which the suspect vehicle was running. Sergeant Powers acknowledges that he has twice removed individuals from an automobile while it was running and that he might have used those experiences as examples in answering questions during vehicle extraction roll call training. He stated that there was no formal "sit-down" classroom training or practical exercise training conducted by him. Since this was informal roll call training, there were no training records to confirm or dispute that this training took place or who might have been present.

When Officer Campbell was questioned if he authored a training lesson plan regarding vehicle extractions, he acknowledged that he had. When asked why he did not redirect Sergeant Brown to his side of the car to assist with the vehicle extraction, as his training material called for, he offered two responses. One was that the sergeant was a superior officer, and the other was, "Because we were not dealt that hand of cards that night."

Sergeant Brown positioned himself on the passenger side of Mr. Samuel's car and had heard Officer Campbell telling Mr. Samuel that there was visible marijuana inside the car. Sergeant Brown also admits to having heard Officer

Campbell tell Mr. Samuel to exit the vehicle for a potential, impending arrest. Sergeant Brown entered Mr. Samuel's car from the passenger side by opening the passenger door and putting his head into the vehicle while the car was in "park," with the engine running. The sergeant reasoned that he chose to do this in order to defuse the situation.

At some point during the traffic stop, Mr. Samuel put the running vehicle into gear and began to drive. Sergeant Brown stated he "jumped" into the moving vehicle, planting both feet onto the floorboard while his head remained above the top of the car. Sergeant Brown said he almost instantaneously slid into the passenger seat. Within one to two seconds, he heard gunshots that he perceived were being fired by Mr. Samuel. Sergeant Brown was adamant that he was inside of the car and not outside of it when the shots were fired. He stated he could not fathom Officer Campbell firing shots at the car with him inside of it.

Detective George Williams began responding to the traffic stop because he believed Officer Campbell might need a backup, given the area of town and something that the dispatcher said making him believe the car was not initially stopping. Detective Williams responded in a normal driving fashion and never activated his lights or siren. As he approached the scene, Detective Williams observed Mr. Samuel's car pulling away at a rapid speed southbound and Officer Campbell standing "in the middle of the road," firing three shots at Mr. Samuel's car as it traveled away from them. Detective Williams then saw Officer Campbell collapse in the street. Detective Williams told the Sheriff's Department detectives, the SAO investigators, and the ASA during two interviews and reiterated in his IAB interview that Sergeant Brown was upset upon having learned Officer Campbell shot at Mr. Samuel's vehicle with the sergeant in it.

Sergeant Brown characterized his feeling in his IAB interview as being "displeased" with Officer Campbell shooting at the vehicle while he was inside of it. When asked, he agreed that it was an "inherently dangerous" thing for Officer Campbell to do. Officer Campbell claims it was legally sufficient and necessary based upon the circumstances. When asked multiple times in multiple different ways, Officer Campbell was steadfast that regardless of the outcome from the traffic stop that night, if he were faced with the exact same circumstances and facts, he would do the exact same thing again. Sergeant Brown felt differently, saying it was possible to learn from mistakes and there were other options he might try if confronted with a similar situation again.

Officer Campbell said that he was on the ground, firing shots at Mr. Samuel's vehicle after it ran him over, despite Sergeant Brown's and Detective Williams's testimony to the contrary. At one point, it seemed as if Officer Campbell acknowledged he might not know for sure if he was standing the entire time or if Sergeant Brown's head was outside of the vehicle the entire time he was firing at the car. His counselor cleared this up during her permitted follow-up questioning at the end of the IAB interview, saying that Officer Campbell was positive the sergeant's head was above the car during each of the shots he took at Mr. Samuel's car.

Officer Campbell stated during his SAO / Sheriff's Department interview that he had informed "them" that his in-car camera system was not working properly prior to the shooting. When asked to explain in his IAB interview who "them" was, Officer Campbell explained that it was his immediate supervisor during inspections, Sergeant Buck Young. Sergeant Young said during his IAB interview that he had told Officer Campbell, not once, but twice, to go get his camera fixed by getting with Mrs. Bright Action from the information technology unit and to get with Officer Jack Dens to be trained on how to operate the in-car camera system. Officer Dens said in his IAB interview that he did not recall having been asked by either Sergeant Young or Officer Campbell to help Officer Campbell with the in-car camera system. Officer Dens did recall Officer Campbell requesting help with the computer and department paperwork, which he accommodated.

When asked to explain why he failed to obtain the training his supervisor ordered him to do, Officer Campbell claimed he did not remember that order. He stated that his vehicle was scheduled for repair, and generally avoided answering by blaming the department and others within the department for their perceived shortcomings in his eyes.

When asked if he recognized an email from Lieutenant Drake Smoke regarding body-worn cameras, Sergeant Brown looked it over and admitted to remembering the email. When asked what the email instructed him to do with the special weapons and tactics (SWAT) team's body-worn cameras, the sergeant responded, "Collect the body cameras and place them in the SWAT locker."

When asked why he would have one of those body-worn cameras in the trunk of his car on the night of the shooting, the sergeant responded that the order was written to not use them for training or operational purposes. Sergeant Brown stated that he used them for demo purposes; therefore, he did not violate the order. Both Deputy Chief Wily Trust and Lieutenant Smoke said that their intention was that the cameras be locked away, so there would not be a legitimate reason for the sergeant to have one in his possession.

When asked how many body-worn cameras had been locked up in the SWAT locker, Officer Campbell said he believed it was "ten." When told that each time the number 10 arose in this investigation concerning the body-worn cameras, it was always associated with him or one news reporter, Officer Campbell responded by claiming many of the investigators had access to his interview. As a way of further denying his involvement in releasing information to the media during an active investigation, Officer Campbell said, "No, I did not, and even if I did, I was given permission to speak to *The Washington Post* by PIO Ward Innocent that came from the Chief two weeks after the shooting, to discuss the shooting. So if I really wanted to give it to somebody, I would have given it to *The Washington Post* with a lot more bite."

The department's public information officer (PIO), Mr. Ward Innocent, was interviewed, and he denied having told Officer Campbell he could speak to any of the media regarding the David Samuel shooting. Mr. Innocent said he would not even know Officer Campbell if he saw him and he and the Chief would have never released anything to the media relative to the Samuel shooting without having discussed it with the SAO or the Sheriff's Department first.

When Officer Campbell reviewed Mr. Innocent's statement, he immediately requested a second interview without counsel present to clarify a statement he had made during his initial interview. He requested that I speak to Lieutenant Sabrina Powers because his communication with the department during the time he was on administrative leave was through her via email.

I interviewed Lieutenant Powers, and she recalled receiving an email from Mr. Ward Innocent regarding a news outlet wishing to speak with the officers involved in the shooting. Lieutenant Powers recalled that she spoke to the Chief regarding the email, and she told her, "Tell them they can talk to them if they want to." Lieutenant Powers said she either emailed or telephoned Officer Campbell and Sergeant Brown in reference to the Chief's response, but she believed she had emailed it.

I had Mrs. Bright Action, the systems administrator of the department's information technology unit, conduct a search on emails between Officer Campbell and/or Sergeant Brown and Lieutenant Powers during the month following the shooting. There are none on the topic. I also had Ms. Action conduct a search on emails between Lieutenant Powers and Mr. Innocent during that same time frame. There are none on the topic. Finally, I interviewed Mrs. Action to ascertain if it was possible to delete emails so that she could not retrieve them, and Mrs. Action informed me that it was impossible for a user to be able to make emails unable to be retrieved by her.

Officer Harley Action was interviewed as the department's armorer and was shown a picture of a rifle found in Officer Campbell's trunk during the Sheriff's Department inventory search of his car postshooting. Officer Action said that the pictured rifle "would not be authorized to be carried." When asked about the high-powered rifle that was photographed as being in the trunk of Officer Campbell's assigned patrol car on the night of the shooting, Officer Campbell acknowledged that it was not a departmentally sanctioned firearm. Officer Campbell said that he "knew better" and did not even have ammunition for the gun. Officer Campbell stated that the firearm was just brought in that night because he wanted to show it to Officer Action on his personal time but did not have the opportunity to do so.

Chief Truth handed the package over to Deputy Chief King at our next staff meeting. Deputy Chief King was less than thrilled with the prospect of the review and the responsibility of reaching conclusions regarding this important case. He told me that he would be calling me often to help him navigate through the morass of paperwork in the file.

CHAPTER 14

Deputy Chief Alex King

Deputy Chief Alex King was an imposing figure. He had to cut the seams of his sleeves under his arms to get his uniform shirts on. The man was not fat. With all that muscle, many people would guess that there were not a lot of brains in the man's equally large cranium, but that would be a mistake. He was extremely thoughtful and thorough, which meant that I should not have been surprised when he called me, telling me he had several questions he wanted answered that I had somehow missed. One of them involved the use of hinged handcuffs, which I did not know the history behind prior to my arrival at the department. The other involved orders given to Officer Campbell involving those hinged handcuffs, which Deputy Chief King had seen a picture of in the Sheriff's Department investigative files following the shooting.

The proper procedure involved Deputy Chief King returning the entire package to the Chief of Police, who in turn would return it to me for updating. Based upon the deputy chief's recollection of the approximate dates, I was able to obtain the following emails from Mrs. Bright Action that supported Deputy Chief King's recollection:

From: Liam Noit
Sent: January (year of the shooting)
To: All Department Supervisors
Subject: Hinged Handcuffs

Good morning!

Please inspect the handcuffs of all officers assigned to you. They should all have chain handcuffs. If any are in possession of hinged handcuffs, they should be collected and returned to Special Investigator Blake Adder. Our policy is being modified to reflect that hinged handcuffs will not be authorized for use at our department.

Please contact Investigator Adder or me should you have any questions or officers are in need of chain handcuffs. As always, thank you for your cooperation in this matter.

Director Liam Noit
Training Specialist and Public
Information Officer

*****

From: Than Campbell
Sent: January (after above email)
To: All Department Supervisors
Subject: Hinged Handcuffs

Please collect all hinged handcuffs and turn into either Director Noit or Special Investigator Blake Adder.

Thank you for your assistance in this matter.

Officer Than Campbell

*****

From: Liam Noit
Sent: January (third relative email on topic)
To: Than Campbell; All Department Supervisors
Subject: RE: Hinged Handcuffs

Than, I know you will be gone as of next week. However, instead of putting this back on me (I will be gone also for two weeks starting Monday), please collect these handcuffs yourself. Today is one rotation, tomorrow another rotation, so we should have them all collected before we leave.

Supervisors: Please collect the handcuffs and document on your rosters that they have been returned. Then make arrangements for Than to take custody of them. Thank you.

I was also able to obtain a copy of the recommendation by Liam Noit to Chief Truth regarding changing handcuffs used by the department. The date on the memorandum was prior to the officer-involved shooting that was the subject of the investigation and prior to Liam Noit's employment by the department. The following is a synopsis of that memorandum:

DEPARTMENTAL MEMORANDUM

To: Chief Rosa Truth
Attention: Deputy Chief Alex King

Ma'am:

The following is an overview and assessment of the current handcuffs issued and utilized by your department.

As you are aware, the department currently issues and allows its officers to use hinged handcuffs. A hinged handcuff has the individual cuffs attached by a hinge joint rather than a chain. This hinge causes the handcuff to be very inflexible and very uncomfortable to wear. This lack of flexibility causes the application of the cuffs to be very difficult and usually causes pain and discomfort during a standard speed-cuffing technique.

The handcuffs are one of the most used tool an officer has at his/her discretion. It is common practice to tell a subject if he/she cooperates with apprehension that he/she will not be harmed, thus encouraging a subject to cooperate as he/she does not wish to be uncomfortable and/or in pain. In most cases, the hinged handcuffs continue to cause pain and discomfort for even cooperative, noncombative subjects. I have personally felt this pain and discomfort as an officer trainer in training scenarios that required myself and other trainers to be handcuffed with hinged cuffs as a part of scenario training.

Therefore, it is our proposal as subject matter experts that the handcuffs issued be changed to chain handcuffs. Upon issuance, the officers will be shown proper speed-cuffing. As they currently have no consistent way of cuffing, this will not cause any issues with retention and application of these techniques.

This change will provide better control of application for your officers and a more humane way of dealing with handcuffed subjects by members of your department.

Respectfully,
Liam Noit
Master Instructor

The department keeps copies of all memorandums that are circulated with the effect of an order. The date on the memorandum was prior to the officer-involved shooting that was the subject of the investigation and after Director Liam Noit's employment with the department. The following was in the department's files regarding this topic:

DEPARTMENTAL MEMORANDUM

To: Chief Rosa Truth
Attention: Deputy Chief Wily Trust
From: Director Liam Noit
Subject: Handcuffing

This memorandum is being authored in response to Officer Campbell's last letter addressing the issuance of chain handcuffs. As you recall, my previous memorandum on this topic recommended the replacement of the hinged handcuffs that were issued by the department, and Officer Campbell has authored a contrary opinion.

Officer Campbell's letter addresses the fact that he was told that the department was carrying the "wrong" handcuffs. As a defensive tactics instructor for twenty-five years and as one of the architects of the current defensive tactics curriculum for the state of Florida, I do feel that hinged handcuffs are the wrong handcuffs for an agency to carry.

As outlined in Officer Campbell's letter, his research has led him to the same conclusion that the selection of the handcuffs "are up to the department." With that said, the department has chosen the chain-style handcuff for issuance to our department personnel. It should be noted that while Officer Campbell was assigned to the

training unit and part of the process of the issuance of the chain handcuff, he never brought his
concerns to my attention.

I do not believe the "chain" handcuff is a
safety issue, as Officer Campbell alleges. I believe
handcuffs are a temporary restraint device and
all handcuffs can be manipulated. The focus
should be on officers properly monitoring subject's attempts at manipulating any type of handcuff. With that said and staying with the current department philosophy of considering the
officers and community affected by these types
of decisions, the decision to utilize the chain-
style handcuffs was made, with both the officer
safety and subject being restrained taken into
consideration.

Therefore, our agency is in the process of
changing the handcuffing policy to prohibit the
use of hinged handcuffs. So at this time, Officer
Campbell's request to carry hinged handcuffs is
respectfully denied.

Respectfully,
Director Liam Noit

The next step required me to go interview Liam Noit (former
sergeant at my old agency) and his partner in the review of the department's hinged handcuffs (former captain Charlie Hernandez at my
old agency). I had known Sergeant Noit when we worked together
at my first agency, and he was one of the most experienced tactical
instructors I have ever known. He had worked on the state's curriculum in devising appropriate defensive tactics techniques, and he
was an experienced SWAT operator. I obtained a copy of his résumé
for inclusion in the investigative file. He is now working at another
police agency in our previous department's city, and the following is
a synopsis of that interview:

ME: This interview is being conducted in another city at a police agency where Sergeant Liam Noit is now employed. Sarge, I would like to take you back to when you were working for Chief Truth at her department in a civilian position. What was your title?

NOIT: I was working as the director of administration and the public information officer.

ME: Okay, and you had several employees that worked for you?

NOIT: Yes, sir. I was responsible for the technology unit, the training unit, and personnel, primarily.

ME: Okay, did you have Officer Campbell or Sergeant Brown working for you during that time?

NOIT: I had Officer Campbell working for me as a training officer when I first got there, and Benjamin Brown was one of the sergeants on the SWAT team and I was in the process of reconditioning and putting them back. I worked in the capacity as a SWAT adviser, so Brown would have also technically reported to me on SWAT. Yes, sir.

ME: At some point you had an issue with the handcuffs that the department was carrying. Can you tell me what the issue was?

NOIT: Yes, sir. Before I was actually employed with the department, I conducted some training with Captain Charlie Hernandez specifically for subject control and utilizing handcuffs. What I found was that Chief Truth's department was using hinged handcuffs, which is something that, in my experience, is very uncomfortable for the subjects that wear them. It is actually hard to train with the handcuffs, and they are just not as effective as the chain handcuffs. After I spoke with the administration at the department, which was the Chief and the deputy chiefs, they agreed that the department would change and would issue all their officers the chain handcuffs. Once I was employed with the department, we provided training to all the department's police officers in the use of the chain handcuffs.

ME: So you have some documents with you that you would like to share with me?

NOIT: Yes, sir. I have two documents for you. The first one I have is the memorandum to Chief Rosa Truth, attention to Deputy Chief Alex King. This talks about the recommendation to change from hinged to chain handcuffs. Along with that, I have an Excel spreadsheet that has the chain handcuff issuance and training roster that identifies each officer, the serial number of the handcuffs they were issued, their ID number, and the actual date that they received the training or were issued the actual handcuffs.

ME: Is Sergeant Brown's name on the training roster?

NOIT: Yes, sir. Right here at the bottom of this page.

ME: How about Officer Campbell?

NOIT: Officer Campbell is not.

ME: And why would Officer Campbell's name not be on here?

NOIT: Officer Campbell was the training officer at that time, and so he would have helped put that Excel spreadsheet together on the issuance of the equipment. Why he would have left his name off the list, I am not sure. I know for a fact we had several discussions as he worked for me that he did not think we should change from the hinged handcuffs. He actually authored a letter to Deputy Chief Wily Trust saying that he did not want to switch from the hinged handcuffs. I wrote a response letter explaining to Deputy Chief Trust that I listened to what his grievance was and, in essence, said we still needed to go with the chain-style handcuffs, and at the bottom I actually have a statement that says, "Therefore, our agency is in the process of changing the handcuffing policy to prohibit the use of hinged handcuffs, so at this time, Officer Campbell's request to carry hinged handcuffs is respectfully denied." Even after all the training we had done, the gist of Officer Campbell's letter was, he wanted to still carry the hinged handcuffs, and as his supervisor and the director of training at that time, I told him we were not going to allow him to carry those handcuffs.

ME: Okay, so you had plenty of the chain handcuffs that he would have been issued a pair?

NOIT: Yes, sir.

ME: Okay.

NOIT: Absolutely.

ME: So it was not a matter of supply, did not have enough?

NOIT: No, sir.

ME: In your mind, he was clear that he was supposed to carry them?

NOIT: Yes, sir.

ME: Okay.

Me: Would you please read into the record this email and tell me if you recognize it?

Noit: I do. Investigator Adder and I were responsible for the issuance of the handcuffs, and I sent this in January to all the supervisors for the department, with the subject being "Hinged Handcuffs." It says, "Good morning! Please inspect the handcuffs of all officers assigned to you. They should all have chain handcuffs. If any are in possession of hinged handcuffs, they should be collected and returned to Special Investigator Adder. Our policy is being modified to reflect that the hinged handcuffs will not be authorized for use at our department. Please contact Investigator Adder or me should you have any questions or officers are in need of chain handcuffs. As always, thank you for your cooperation in this matter." And it was signed by me.

Me: And was that the same date when Officer Campbell put his letter up the chain?

Noit: That is correct, sir.

Me: All right, and there is another one from you—that would have been in January—in a response to an email Officer Campbell wrote.

Noit: Yeah. I had directed Officer Campbell to collect the hinged handcuffs that were still out there, and what he had done was, he responded by pretty much putting it back on myself and Investigator Adder, which I found to be unacceptable, so I sent him this email. It was from me in January to Than Campbell and all the supervisors for the department, with subject being "Re:

Hinged Handcuffs." "Than, I know you will be gone as of the next two weeks." As of next week, he was getting transferred back to patrol. "However, instead of putting this back on me"—I was also going to be gone, I was going on vacation—"please collect these handcuffs yourself. Today is one rotation, tomorrow another rotation. We should have them all collected before we leave." Then I continued the email, to the supervisors. "Please collect the handcuffs and document on your roster that they have been returned. Then make arrangements for Than to take custody of them."

ME: Okay, so you had training with the new chain handcuffs. You showed people how to use them. You went through exercises with them, and you gave them the new pair and had them turn in the old hinged cuffs at that time?

NOIT: Yes, sir.

ME: But then you also found the need to have a supervisor go back and check because, what, people had backups or…?

NOIT: Correct, they had backup hinged handcuffs. There was an issue…yes, sir, there were some people still in possession of the hinged handcuffs as a second pair, and so when word got back to me, that was why I had the supervisors go back and inspect again, to make sure that that was all taken care of.

ME: Okay, and so by the time you left the department, it was your belief that all the hinged handcuffs had been removed from the department's inventory.

NOIT: That is correct, sir.

ME: Okay, and that was an order not only issued by you but also from staff, from the Chief of Police herself?

NOIT: That is correct, sir.

ME: Okay. I want to deviate to another topic. Had you left the department prior to the officer-involved shooting of Mr. David Samuel?

NOIT: Yes, sir. About one or two months before.

ME: Officer Campbell fired at a vehicle as it was fleeing, and his reasoning was to help protect the life of his sergeant, who he perceived to have been in the car or be dragged by the car, and his testimony was that he could see his sergeant's head above the roof of the car as the sergeant was hanging on. He fired three shots after having been run over by the front door of this car. Would you take a look at these pictures that show the shot placement in Mr. Samuel's vehicle?

NOIT: Yes, sir.

ME: Now, you have been a SWAT operator for how long?

NOIT: Twenty-one years, sir.

ME: And you have done all sorts of specialized training. Are you a sniper?

NOIT: Yes, sir. I am not a certified sniper, but I do sniper training, yes, sir.

ME: Okay. Do you guys train to shoot like that?

NOIT: No, sir. Barring any other facts here, if there was a possible backstop issue, which is what I would call it, with another police officer in the proximity to the friendly fire in the same direction, especially where these shots are grouped…it seems like it would be something that would put that officer, the secondary officer, in jeopardy.

ME: So to try to save the officer's life by firing at a car that he is in would not be a prudent thing to do?

NOIT: No, sir, I do not think it would be prudent or appropriate.

While I was in that city where I used to work, I needed to interview a captain that I had known when we worked together at my previous agency. His name was Charlie Hernandez, and he was another highly respected and experienced tactical trainer. I obtained a copy of his résumé for inclusion in the investigative file. The following is a synopsis of our interview:

ME: This interview is being conducted at my old agency in another city where I used to work. I am the major with my new department, in charge of the Internal Affairs Bureau, and I am conducting an interview with Captain Charlie Hernandez of my old department. Captain, the reason I have come to talk to you today is that you helped Sergeant Liam Noit, who had been asked by Chief Truth of my current department to conduct a review of their hinged handcuffs, correct?

HERNANDEZ: Chief Truth had asked us to do an initial assessment of their current civilian interactions. We had been trainers at our agency for many years, so Chief Truth wanted to have an overall look at how the officers were performing some basic things, such as, you know, stance and body movement, handcuffing, and overall how they were addressing citizens daily.

ME: What was one of the first things you noticed about their handcuffs?

HERNANDEZ: One of the first drills we did was to just get a view of how people approach subjects that they intend on taking into custody.

ME: Okay.

HERNANDEZ: One of the very first drills before any instruction is, we set up a role play of an officer and a subject that they intend on arresting. We say that they have a warrant, and we just say, "Go ahead and arrest him," the actor. "Put him under arrest and do whatever you would do. The person is going to be compliant, go ahead and arrest them." So we set up a very simple drill. They are about ten feet apart, and we just observe, looking for how they approach the subject, the type of verbal direction they give to the subject, and how they go about handcuffing them. That gives you a good overall view of their officer safety practices, the verbiage that they use, whether somebody is saying something appropriate or inappropriate, etc. It is a very simple drill, but it allows you to see many things if you are paying attention. One of the first things that I did see that I immediately told Liam Noit of was that one of the officers had hinged cuffs, and then another, and another, so I thought, you know, several of the officers had hinged cuffs, so I knew that was going to be an issue right away.

ME: And when you say it is going to be an issue, can you please explain to me what issue you see when you see hinged cuffs?

HERNANDEZ: Well, I had been a defensive tactics instructor for thirteen years to that point, and in my experience as not only a lead defensive tactics instructor but also as a role player, I have worked with hinged handcuffs before, just in a training scenario, to see how they worked. In the past, what we have discovered is that they are very inflexible and they put a lot of strain on shoulders and wrists. They have no flexibility, and they are just attached by a hinge so that, through our own personal experience as well as teaching experience, these are very generally discouraged among those who teach handcuffing and defensive tactics. In my opinion, I would not have them used, because it just puts undue pressure and pain on even a compliant subject. So imagine some of the people that do on occasion resist us, even if not violently. Applying those handcuffs is going to be very, very painful.

ME: Did you share your observations with Chief Truth?

HERNANDEZ: Yes. It was one of the first things we spoke about.

ME: And what was her reaction?

HERNANDEZ: She asked both of us to put together a letter of recommendation and explain why we felt the way we did, which Liam Noit did.

ME: Were you there when the department transitioned over to the new handcuffs?

HERNANDEZ: Yes, sir, I was.

ME: Okay, so you helped with the training on that day?

HERNANDEZ: Yes, sir.

ME: The department's lead training officer at that time was Than Campbell. He would have been out there, helping, as well?

HERNANDEZ: Yes.

ME: Okay, was everybody that attended the training issued the chain handcuffs?

HERNANDEZ: Yes.

ME: Was it your understanding that the directive was for all the hinged cuffs to come off the street?

HERNANDEZ: Yes.

ME: Okay, were there any exceptions to that rule that you saw?

HERNANDEZ: Not that I saw, no.

ME: Okay, at your current agency, you have been on the SWAT team, correct?

HERNANDEZ: Yes, sir.

ME: What roles have you been assigned on SWAT?

HERNANDEZ: I became a member of the team, and shortly thereafter, I became one of the department's lead defensive tactics instructors for the team, as well as the administrative officer, scheduling training days, making sure we had all the necessary equipment that we needed and ranges for us to do that.

ME: One of the things the team does is practice a lot, right?

HERNANDEZ: Tremendous amount of practices.

ME: And the practices often involve scenarios?

HERNANDEZ: Yes.

ME: Okay, have you ever seen a scenario where an officer gets run over by a car and tries to shoot the driver of the other automobile with another officer in the car?

HERNANDEZ: No, sir.

ME: I just handed you a picture that shows the shots that were fired at Mr. Samuel's automobile from behind, and there are three shots. One on the driver's side and two on the passenger side. Understanding that Officer Campbell said that he could see the sergeant's head above the roof of the car as he was hanging on the front passenger side and his shots were to help save the sergeant...looking at that picture and that shot grouping, what is your impression?

HERNANDEZ: Well, it would appear that the shots came from behind the car, so the person who was shot at...this was Officer Campbell shooting at the threat of the car to them or somebody else? The only time you can use deadly force is when there is an imminent threat of death or great bodily harm to you as an officer or to another person. So if the thought was, "I'm going to," what was the target I would have to know?

ME: The driver, Mr. Samuel.

HERNANDEZ: You know, if the target was the driver, these shots are definitely, you know, nowhere near that, and actually, they would put the other officer in danger, the sergeant in danger.

ME: As a tactical expert, you would say?

HERNANDEZ: It would be very discouraged, actually. That is not an effective way to neutralize the threat, if the threat is the driver and that he is going to cause harm to the other person that is on the car or in the car. That is actually putting the second officer in more danger, to actually take that shot.

ME: Because?

HERNANDEZ: If the goal…the goal of any use of
force is to neutralize the threat or stop the
threat. That is not the target if the target
is the other driver. Now, he is operating a
roughly 3,500-pound vehicle with an officer on the other side of that. That is not the
best way to go about it.

ME: Okay, so it's an inherently dangerous thing
to do to try to shoot the driver to save the
sergeant?

HERNANDEZ: Absolutely.

ME: What if you were the sergeant in that car?

HERNANDEZ: I would be… I would have some
words with the officer, because what he is
shooting at is directly where I am at. If that
is what you are telling me happened, that
the sergeant was on the passenger side of the
vehicle. I am in harm's way. I am in his line
of fire.

The road trip to my old city was fruitful in that it answered
the questions that Deputy Chief King had asked. Now I had to call
Sergeant Brown and Officer Campbell back in to review the new
interviews prior to handing the package back over to Chief Truth
for Deputy Chief King's final review. As I expected, Sergeant Brown
reviewed both interviews and the additional materials that were collected, then declined a reinterview. Officer Campbell reviewed them
and wanted to make another statement without his attorney present
but with the presence of a union representative (a fellow officer). We
agreed again to stay focused on the subject of the latest interviews.
The following is a synopsis of that interview:

ME: I am the major in charge of Internal Affairs
Bureau and the lead investigator for the
police department's administrative review
of the officer-involved shooting case involv-

ing Mr. David Samuel. Also present with me, representing the department's IAB, is Detective Felicia Direct. The interview we will be conducting is with Officer Than Campbell at his request after having read two follow-up interviews and reviewing some additional material collected in this case. Is this correct, Officer Campbell?

CAMPBELL: Yes.

ME: Okay. By contract you are entitled to a representative. You have elected to forego counsel for this interview and utilize a union representative. Is that correct?

CAMPBELL: Yes, sir.

ME: Okay. Also present is Detective Felicia Direct with the Internal Affairs Bureau, who will be participating in this interview. According to the Police Officer's Bill of Rights, only one interviewer is allowed to ask questions during the interview. Do you waive this right so that Detective Direct may ask questions?

CAMPBELL: She cannot ask questions.

ME: Prior to this interview, there are several items that you must be advised of. The complainant in this case is the Chief of Police. You are the subject officer of this investigation. The allegations are as follows: There are no specific allegations. This is an administrative investigation required by policy as a result of an officer-involved shooting. You understand that?

CAMPBELL: Yes, sir, I do.

ME: Do you understand that this interview is a part of an official proceeding per Florida state statute?

CAMPBELL: Yes, I do.

ME: This is an administrative and not a criminal investigation. You have been given and have signed copies of the Police Officer's Bill of Rights, the Garrity statement, and the perjury form. Do you understand your rights?

CAMPBELL: Yes, I do.

ME: Do you have any questions concerning these forms?

CAMPBELL: No, sir, I do not.

ME: Okay, you have been given an opportunity to review all evidence and interviews to date. Have you had sufficient time to review the evidence and interviews?

CAMPBELL: Yes, sir, I have.

ME: Would you please raise your right hand? Do you swear or affirm that the statement you are about to give will be the truth, the whole truth, and nothing but the truth, so help you God?

CAMPBELL: Yes, sir, I do.

ME: Okay. You asked to have this interview after having reviewed some recent materials that were submitted.

CAMPBELL: Yes, sir.

ME: And you wanted to make a statement.

CAMPBELL: Yes, sir.

ME: Go ahead.

CAMPBELL: Uh, first, Captain Hernandez with the other police department stated that I was at their training when he and Liam Noit came over as contract employees to instruct the training. I was not and did not attend their training. I was not in charge of any training when Chief Truth took over here. She canceled training when she got here. I was placed under Special Investigator Adder. He was my supervisor. He was the one that scheduled all officers. I was not scheduled to attend that training. Second, I did not notice in either Hernandez's or Noit's résumés that they are proprietary handcuff instructors to any handcuff brands, as stated in their interviews. They just stated that they were instructors. Their résumés do not state that they have been taught by a specific company, as stated. The third aspect is, in their résumés, there is nothing stating that they are experts in testimony as far as any state attorney or judge making them subject matter experts in those areas. And then also I did, I was issued chain handcuffs. I was not asked why I did not use them on that scene. Prior to that evening, probably about two hours or so—I am not sure of the time, I would have to go back and look at the CAD and the arrest reports—I arrested a prostitute. She was a heroin or opium addict. She actually had blood on her wrists. I did not have a chance to sanitize the chain handcuffs. I deemed them biohazard until I had a chance to go get them cleaned at the hospital properly. I did not want to use them that night. I did have a spare set of hinged handcuffs in my trunk, which I used.

ME: Okay. You are a part of an email chain that spoke about collecting all the handcuffs.

CAMPBELL: Collecting all department-issued handcuffs, yes, sir.

ME: So it was your understanding that the department was not going to be using or authorizing the use of the hinged handcuffs anymore after that.

CAMPBELL: That policy was not written at that time, so until that policy was written, I did have extra handcuffs in my trunk, or else I would not have been able to effect an arrest until properly cleaning my handcuffs. They were a biohazard.

ME: Were those personally owned?

CAMPBELL: Yes, sir.

ME: Hinge handcuffs? And you are aware of the policy that you are not supposed to use equipment that is personally owned that has not been approved?

CAMPBELL: Yes, sir. Those were approved by the prior chief, and there was not a policy change given by the new chief yet, so they were approved. I am also a specific brand handcuff instructor, trained on hinged, chain, lockable hinge, and zip cuffs.

ME: And you disagreed with the change of the policy?

CAMPBELL: Yes, sir. According to Noit's statement and according to the statement the chief made directly to human resources, we were issued and were carrying the wrong hand-cuffs, but that was not correct. If we were carrying the wrong handcuffs, 95 percent of the other agencies in the state of Florida and throughout the United States would also be carrying the wrong hinged handcuffs. I dis-agreed with them, yes, but the policy had not been written yet, so...

ME: But a directive or an order can be given until a policy can be changed. Correct?

CAMPBELL: Yes, sir.

ME: Okay, and you were at least aware that Director Noit had said to have all the hinged handcuffs removed from the street, right?

CAMPBELL: Department-issued hinged hand-cuffs, yes, sir.

ME: Okay, so you are trying to differentiate between department-issued and your own personally owned?

CAMPBELL: He asked me to collect all depart-ment-issued hinged handcuffs and return them to supply.

ME: You understood the gist of the order was, they were removing them from the street, correct?

CAMPBELL: Yes, sir. They were removing depart-ment-issued handcuffs from the street.

ME: The hinged handcuffs specifically.

CAMPBELL: Yes, sir.

I had gotten used to Officer Campbell's obfuscations by then and saw no reason to prolong his interview. Nothing was ever his fault, and he liked to cast dispersions on others while pointing out all his real or imagined accomplishments. He enjoyed wordplay, and "issued" versus "personally owned" was one of those he delighted in. I was ready to hand this back over to Chief Truth so that Deputy Chief King could do what he needed to do.

CHAPTER 15

Sergeant Powers Update

While other things were happening on the department, the investigations involving Sergeant Powers were continuing on. We had gotten to a point wherein we felt comfortable turning the cases over to the Chief of Police. The following is the synopsis of the investigative summary in the Masters case:

Investigative Summary

Sergeant Ethan Powers conducted a traffic stop on a vehicle that he observed speeding. According to Sergeant Powers, after verifying the suspect vehicle was traveling sixty-four miles per hour (mph) in a forty-mile-per-hour zone, he pulled out to attempt to stop the suspect vehicle, which committed an illegal lane change prior to stopping.

The driver of the vehicle, Mr. Jose Masters, came to a stop. According to Sergeant Powers's Internal Affairs Bureau (IAB) testimony, he approached Mr. Masters's window, offering him a greeting and explaining to Mr. Masters that he was being stopped for speeding. According to Mr. Masters, Sergeant Powers never explained the purpose for the stop. The video supplied by Mr. Masters does not appear to have the sergeant's initial approach recorded. The sergeant is unsure if he identified himself by name and rank.

The ensuing conversation between Mr. Masters and Sergeant Powers has been characterized by Sergeant Powers as "bantering" and Mr. Masters as "bickering." Both admit that they were speaking when the other party was speaking, which meant that neither heard what the other person was saying. Sergeant Powers was focused on collecting the information he needed to complete the traffic stop, and Mr. Masters was focused on recording the traffic stop and sharing his understanding of how a traffic stop was supposed to be conducted.

Sergeant Powers wanted Mr. Masters to roll down his vehicle's windows so that he could check the legality of the tint on them. According to Sergeant Powers, his training and experience caused him to believe the tint was not legal and caused officer safety concerns since one could not clearly see inside the vehicle during the traffic stop. Mr. Master's position was that he only needed to roll his windows down far enough for them to be tested, and no more.

Officer A, who was on scene, described Sergeant Powers as seeming "a little perturbed" at the scene of the traffic stop, and Officer I, who has worked for Sergeant Powers for four years, characterized him as "upset" or "frustrated." Sergeant Powers agreed with those characterizations, adding that he was a "little upset" because Mr. Masters would not just cooperate, take his tickets, and go about his day. He said, "And it was just, there was bickering, and you're absolutely right. There were two of us, he was stuck on how he knew his rights and this and that and the other, and I was stuck on 'You need to obey my commands.'" Mr. Masters characterized Sergeant Powers's attitude as "angry" from the beginning of the traffic stop.

Sergeant Powers said that it had been his experience that some people cannot be reasoned with, and Mr. Masters was one of those people. In attempting to effectively deal with the situation, Sergeant Powers said that he informed Mr. Masters what he needed to know and retreated to his vehicle to begin writing the citations he intended to give Mr. Masters.

At one point, Lieutenant Chance Bennett arrived at the traffic stop. Lieutenant Bennett said that he attempted to speak with Mr. Masters but got more of the same thing Sergeant Powers had gotten. Lieutenant Bennett said that Mr. Masters was "not paying attention" and was "not complying." Lieutenant Bennett determined at that time that Mr. Masters needed to be arrested and instructed the officers on scene to make the arrest.

Both Sergeant Powers and Lieutenant Bennett were on scene when Mr. Masters was taken into custody. They both witnessed the extraction from the vehicle and the subsequent handcuffing. They contradict Mr. Masters's accusation that stated, "About six officers, I swear I could feel everybody's knee from my neck to my ankles, all the officers on my back putting heavy pressure," during his arrest. The police in-car video camera also contradicts that accusation.

Lieutenant Bennett said that Sergeant Powers seemed "a little annoyed" at the scene of the traffic stop. The lieutenant said the purpose of his being there was to try to defuse the situation, if he could. Lieutenant Bennett said it was unusual to have to break the car window at the scene of a traffic stop, saying that it was the first time he had seen it done in his twenty-two- year career. Due to the unusual circumstances, he felt the need to notify his superiors.

Mr. Masters alleged that Lieutenant Bennett tried to erase the video from his phone. Lieutenant Bennett denied ever touching Mr. Masters's phone. While he could not remember who collected the phone, the lieutenant was adamant that he would not have allowed anyone to try to erase the video on the phone in his presence.

In discussing the missing information from the report, Sergeant Powers said that there was an "unwritten rule" on his squad, that his officers know if they take someone to the hospital, they are supposed to take pictures of that individual to document visible injuries or the lack thereof. Lieutenant Bennett said that he would have been responsible for editing the report but that the sergeant was still responsible for making sure everything that needed to occur at the scene did in fact occur (impounding the car, taking pictures, etc.). The lieutenant said that he would share in the blame if those things did not occur, since he was the ranking department member on scene. However, "the sergeant would still do sergeant's responsibilities."

In the internal affairs case involving Mr. Billy Bad, Officer SS testified that there was indeed an "unwritten rule" on Sergeant Powers's squad requiring officers who take prisoners to jail who are claiming injury to photograph them. Officer

Stroller said he did take pictures of Mr. Masters once he arrived at booking. Officer Stroller said he attached them electronically to the field interview form in the report.

Detective Felicia Direct was able to access those pictures and print them out, which Officer Stroller verified were the images he took that day. Officer Stroller said he was unaware of any "unwritten rules" on Sergeant Powers's squad but explained that he was still new to the squad at that time.

The entire file had been shared with Wendy Late's young attorney, who had successfully prosecuted Mr. Masters in criminal court. In fact, the young attorney was appreciative of our investigative efforts, which made his job much easier. The following is the investigative summary from the Billy Bad case:

Investigative Summary

Sergeant Powers conducted a traffic stop on a vehicle that he observed speeding. According to Sergeant Powers, he verified his observations of excessive speed by checking his radar, which gave a speed of fifty-six miles per hour. The sergeant made a U-turn. The suspect vehicle immediately turned into the beach park and continued along the dirt road until the sergeant activated his overhead lights. The driver, Mr. Billy Bad, immediately pulled over, and the sergeant greeted Mr. Bad, explaining the purpose for the stop, and requested Mr. Bad's driver's license, registration, and proof of insurance.

Sergeant Powers said it was readily apparent that Mr. Bad did not have a driver's license with him, so the sergeant asked Mr. Bad if he had a

license. Mr. Bad replied, "No, it is suspended."
Sergeant Powers obtained Mr. Bad's name and
date of birth by writing the information verbally
supplied to him on a notepad. Sergeant Powers
returned to his patrol car and verified that Mr.
Bad's license was suspended as he was a habitual
offender.

Sergeant Powers returned to Mr. Bad's car
and found him eating from a container of food
that had previously been on the seat. Sergeant
Powers ordered Mr. Bad out of the car in order to
make the arrest, and Mr. Bad replied, "No, I am
eating." Sergeant Powers removed the tray of food
from Mr. Bad's hands, and Mr. Bad picked up a
drink instead of getting out of the car. Sergeant
Powers saw an opportunity to extract Mr. Bad
at this point using a shoulder lock. Mr. Bad's
account is that the sergeant grabbed a handful
of his hair to extract him from the vehicle. Mr.
Hank Marry and Mrs. Christy Jones were civilians visiting the beach that day, and they support
Sergeant Powers's version, with both testifying
that Sergeant Powers extracted Mr. Bad by an
arm.

Sergeant Powers immediately put Mr. Bad
up against the suspect vehicle to attempt to complete the handcuffing, but Mr. Bad was tensing
up and resisting the attempt. Sergeant Powers
transitioned to a hip toss, while Mr. Marry came
to the sergeant's aid by pulling Mr. Bad's feet out
from under him. Sergeant Powers said that they
all went to the ground and he believes his knee
might have made contact with Mr. Bad's cheek
during the fall.

During the ensuing struggle, Sergeant
Powers was attempting to gain control of Mr.

Bad's arms to apply the handcuffs, and Mr. Marry restrained Mr. Bad's legs. Mr. Willie Jennings saw what was going on and came to aid the officer by grabbing Mr. Bad's left arm, pulling it out from under Mr. Bad's body, and holding it while the sergeant applied handcuffs. The sergeant was then able to gain control of Mr. Bad's right arm and complete the handcuffing.

Mr. Bad claimed repeatedly that he did not resist Sergeant Powers. Ms. Babs Schultz was driving by when the incident occurred, and she described what she saw this way: "I could tell that there was some kind of altercation, because the driver [Bad], his fists were coming out of the car, and the policeman [Powers], at the same time, was trying to…looked like he was trying to grab to subdue this, uh, person." This caused Ms. Schultz to have concern for the sergeant's safety and to call 911 to try to get him some help. Ms. Christy Jones said that the sergeant was struggling to gain control of Mr. Bad and others came to help because, as she said, "this man [Bad] would not…he [Bad] was resisting quite heavily." Ms. Carol Black characterized Mr. Bad's actions in the following manner: "The officer [Powers] was trying to contain him [Bad] because he [Bad] was fighting like crazy."

Mr. Willie Jennings said he saw the sergeant struggling with Mr. Bad on the ground and explained why he came to help the sergeant. "The officer [Powers] was having trouble getting control of the person [Bad] that came out of the car." Mr. Marry said he saw the sergeant struggling to control Mr. Bad and explained why he went to assist the sergeant: "He [Bad] was actually almost at the point of turning the officer [Powers] around, and he [Bad] was fighting and kicking." These five independent witnesses all corroborate Sergeant Powers's characterization of Mr. Bad's behavior while debunking Mr. Bad's claim that he did not resist.

In describing the one time he utilized a "hair pull" to control Mr. Bad, Sergeant Powers said, "I sat him up on his duff, on his rear end. He got his legs completely extended. I was explaining to him, 'Bring your leg in.' I said, 'I am going to get you up,' and he was not getting up at all. He made a comment that I broke his jaw… I tried to get him to come forward, and he was not getting up. He was complete dead weight. I reached in behind the little tuft of hair underneath, and I pulled it and he came straight up like a rocket ship."

In explaining why he chose to utilize a tactic that is not taught nor can it be found in the state of Florida's curriculum of accepted control tactics for escorts and transports, Sergeant Powers said, "I, too, am a defensive tactics instructor. I improvised, utilizing a method that might be unconventional but effective, does not cause permanent injury, and the pain does subside as quickly as it is placed, like a wristlock or a fingerhold. I was not going to do a mandibular lock on him or place a pressure point to the ear, because he was stating that I broke his jaw. I do not know which side. I am not going to reinjure or aggravate any injury that he had that he was constantly complaining about, because if not, I would usually do a mandibular lock and get him up, so I improvised."

When the department's lead defensive tactics instructor and certified use of force expert witness Sergeant Ethan Quick was asked about the use of a tactic that is not covered by the state's guidelines, his response was, "A hair pull or using somebody's hair is an improvised technique in the middle of combative-type situations. So in other words, if you were fighting with somebody and they put you in a headlock, or you are fighting with somebody that you can use a hair pull on in a combative-type situation to control someone, if it is in the middle of a fight, if I am using a hair pull as a punishment, then that is not acceptable."

Mr. Bad told investigators several times in his interview that he gave his name to Sergeant Powers when the sergeant asked for his license. Toward the end of the interview, Mr. Bad claimed that he gave Sergeant Powers his Florida identification card and the card was never returned to him. Sergeant Powers unequivocally denies Mr. Bad ever giving him an identification card.

Sergeant Powers collected the names of the two men who assisted him in gaining control of Mr. Bad during Mr. Bad's violent resist of the sergeant's efforts to handcuff him in completing the arrest. He also had the name and contact/telephone number of the person who drove by and called 911 to get him some assistance. Sergeant Powers did not conduct interviews with these witnesses and said he gave their names to Officer JL to place into the report.

Officer SS was Officer JL's field training officer on that day, and Officer JL was new to the department by about one month. Officer SS said he was not present with Officer JL the entire time they were at the scene of the traffic stop and did not see Sergeant Powers provide Officer JL the witnesses' names and contact information.

Officer JL does not recall having been given the names by the sergeant.

Officer SS did transport the prisoner to the hospital after the affidavit was completed. He accepted responsibility for failing to take photographs of the prisoner, who was complaining of injury, and says that it is an "unwritten rule" on Sergeant Powers's squad that officers who take prisoners to the hospital take pictures as required by department policy.

Sergeant Powers denies "boasting" about the fight and eventual arrest of Mr. Bad. The sergeant said that he, Officer SS, and Officer JL were under the bridge, completing paperwork, and he did tell them about the incident because he was asked. Sergeant Powers specifically denies laughing and joking about the struggle to complete the arrest of Mr. Bad but does acknowledge that he said "Good" when Mr. Bad complained about the possibility of having broken ribs as a result of the struggle. Sergeant Powers said he did not mean it when he said it; he was just frustrated by Mr. Bad's continued belligerence while they were completing paperwork. Officers SS and JL remember Sergeant Powers recounting the events but remember him being professional and unemotional.

When asked if he notified his immediate supervisor after the resist, Sergeant Powers could not recall when exactly that he had notified him. Sergeant Powers said, as someone involved in the arrest, he was only responsible for completing the affidavit. When investigators pointed out that the affidavit appeared to be "cut and pasted" into the report, Sergeant Powers admitted that could be the case, including that it was his understanding that the affidavit should be the "facts" and the report should be the "buffet."

Lieutenant Chance Bennett was Sergeant Powers's immediate supervisor on the date in question, and in a separate IAB interview (in the Masters case), he said he was in a meeting during this incident. Lieutenant Bennett said he was informed "long after it happened." The lieutenant said, after the meeting was over and he answered an alarm call, the sergeant met with him and told him about it. When asked if he had told his commanding officer about the second arrest (Bad was arrested after Masters on the same day), Lieutenant Bennett said that was not something he would normally tell his commanding officer. When questioned if one officer having two resists in one day wherein both subjects had to go to the hospital was unusual, Lieutenant Bennett admitted that would be highly unusual, but "at that time that he [Powers] told me [Lieutenant Bennett] about the second arrest, there was no mention of him [Bad] going to the hospital."

Based upon my experiences in law enforcement to this point, involving IAB cases, these did not appear to be problematic for Sergeant Powers, but that is simply my educated guess. To be sure, there were some minor reporting mistakes, but those do not typically eat a job. The sergeant was still on administrative duty and would be until the conclusion of both the formal cases. This did not make for a happy employee, and it is my strong suspicion that he took his anger out in similar ways to Than Campbell. We started getting media requests regarding uniform crime reporting classifications and "notes" that were internal only in some of the reports. The only way a reporter would know about the existence of such notes would be if someone with access to the restricted portion of the department's records shared them with that reporter. Since Than Campbell and

Benjamin Brown did not have access to the department's records and one of the requested records involved notes that Sergeant Powers had placed into the restricted area, logic follows that Powers was dropping the proverbial dime.

Reaching a Conclusion

Deputy Chief Alex King conducted an exhausting review of all the material I had supplied to him via an electronic thumb drive. To be sure, Alex called me multiple times and had me come to his office on more than one occasion to help him locate files within the morass of file folders/subfolders. Because I was so familiar with the files and where they were located on the drive, I gladly helped him navigate through them. Even though Alex was a "cop's cop" (meaning, he defended officers whenever/wherever he could, even if they were a little wrong), he ultimately reached the following conclusions that were provided to Chief Truth:

> **Recommendation of Deputy Chief Alex King in the Case Involving Sergeant Benjamin Brown and Mr. David Samuel**
>
> After consideration of applicable department policies and procedures, photographs, video, formal and informal audio statements, and the investigations conducted by the State Attorney and our department's Internal Affairs Bureau, the following findings have been made: Sergeant Benjamin Brown has been an officer with our department for fourteen years. He is also trained

as a special weapons and tactics (SWAT) officer, with approximately two thousand hours of training. During this traffic stop, Sergeant Brown arrived as a backup unit.

As Sergeant Brown approached the vehicle, he overheard Officer Campbell tell Mr. Samuel that he could smell and see marijuana inside of the vehicle. He arrived at the front passenger door and opened it, placing himself between the open door and the body of the vehicle (while the vehicle was still running). Sergeant Brown placed himself in an unsafe position, which later contributed to Sergeant Brown's fear of being trapped between the door and the body of the vehicle.

During this investigation, it revealed that Sergeant Brown was in possession of an unauthorized body-worn camera (BWC) system that was purchased for SWAT several years ago. Sergeant Brown was directed by a commanding officer to collect all the body-worn cameras and place them into the SWAT storage locker.

Sergeant Benjamin Brown is in violation of department policy regarding the Code of Conduct—namely, insubordination—which states, "Employees will promptly obey any lawful order or direction of a supervisor. This includes any lawful order or direction relayed from a supervisor by an employee of the same or lesser rank. If an employee does not understand the direction given to them, the employee will seek guidance from a supervisor."

Calling an officer wrong in an internal investigation is not easy for an administrator, especially for one with a heart as big as Deputy Chief King's. When you consider that Brown had been elevated in rank to sergeant, it becomes even harder. While Alex and I did not have any conversations about his feelings on the matter, because that would have been the wrong thing to do, given our positions in the department, I could tell his decision weighed heavily on his mind. The following was his decision referencing Officer Than Campbell:

Recommendation of Deputy Chief Alex King Regarding Officer Than Campbell and Mr. David Samuel

After consideration of applicable department policies and procedures, photographs, video, formal and informal audio statements, and the investigations conducted by the State Attorney and our department's Internal Affairs Bureau, the following findings have been made: Officer Than Campbell has been an officer with our department for fourteen years and is trained as a special weapons and tactics (SWAT) officer. He was also former training officer for six (6) years, with approximately three thousand hours of training.

In this case, Officer Campbell conducted a legitimate traffic stop. During this contact, Officer Campbell detected the odor of marijuana and observed suspected particles of marijuana on the "cluster" gauge of the vehicle. At this point, Officer Campbell failed to ask Mr. Samuel to turn off his vehicle. When Officer Campbell reached into the running vehicle and opened the door, he created a dangerous situation, which later contributed to Officer Campbell's being struck by the vehicle as Mr. Samuel unlawfully fled the scene.

During this investigation, it revealed that Officer Campbell was in possession of unauthorized equipment: a pair of hinged handcuffs (located at the scene) and a personally owned .308-caliber long gun / rifle (in the trunk of Officer Campbell's patrol vehicle).

Before this event, Sergeant Young testified that on two separate squad inspections, Officer Campbell told him that his in-car camera system was not functioning properly. Officer Campbell was ordered by his sergeant to have his in-car camera system checked by the IT manager. Officer Campbell related that he informed his supervisor that he did not know how to properly utilize the in-car camera system. Sergeant Young ordered Officer Campbell to get with the field training officer to receive proper training on how to use the in-car camera system. Officer Campbell failed to follow up on these orders.

Officer Than Campbell is in violation of department policy and procedures: Authorized Firearms/Ammunition (one count); Code of Conduct / Knowledge and Performance (one count); Knowledge of Rules, Regulations, and Procedures (one count); Failure to Follow Policy (one count); Insubordination (two counts); Neglect of Duty (two counts); Knowledge and Performance / General Proficiency (one count); and In-Car Camera System/Inspections (one count).

Chief Truth then met with her two deputy chiefs to discuss possible disciplinary measures. I was not privy to that conversation. I was asked to attend a meeting with the city manager, the city's human resources director (Carl Dolt), the city attorney (Paul Fibber), one of the assistant city attorneys (Lola Cooley), Chief Truth, and the two deputy chiefs. The purpose for my presence was to answer any questions regarding the IAB files. Mr. Fibber opened the meeting by telling Chief Truth, the deputy chiefs, and me, "Chief, I assure you that my attorneys and I have all the department's legal needs

covered should any be required regarding the outcome of the Brown/
Campbell administrative investigation." I was reminded of the old
adage "How can you tell when an attorney is lying? His lips are moving." I was dismissed from the room before the end of the meeting, which was likely so that they could discuss possible disciplinary
measures.

CHAPTER 17

What's Next?

Chief Truth had Deputy Chief King provide notice to both officers of her intention to move forward with discipline. The notice had each of the violations listed, explaining that each officer was being notified of the findings of the administrative investigation, proposed disciplinary action, and the offer of a predetermination hearing. The notice included the following verbiage: "Pursuant to Florida statute 112.532, the proposed action has yet to be determined and can range from suspension, demotion, and/or termination from employment. Prior to finalizing a decision on disciplinary action, I will provide you with an opportunity to address the findings and pending discipline in a predetermination hearing." Deputy Chief King then provided the date for that hearing.

I was tasked with serving these notices and had Detective Direct contact each officer to have them report to the department for service. Sergeant Brown was quick to respond and received his notice. Officer Campbell did not, telling Detective Direct that he was "getting on a plane" and it was not reasonable to expect him to report on short notice. That was a wholly unacceptable response. Officer Campbell had not requested any leave, as explained previously, and was being paid by the department to be available within one hour of any request of his presence by the department. When I explained this to Chief Truth, she requested Carl Dolt to make another call to Officer Campbell in my presence on a recorded line.

Mr. Dolt then requested Officer Campbell to report in person to city hall, and Officer Campbell explained to Mr. Dolt that he was more than an hour away so he could not comply with the request. Officer Campbell then told Mr. Dolt that he could report to the department in two weeks. Chief Truth instructed me to open another internal affairs formal investigation into Officer Than Campbell's Absence Without Leave.

I really was not surprised by Officer Campbell's behavior, based upon how I had seen him operate during our interviews and what I suspected he was doing outside of the agency with the media. Chief Truth then tasked me to look into the disciplinary history of each of the officers and provide her the information for the executive staff's consideration during disciplinary deliberations for Brown and Campbell. Since I had access to all the department's internal affairs files, it was logically my chore to complete this task. What made it difficult was an oddity that I had discovered when I first arrived at the department. The department had leased a computer software program for use in internal affairs cases and, at some point, decided that they no longer wished to pay for the service. Unfortunately, no one thought to convert the files into a usable format outside of the computer software program, and all the old files were gone. There were other files in readable formats that were bread crumbs I could follow, but they were spread out among multiple file folders in the vast internal affairs program. I was reduced to opening folder after subfolder, looking at each individual document within to find what I needed. I was really surprised by what I found.

CHAPTER 18

The Past

Sergeant Benjamin Brown was a Boy Scout. Early on in his career, when he was a patrol officer, Sergeant Brown had missed an off-duty work detail and there was no record in the file describing the circumstances, but he received "counseling" for the mistake. Counseling is not considered formal discipline per our agency's rules and regulations and is only placed in an officer's file for reference should the behavior repeat itself within one year of the initial occurrence. The sergeant was also counseled for performing an inadequate vehicle inspection on a patrol officer's car. Several years after that, the sergeant missed another off-duty work detail, which he said he simply forgot about. He received counseling for that instance too. Three minor infractions over the span of a career is fairly remarkable.

Officer Than Campbell was the polar opposite. I found that Campbell had been a US Marine prior to coming to work for our agency. He was demoted in rank from sergeant to corporal because he fraternized with enlisted women while at a training program and they were all late returning to post. Campbell had also worked for the local sheriff's office at their jail facility, and he called out "sick" so that he could attend a professional football game on his birthday. When contacted regarding his failure to show up for a mandatory work assignment, he lied, telling them he was sick. He later admitted this was not true (a rarity) but blamed it on another deputy sheriff that he had allegedly asked to switch work assignments with him.

Both of these were in Campbell's file, which also included a young then-lieutenant's recommendation that Campbell not be hired. That young lieutenant was Deputy Chief Wily Trust. The senior staff at that time ignored the lieutenant's recommendation and hired Campbell anyway. Having sat on many hiring boards in my career, I can tell you that those would have been red flags that would have swayed my vote away from hiring such an individual. Knowing someone is dishonest or has a proven history of such behavior would normally preclude that person from consideration in a law enforcement career. The following was Campbell's internal affairs history, starting with the oldest and working toward the most recent: (1) Discourtesy (Not Sustained) and Neglect of Duty (Sustained, receiving a Written Warning) (no record on file); (2) Excessive Force (Not Sustained) and Neglect of Duty (Sustained, receiving a Reprimand) (no record on file); (3) Harassment (Sustained; Reprimand), Code of Conduct (Sustained; ten-day suspension), and Conduct Unbecoming (Sustained; Training); (4) Neglect of Duty (Sustained; counseling); (5) Neglect of Duty (Sustained; Written Warning); (6) False Arrest (Sustained; Counseling) (no record on file); (7) Neglect of Duty (Sustained; Counseling) (no record on file); (8) Neglect of Duty (Sustained; Reprimand) (no record on file); (9) Too Many Hours Worked (Sustained; No Discipline); (10) Missed Detail (Sustained; Warning); (11) Harassment (Sustained; Counseling); (12) Vehicle Operations (Sustained; Counseling); (13) Inattention to Duty (Sustained; Counseling); and (14) Social Media Policy (Exonerated) and Misuse of Personal Web Pages (Sustained; No Discipline).

Considering that the first four instances listed above occurred within the first year of his being hired, I was amazed that Officer Campbell still had a job. Especially troubling was the instance that garnered him a ten-day suspension. Officer Campbell had been dating, and later cohabiting, with a lady named Kayley Wright, who (by some accounts) might have been underage when they began their sexual relationship. Regardless, Ms. Wright was hired after Campbell, and they were living together at that time. They broke up, and Wright saw Campbell "sneaking up" the side of a hill near her apartment. She called out to him, saying she could see him, and asked him what he thought he was doing. Campbell stood up and said, "Oh, I was just checking on you." According to Wright, Campbell did not take the breakup very well. A short time later, Campbell was showing nude photos of Wright with another woman to several officers, which was what began the complaint. Wright kept those photographs in the top of her closet, and she was adamant that Campbell did not take them with him when he moved out, because she had seen them after he left. It took Campbell several days to return the apartment keys to her, and Wright surmised that he must have come back to the apartment after their breakup, using a key to go inside, taking them without her permission.

A sustained case of sexual harassment in the workplace is typically a job eater. The only way that Campbell survived had to be because "someone up there" liked him. One of the names that kept resurfacing with many of the files was Lieutenant Drake Smoke's. I knew that Drake had been the SWAT commander and that Campbell and Brown had been SWAT operators. From years in law enforcement, I also knew that SWAT members have an unspoken code of "Brothers for life," which means they stick together regardless of what one of them has done.

Another file that caught my eye was of an officer-involved shooting of an unarmed motorist wherein Campbell had been the one that shot the motorist. This occurred just before Officer Campbell left the street to be the department's training officer. Lieutenant Smoke had been in charge of the internal affairs investigation that cleared Officer Campbell, which was not surprising, but what I found dubious was the award recommendation written by the lieutenant after the case clearance. As part of the Heroism Award submission justification, Lieutenant Smoke wrote, "During a pursuit, the suspect used his vehicle as a deadly weapon against the officers trying to stop him. Officer Campbell *left the safety of his vehicle* [emphasis mine] and stopped the suspect by firing his service weapon." The suspect was in an open field, doing doughnuts with his truck, when Campbell shot him, despite there being an innocent female passenger beside the suspect! That emphasized comment begged the question, "If it was safe in their vehicles, why did anyone need to leave their vehicle?"

It also brought to mind Geoffrey Alpert's "officer-created jeopardy" theory. Needless to say, Campbell did not get the Heroism Award for that case.

Lieutenant Whit Singer was the sergeant in charge that night of the pursuit. He confided in me that he thought at one point that night that they were all going to lose their jobs over the pursuit of this subject whom they had interrupted while the suspect was buying drugs. The suspect had hit several police vehicles, and it was "assumed" the collisions were done intentionally (thus the aggravated assault allegation, which allowed the pursuit). Singer was relieved when their former chief showed up and immediately praised everyone for doing a "good job" without questioning any of the details of the incident.

I also discovered a secondary recommendation that did result in Campbell's being awarded the Heroism Award. Campbell allegedly saved three teenage girls from drowning. When I spoke to several officers in the department, they all rolled their eyes skeptically, and one even confided that the two deputies and the Marine Patrol officer who responded to help in the rescue were pissed off with Campbell receiving the award. According to the sergeant that shared this with me, the other law enforcement officers involved had to actually save Campbell, who had gotten himself into a pickle by jumping into the water without planning his extraction. Yet none of those officers' names were mentioned in the award nomination!

I had not known Campbell or anything about his past prior to the completion of the Samuel internal affairs investigation, but now I was beginning to get a picture of a man who probably should not wear a badge. I have worked around many "glory hounds" throughout my career, and they are the type that can get other officers hurt (or worse, killed). Given the agency's and city's disciplinary rules, all this information was available to Chief Truth and the deputy chiefs in making their decision. Deputy Chief Wily Trust knew most of it without having to be told.

CHAPTER 19

The Decision

Detective Direct hounded me for days about the Chief's decision. She even accused me at one point of lying about knowing what the outcome was going to be (I honestly did not). To be sure, the Chief and I were friends, but we both knew the mandatory separation of internal affairs and the final decision by her executive staff.

I, like others, had my thoughts on what might be appropriate, but I did not know what Chief Trust's final decision would be. I could see the termination of Sergeant Brown only as a slight possibility, based upon the well-established tenet that the immediate supervisor on scene is responsible for all the actions of his/her subordinate. Campbell openly defied policies, and those, like Brown, who knew him knew what violations (like hinged handcuffs) he routinely committed. Sergeant Brown was well-liked among the department's employees, and there would be broad sympathy for him regardless of the punishment. Campbell did not share in the sergeant's popularity, and plenty had negative things to say about the arrogant, better-than-you personality that Campbell displayed.

The question of Campbell seemed obvious to me. I mean, how could you put a man back to work as a patrolman when he has killed two unarmed motorists in the past and says in his internal affairs interview that he would do it again (despite the numerous opportunities I gave him to change that stance)? What would the department's liability be in the next shooting? I was glad my sole part was the investigation, and I did not envy Chief Trust's obligation to make a decision.

The day that Chief Trust intended to serve the discipline she had determined was appropriate given the circumstances, she called the on-duty department supervisors and managers into the conference room. She announced her decision to terminate both Brown and Campbell for the administrative infractions and officer safety violations uncovered by the administrative investigation. Several in the room were visibly upset, and one even cried out, "Bullshit!" before storming out of the room. Others, like me, were in a state of disbelief.

The boss had made her decision, and it was far from over. She had to make a public statement, which she had arranged with the media immediately following her informing all her supervisory/managerial staff. At a senior police school that I had attended as a lieutenant at my prior agency, I took a law class wherein the law professor explained to the future heads of agencies in the room, "The courts do not care how you run your railroad as long as you run it consistently." With the dismissal of these two officers, Chief Truth had drawn a line in the sand of what would be considered acceptable behavior. It was a tough decision, but she made it. I was (and am) proud of her.

C H A P T E R

The Aftermath

Than Campbell reacted by throwing public punches at those he deemed responsible for his demise, while Benjamin Brown was the consummate gentleman. Campbell filed an internal affairs complaint against the city manager, the chief of police, and me. Then he went to the city commission meeting that same night and read his complaint aloud during the public speaking portion of that meeting (despite an active internal affairs complaint being protected as confidential by law, the violation of which is a misdemeanor). The city clerk, Lisa Cook, who was also the assistant city manager, wanted a copy of the internal affairs complaint to release to the media. I informed her that I was one of those people being complained about, and as such, I had the right to anonymity under Florida laws until the investigation was complete, even though the chief and city manager were exempt from those laws.

Ms. Cook suggested I contact my attorney, Lola Cooley, who was an assistant city attorney. In the meantime, she asked for a redacted copy of the complaint that did not contain my name. I provided that information to Chief Truth, who can release active internal affairs information if she chooses, per law. I called Ms. Cooley, who immediately announced she was putting me on speakerphone and that she had another assistant city attorney in the room with her. She told me repeatedly that she was **not** my attorney (emphasis hers). Then I got her to agree to answer a hypothetical question regarding the release of an active internal affairs complaint, and she got cute with her answer, suggesting that it might not be considered a complaint since the chief had not yet issued it a case number.

Paul Fibber addressed the next city commission meeting, and during it he provided the following letter:

> To: The Honorable Mayor and City
> Commissioners
> From: Paul Fibber, City Attorney
> Re: (1) Pending Arbitration of former officer Campbell and former sergeant Brown
> (2) Authorization to forward the sworn complaint of former officer Campbell to the Florida Department of Law Enforcement
>
> (1) Pending Arbitration of former officer Campbell and former sergeant Brown. As stated in the sworn complaint of former officer Campbell, the cases of terminated city police officer Campbell and sergeant Brown would appear to be headed toward an arbitration proceeding. Rather than discuss this problem at a later date, I believe it advisable to obtain guidance and concurrence from my client, the city commission, at the earliest possible time.
>
> The sworn complaint of former officer Campbell has precipitated this issue. Section 45 of the city charter states that the city attorney "shall act as the legal adviser to, and counselor for, the city *and* all of its officers in matters relating to their official duties." This means that I represent two clients: the city *and* city officers. Sometimes the interests of each client are aligned, and sometimes the interests are adverse or in conflict.
>
> Former officer Campbell's sworn complaint raises just such a conflict: it creates substantial

risk that my duties of loyalty, confidentiality, and candor would be compromised by my representing both the city and its officials in the arbitration. Thus, I am ethically forced to decline the representation at the outset.

I can ensure that the interest of the city will be adequately represented by outside counsel at the arbitration, while I remain able to provide counsel to the city commission on this or any other personnel matter springing from it.

Rule 4-1.7 of the Rules Regulating the Florida Bar, which are the rules of professionalism governing members of the Florida Bar, states that a lawyer is prohibited from representing a client if representation of one will be directly adverse to another or there is a substantial risk that the representation of a client will be materially limited by the lawyer's responsibility to another client.

An attorney's duty of loyalty to a client is the motivating factor behind this rule and requires that an attorney decline representation in such a case. In short, I should be loyal to the city commission, not the individuals named in the complaint.

Comments to the rule explain that "loyalty to a client is impaired when a lawyer cannot consider, recommend, or carry out an appropriate course of action for the client because of the lawyer's other responsibilities or interests. The conflict in effect forecloses alternatives that would otherwise be available to the client." Thus, the comments to the rule state, when an impermissible conflict of interest exists, "before representation is undertaken…the representation should be declined."

Here, actions of the city *and* its officers are the subject of the pending arbitration. The city has received a sworn complaint, under penalty of perjury, from former officer Campbell that alleges serious violations by city officers in their individual capacities relating to the same incident.

Based on this sworn complaint, I am alerted at the outset that there is a substantial risk that my representation will be materially limited because of the adverse position of each client. My duty of loyalty to each client forces me to decline representation in this instance. I will be impaired from recommending an appropriate course of action to the city commission because it may be adverse to one of the named individuals in the complaint.

This is why rule 4-1.13, the rule governing a lawyer's representation of a city, states that a lawyer employed by a city may represent any of its directors, officers, or employees, but the lawyer is subject to rule 4-1.7, the rule governing conflicts between two clients, detailed above.

Similarly, my duty of confidentiality to each client prevents me from representing both. Rule 4-1.6 states that "a lawyer must not reveal information relating to representation of a client except" for a few specific situations, such as to prevent a client from committing a crime or to prevent death or substantial bodily harm to another.

If I represent both the city and its officials, information I learn during the course of preparing for the arbitration may benefit one client while, on the other hand, prejudice my other clients. However, my duty of confidentiality and duty of loyalty to each client prevent me from using or revealing this information to the city commission.

Regardless, the sworn complaint under penalty of perjury will be resolved in some manner. There is either some truth to the allegations or Officer Campbell has committed a crime by perjuring himself.

Additionally, rule 4-2.1 states that "in representing a client, a lawyer shall exercise independent professional judgment and render candid advice." In other words, I must render truthful advice. Where a conflict exists between my clients, my duty of loyalty and confidentiality prevents me from rendering candid advice.

An analogous example of this conflict is the situation where the Attorney General of the United States cannot participate in a legal proceeding because he cannot represent both the President of the United States and the Department Heads the President appoints without an ethical conflict.

This memorandum is an effort to educate everyone on a complicated issue that we have never had to deal with before. Hopefully, this explanation will enable us to reach an expeditious resolution when I bring this matter to the attention of the next city commission meeting.

RECOMMENDATION

1) That the city attorney be authorized to hire outside counsel to litigate the pending arbitration only.

2) Authorization to forward the sworn complaint of former officer Campbell to the

Florida Department of Law Enforcement. On a related note, yesterday I received a copy of the sworn complaint by former officer Campbell. I have contacted the office of executive investigations of the Florida Department of Law Enforcement and have been informed that they are the correct agency to resolve the issues raised in the complaint.

Remember that meeting wherein Mr. Fibber assured Chief Truth that he had all her and her employees' legal needs covered regarding this issue? Not only that, but there are also several avenues where people can get in trouble in law enforcement. The first (and most concerning) is a criminal allegation. The next is an administrative complaint, and arbitration can be part of that process. The final one is civil suit.

I had no doubt that all three avenues were going to be pursued in this case, but my most immediate concern was obtaining legal counsel regarding the criminal investigation that the Florida Department of Law Enforcement was going to undertake. Sure, I knew that I had not done anything wrong, but having a lawyer present with you that is looking out for your best interest can keep you out of unintended trouble (just ask General Michael Flynn). When the city decided to meet with the outside attorney assigned to be the city's attorney in the arbitration cases, I was asked to come to a meeting with Chief Truth and Mr. Claus. The purpose of my presence was to answer questions about the administrative investigation for Officer Campbell and Sergeant Brown.

In my mind I had a quagmire. The Florida Department of Law Enforcement was still investigating Officer Campbell's criminal allegations against me. Anything I said to the city's attorney, who was looking at the arbitration cases, could be used in a criminal case. Finally, I was an at-will employee, so failing to respond favorably to the request of Mr. Claus could cause my early termination. I requested my own attorney from Mr. Claus through Chief Truth. Mr. Claus's response through his secretary was, "If the major needs an attorney, he can have one." Of course, when I asked to be reimbursed for the expenses involved in hiring an attorney, Mr. Claus balked at the city paying me back (but that is a separate fight).

Ultimately, the Florida Department of Law Enforcement determined there had been no criminal wrongdoing by me, Chief Truth, or Mr. Claus. The next chapter would be arbitration.

CHAPTER 21

King Solomon

For those who do not know one of the Bible stories involving King Solomon, I will give you a *Reader's Digest* version. For those who do, please indulge us. Two women were brought before King Solomon to settle an argument over which of the women was the mother of an infant. Both women claimed the child was theirs. King Solomon ordered a swordsman to chop the baby in half so that each woman could have half of the child. Just as the axman was about to swing, one of the women relented, saying, "Please do not harm the child. Just give it to the other woman." King Solomon then knew who the real mother was and gave the child to the woman who had spoken up to save the child. Such was the renowned wisdom of King Solomon.

It has been my experience with arbitrators that they tend to want to split the proverbial baby, giving each side a win even if neither side is truly happy with the result. The arbitration hearings involving Sergeant Brown and Officer Campbell were split, with each held independently of the other. Officer Campbell continued to hold court on television with his news reporter friends that he had been tipping off the entire time. Now that he was no longer employed by the agency, he could openly appear on the news and spew his version of the truth. He continued to make his allegations about mismanagement in the city, but those were unfounded. It did not stop him from continuing to make them.

Sergeant Brown was returned to work by the arbitrator at his previous rank and was to be "made whole," which meant the pay that he lost during his termination, he would receive (and any raises that were gotten, he was entitled to), except for one day of suspension that would be his punishment for his insubordination. Officer Campbell's arbitration ended a little differently.

On the topic of how Officer Campbell attempted to make the arrest of Mr. Samuel, the arbitrator wrote, "It is important to note that this is a highly decorated police officer who has thousands of hours of training and at one time was also instrumental in teaching extraction techniques to his colleagues." Furthermore, the arbitrator said, "Officer Campbell's methodology of attempting to subdue and extract this individual put him in harm's way and was ultimately the reason he was permanently injured when the suspect drove off. I would expect that someone with his experience would use a bit of creativity to extract the individual and minimize the already-heightened tension. He showed poor judgment in the actions he took."

Regarding the unauthorized rifle in Officer Campbell's trunk, the arbitrator said, "I do question the judgment of the grievant in having said weapon in his patrol car." Furthermore, in questioning Campbell's excuse for having the rifle, the arbitrator said, "The grievant's credibility comes into question here if he expects to have this arbitrator believe that the armorer would be at the police station at the end of his late-night shift or on a Sunday morning, waiting for the weapon so he/she could inspect it."

Regarding the unauthorized hinged handcuffs used by Officer Campbell, the arbitrator said, "Make no mistake: Officer Campbell did comply with the change, albeit begrudgingly, but he seems to cite policy when it benefits him personally and disregard it when it does not. I have serious concerns about his attitude and behavior regarding this matter. A long-term senior employee should adhere to a higher standard and should be keenly aware that his behavior, knowledge, and judgment are constantly on display for others, whether he realizes it or not. He sets the standard for others to follow."

Furthermore, in analyzing Officer Campbell's decision to continue to carry unauthorized hinged handcuffs despite knowing the department's intent to change to chain handcuffs, the arbitrator said, "His disdain for the decision was evident on the night of the incident, more than two (2) months later, when he was in possession of his personal set of hinged handcuffs and not the standard-issue chain cuffs. His defense was that the authorized set had bodily fluids and were not available for use. If he had been successful in effectuating an arrest, he would not have been in compliance with the city's policy. This notwithstanding, I find it difficult to believe that he could not have obtained a standard-issue backup set of cuffs in his possession once his original issued set was contaminated. It is evidently clear that he was not in agreement with the policy change, not initially and not at the time of the incident. By his own admission, Officer Campbell has worked for several different chiefs during his fourteen-year tenure with the city. As a veteran on the force, he has observed firsthand that with a different leadership comes different policy decisions, different styles of management, as well as different styles of community involvement. He recognizes this, but on this issue, he chose to indirectly disregard it with his actions."

Regarding Officer Campbell's failure to get the necessary training in the use of the in-car video system, the arbitrator found that it did not rise to the level of insubordination, but said, "This, however, does not excuse the grievant from his ability to know better and to act to rectify the situation. This goes to his knowledge, skill, and ability as a fourteen-year veteran of the police force. Here again he showed a lack of judgment, lack of common sense, and at the very least, indifference toward having a properly operating in-car camera system."

Furthermore, regarding Campbell's testimony concerning the in-car video system, the arbitrator said, "On direct examination, he was asked if the in-car camera system had a simple push button saying Record on it. He stated twice that he did not remember in response to this question posed by city's counsel. I find this lapse of memory convenient, considering his vivid recollection as to how he returned to road patrol from marine patrol and about a shooting incident he was involved in a week before the incident in question."

In discussing Campbell's memory (or lack thereof), the arbitrator wrote, "On cross-examination by his own counsel, Officer Campbell described in detail how he came back to the squad. For all his lapse in memory during the direct examination, Officer Campbell remembered vividly that on a given Sunday, he was working in conjunction with the local sheriff's department on his boat. He also remembers that he received a call from Director Noit stating, 'I told you to be at a SWAT demonstration with the MRAP. The MRAP is the armored vehicle that we received from the government.' His response was that he had not received a letter or acknowledgment from the chief or, for that matter, his SWAT commander. According to the grievant, the notice would have come from either of them, as it was **policy** and that, by federal government standards, the armored vehicle is only supposed to leave the compound at their direction."

In further explaining the arbitrator's rationale in relying on Campbell's testimony, he wrote, "The next day, he was off marine patrol and back on the squad. In the above exchange, he cited **policy** when he was asked why he was not at the SWAT demonstration. He apparently was notified to be there ahead of time and ignored the request because *he was following city policy.* He cannot use **policy** in his defense in one instance and then argue that there was no policy when it comes to the alleged violations relating to the hinged handcuffs."

Additionally, Campbell's behavior at the arbitration is described by the arbitrator: "The resignation from marine patrol also highlights to this arbitrator the temperament of Officer Campbell when dealing with his immediate supervisor at that time. It is concerning that he displayed a short temper and a pattern of behavior that may also be attributed to the alleged policy violations."

Continuing his observation of Campbell's testimony, the arbitrator wrote, "I mentioned his earlier 'selective' memory when asked if his patrol car had a Record button on the in-car camera system, yet he could not remember. This is a patrol car he drove every shift for two months, and he expects this arbitrator to believe he cannot remember this minor detail. Yet on cross-examination, he remembered vividly the shootings that were occurring at that time in the same residential neighborhood where the tragic incident occurred. Furthermore, he described in detail how he keeps his windows down when patrolling to hear the gunshots and where they are coming from. Finally, he recounts in detail an incident that occurred a week or so earlier. Upon hearing a couple of gunshots, he drove toward the residential neighborhood in question, whereupon he saw 'smoke emanating from a particular house.'"

After recalling Campbell's testimony regarding an incident that occurred one week before the Samuel shooting, the arbitrator wrote, "My point in citing this incident is two-fold: first is his vivid recollection of the incident; second is how he took control in a situation where shots were fired, where a number of individuals were present, and where a loaded weapon was found. To his credit, he handled this incident with authority and without further incident. This shows this arbitrator that he is more than capable of defusing a difficult situation and not letting it escalate out of hand."

The arbitrator concludes Campbell's testimonial credibility issue with, "In comparing how he handled this situation with the unfortunate incident in question, it is quite apparent that he is more than capable of taking control of a dangerous situation and asserting his authority. However, I am still troubled by his lapse in memory when it does not benefit his position. His credibility again comes into question when this occurs."

Regarding the in-car video system malfunction, the arbitrator wrote, "However, Officer Campbell should have basic, common-sense knowledge that performing his duties with faulty or inoperable equipment is a risky proposition. He certainly would not tolerate it with his weapon, and it should not have been tolerated with the video equipment. It has been noted that when he feels strongly about an issue (hinged handcuffs), he makes sure that his point is made to higher authority in writing. Why he did not apply the same standards to another piece of equipment is baffling to me. It shows selective complacency and contempt for authority."

When attempting to explain that the city failed to provide time for the union to review the entire case, the arbitrator wrote, "For purposes of this case, I will enumerate the question where this arbitrator

believes the employer is not on solid ground to terminate the grievant. The fourth (4th) question as posed by the arbitrator is, *'Was the
company investigation conducted fairly and objectively?'* Clearly,
as noted earlier, the city failed to meet this standard when it did not
give the union ample time to review the investigative file of the grievant prior to conducting the predetermination hearing."

The arbitrator concluded, "Based on the testimony of the union
representative regarding the actions of the city in conducting the predetermination hearing, and for which there was no substantive challenge to her testimony on this matter, I find that the grievant was
not afforded due process by the conduct of the city, and this should
mitigate the discipline imposed."

What was missing was that the original union representative
had previously reviewed the entire case with Campbell prior to his
providing a statement, and Campbell had an opportunity to review
each time he came back prior to the case's conclusion. Just because
the union changed representatives should not negate the city's fulfill-
ment of their obligation to provide the union what it is allowed to
review prior to the predetermination hearing. The only documents
that were "new" to Campbell and the union prior to the predetermination hearing were my summary and Deputy Chief King's disposition letter. A few pages that could have easily been reviewed prior to
the predetermination hearing by any competent counsel. However,
I had left the agency prior to this hearing, and the city's attorney
trying the case opted not to call me back to refute this allegation of
wrongdoing.

In talking about Deputy Chief Trust's testimony, the arbitrator said that his testimony was credible and included, "The standards for a fourteen-year veteran are much higher than for a newly
hired officer. I agree with his assessment." The arbitrator said about
Deputy Chief Trust's testimony, "It is perfectly within management's
right in deciding what discipline to review, the entire work history
for mitigating and aggravating factors in making a final decision."
Yet the arbitrator would not allow testimony concerning Campbell's
disciplinary record? The arbitrator further opined, "By inference or
implication, he was stating that Officer Campbell did not. He there-

fore recommended a suspension or demotion for the second officer. The deputy chief was well within his management right in the way he analyzed the entire work and disciplinary history of the grievant and the other officer involved in the incident to make a final recommendation on the discipline recommendation."

In discussing Campbell's decisions regarding the traffic stop and resulting tactical errors, the arbitrator wrote, "It is incredulous to believe that in the heat of the moment, Officer Campbell did not fall back on his own training that he provided to new officers. Any individual who is part of a paramilitary organization instinctively relies on the training he has received over the years when making split-second decisions, and this situation is no exception. Although the testimony did not go into detail as to what he did differently than what he normally does when training others, it is given weight in terms of his judgment in this situation."

In covering the three alleged policy violations, the arbitrator concluded in general, "Furthermore, the city alleged he violated city policy in three areas thoroughly discussed above based on an internal investigation. In all three, this arbitrator finds a systemic pattern of behavior by the grievant that could be best termed as *indifference* to the policies in question."

The overall discussion of Campbell as an officer is summed up by the arbitrator in the following paragraph: "He displayed questionable tactics in extracting the individual from the vehicle. As a result, two significant, life-changing events occurred. The first has already been addressed, the death of the driver. The second one is the career-ending injury he sustained because of his actions. Furthermore, he showed a lack of judgment, and his credibility is questioned when addressing the issue of the unauthorized weapon in the trunk of his patrol car, he showed disregard for changes in policy relating to the handcuffs, and he showed indifference to multiple requests to have his in-car camera system looked at. As a result, his credibility comes into question when this arbitrator considers the final decision and award."

The arbitrator's ultimate ruling was, "For the reasons set forth in the analysis and opinion above, the grievance is sustained in part and denied in part: (1) the grievant is to be reinstated with full benefits and seniority; (2) since the grievant is medically unable to return to his patrol duties, it is directed that he be put on paid administrative leave until his application for disability retirement is approved; and (3) the grievant is to be reinstated without back pay."

It is important to note that if Campbell were physically able to return to work, he would not have been able to function as a police officer. A police officer's honesty and integrity are paramount in his ability to provide truthful testimony in a court of law. With all the suggestions by the arbitrator that Campbell was less than truthful in the arbitration hearing, his ability to testify under oath would have been impugned, thus crippling his ability to function as a sworn police officer.

It is also important to understand that most arbitrators will not find solely for one party or the other in an arbitration hearing, opting instead to "split" the proverbial baby. This can be seen in the arbitrator's final ruling regarding finding in part for the grievant (Campbell) while also denying in part. The fact that Campbell did not receive "back pay" for the time he had been terminated is indicative of the seriousness of the flaws in Campbell's case against the city. Campbell was not "made whole" like Brown was.

CHAPTER 22

Civil Litigation

After anything criminal, then the administrative investigation, the final step in law enforcement sagas such as these is the civil lawsuit. The mayor, city manager, and chief of police were all named in the ensuing lawsuits as potential litigants. The following is the letter that was sent by the plaintiff's attorneys:

> Dear Mayor, Mr. Clause, and Chief Truth:
>
> The law firm of Dewey, Cheatum, and Howell has the honor of representing Eric Samuel as the personal representative of the estate of David Samuel, and we are hereby presenting this demand against the city. David was a loving son, a loyal friend, and a hardworking young man with no criminal record. On the night your officer Campbell stopped David Samuel, who was unarmed, David was tragically shot in the back and killed by Sergeant Benjamin Brown. While providing backup to Officer Campbell, Sergeant Brown unlawfully entered David's vehicle unannounced, which led to the chain of events that ended in David's death.
>
> We intend to seek damages pursuant to 42 USC § 1983 and 1985 for violations of David's

civil rights under the Fourth and Fourteenth Amendments to the United States Constitution, including the unnecessary use of deadly force, use of excessive force, and unlawful search and seizure by the police department and Officers Campbell and Brown and other agents and employees of the city during the course and in the scope of their employment. These federal causes of action provide remedies for which, despite the statutory cap on damages in Florida under waiver of sovereign immunity, there is no cap on damages, and there is the availability of attorney's fees.

The city's exposure comes from maintaining—well, before the current police chief's tenure—a custom and practice of failing to adhere to proper and accepted policing procedures, both internal and widely recognized, that was "the moving force of the constitutional violations." See Polk County v. Dodson, 454 US.312, 326 (1981), quoting Monell v. New York Dept. of Soc. Svcs., 436 US 658, 694 (1978); see also Grech v. Clayton County, 335 F.3d 1326, 1329 (11th Cir. 2003); See also Vineyard v. County of Murray, 990 F.2d 1207, 1211 (11th Cir. 1993). By failing to maintain and adhere to proper policies and procedures, the city and the police department created a culture of noncompliance that predates the police department's current leadership. The existence of this culture is evidenced by the subject officers' violation of a laundry list of procedural violations during the incident. Being as it is highly unlikely that properly supervised and trained officers could ever commit so many serious violations in just a single incident, the officers' conduct is strongly indicative of indifference to procedure borne out of the department-wide culture of indifference to such.

The department's failure to police their own as it pertains to following procedure caused their officers to be improperly equipped and trained to be cognizant, respectful, and protective of the constitutional rights of their citizens and of David Samuel in particular. The Supreme Court of the United States, almost thirty years ago, determined that a city's failure to adequately train and prepare its police officers may give rise to municipal liability. *City of Canton v. Harris*, 489 US 378, 388 (1989). The court reasoned that the inadequacy of police training may serve as a basis for section 1983 liability when the failure to train amounts to deliberate indifference to the rights of persons whose rights are protected during interactions by virtue of the officers having been trained on how to properly interact with them. Id.

The Eleventh Circuit has decided that, in addition to imposition of municipal liability because of its failure to train, a city may be liable, under section 1983, where it fails to adequately investigate allegations of police misconduct. Samples ex. rel. *Samples v. City of Atlanta*, 846 F.2d 1328, 1333 (11th Cir. 1988). The "cherry-picking" of facts disclosed during the investigation of the subject shooting and, historically, "turning a blind eye" to the performance records of officers in officer-involved shooting fatalities are symptomatic of the city's past practices that failed to pay necessary attention to the proper use of force and proper training of officers. Indeed, the city's public records are bereft of any showing that the police department, in the past fifteen years, decided that an officer-involved shooting was unjustified or that it terminated the employment of one of its officers for unreasonable use of force.

The impact of the police department's flawed culture resulted in the tragic death of a particularly bright and gifted young man. Every person who knew David Samuel offers a noticeably similar refrain: "He was a good kid. A really good one." Many add a comment about him being a good son to his mother, a football star, or a budding young musician. He had a clean record and attended college in Washington on a football scholarship. After a year, David decided that Washington's winters made it no place for a Florida son. He returned home, with a goal of pursuing his music career. While he did, David did not sit on his hands but also held steady jobs, working in a bank for six months and, following that, in a call center without missing a beat.

The opinion expressed by the government's expert, Geoffrey Alpert, lays to rest any doubt as to the improper procedure followed by the officers as well as what caused the chain reaction that led to David's death. Geoffrey Alpert, an expert in use of force, characterized Brown's initial actions as having "ultimately led to circumstances that result in his need to use deadly force as self-defense." (Geoffrey Alpert report, dated, ¶ 18.) The findings from the police department's investigation announced by the chief of police echoed this point and noted that **the officers could have prevented the shooting.**

Mr. Alpert criticizes the "tactics" used by the officers time and again, while the department's investigation found a total of fifteen violations of policies and procedures by the officers during this incident. Most notably, Mr. Alpert further criticized Officer Campbell's training, noting that his inappropriate conduct—more specifically, forcing his way into the vehicle—was indicative of "poor training." (Geoffrey Alpert report, date, ¶7 & 8.) Elsewhere, he lodges similar criticism of Sergeant Brown's action of forcing himself into the vehicle. (Id. at ¶18,22.) His assessment demonstrates that our attempts to prove the department's training was inadequate in the face of the facts before us would almost surely be successful.

David Samuel fled after Sergeant Brown executed an illegal and unannounced entry through Mr. Samuel's passenger-side door, followed by an incursion into the vehicle. Mr. Alpert's report illustrates the degree of severity of this transgression with a litany of adjectives and phrases used in his report (Geoffrey Alpert report, date, ¶. 9,18,22): "inappropriately," "unfortunately," "not proper police procedure," "poor tactics," "put him in an unnecessarily dangerous position," "did not need to," and "put himself in harm's way."

It is abundantly obvious that Mr. Samuel, a young Black man who had been pulled over at midnight by cops, was legitimately and reasonably afraid. He also had marijuana in a small amount visible, which he knew Officer Campbell could observe, and that surely only heightened his anxiety. It is certain that he was never expecting to hear the voice of a mystery person from the seat next to him as he looked the other way toward Officer Campbell during the stop. Then, after the startling sounds of a person beside him reached his ears and he swung his head to discover your officer there, one can only imagine the myriad of thoughts and fears that ran through this young man's head: *"Why is he there? Why did he sneak in? Does he want to shoot me like all the others killed by police? How can a cop sneak in my car like that? Doesn't he need to announce himself? Did he not follow the law and announce himself because he does not care about following the law? If I get out of the car, will I die? Should I run for my life? Should I try to drive away instead?"*

Sergeant Brown's interview is illustrative of what one would expect from a dishonest person trying to get out of killing an innocent person. Brown details on page 13 of his interview, which illogically was not taken until three days after the shooting, approaching David's vehicle on the passenger's side without as much as announcing himself. In fact, his testimony reflects he was sneaking up: "I made my way over to the passenger-side door, then opened up the car door, and I stuck my head a little bit down so…cause I think I was on a curb. I had a little room, one leg was down, one leg might have been up. But I was peeking in the car because I wanted to get a look in the back seat and make sure there was no one else in the vehicle. I can tell when I drove up there was only a driver in the front seat" (p. 13, interview of Sergeant Brown, date).

Considering the department's finding of a staggering number of violations of protocol and procedure, the chief's recognition of these violations in a public press conference, the findings of the government's expert, the department's investigation, and the public's sentiment following this police shooting and similar ones nationwide, I see no reason to belabor the obvious merits of our case. Rather, my preference is to simply touch on a handful of items and refer you to the complaint we will be filing at week's end for further detail.

That said, it is difficult to refrain from making a pejorative comment regarding the stark contrast between the autopsy report and Sergeant Brown's testimony regarding the direction Mr. Samuel was facing when he was shot. Neither logically nor succinctly offers a viable explanation of how a bullet entered David's back if his front was facing Brown, and the jury will not be fooled into believing such absurdity. The defense that the city has attempted to set up has the deceased running in several directions: toward the officer with his hands up, toward him with one hand outstretched, from left to right, away, and lest we forget, running while "contorting and twisting," but not running straight. There is certainly "contorting and twisting" at play here, but it has nothing to do with the manner in which David ran for his life.

Almost unbelievably, Sergeant Brown's magic bullet is not the only aspect of his version of the incident that is metaphysically impossible. After agreeing during his interview that "from an officer's safety perspective, your number 1 concern and focus has gotta be on the hands of the driver," Brown somehow lost track of how many things one can do with two hands while telling his contrived story. On page 64 of his interview, he testifies that as he jumped into the car, then Mr. Samuel drove off with one hand on him, pushing.

Clearly, Mr. Samuel's left hand was driving the car, a fact Brown confirms multiple times in his statement. Brown also confirms specifically that David was not holding a weapon, only to shift a few lines later and say that he did not see

David's left hand. Brown was right next to Mr. Samuel as he drove the car with his left hand while grappling with him with the other. Both officers concede that they never saw a gun. This was because there never was a gun, as the investigation confirmed. Brown's claim that he believed David was firing some invisible gun while pushing him with one hand and driving with the other is pure nonsense that would embarrass the city if it comes to light and aggravate the jury should they hear of it.

Notwithstanding the subject "test" performed by a police officer from a neighboring department after the FBI refused to assist with an expert, nobody, least of all a reasonable, experienced officer trained in the use of firearms, would ever reasonably mistake three gunshots being fired from arm's length in a car with shots fired from a healthy distance outside the car. In addition, one of the officers who came to the scene noted the prevalence of gunpowder inside the car would have erased all legitimate doubts of even the most skeptical policeman as to who fired the shots.

Brown was not just some unreliable historian. On page 66 of his interview, Brown said he heard gunshots and then threw his body against Mr. Samuel. Then after three short answers describing the melee that followed, Sergeant Brown testified to then hearing the gunshots... again. These are not minor inconsistencies that a jury might be convinced to simply disregard.

To add to the officer's lack of credibility, Brown's story at his interview three days after the incident was that he believed Mr. Samuel shot a gun at him inside the enclosed vehicle, and he responded by employing a Taser. We share in the confusion expressed by the government's expert, Geoffrey Alpert, who stated on page 10 of his report, "It is not clear why Sergeant Brown used a Taser if he believed Samuel had a firearm" (Geoffrey Alpert report, date, ¶24). Sergeant Brown, a trained SWAT officer, claimed in the version of events he was allowed to give three days after the incident that he instinctually reached for his Taser after believing he was shot at three times by the suspect next to him. A specially trained tactical officer engaged in hand-to-hand combat in a confined space is not trained to reach for his Taser when his opponent pulls a gun and starts shooting at him at point-blank range. Sergeant Brown's SWAT training developed his instincts and reflexes to respond to attack with a measured response. As Mr. Alpert also pointed out in his report, no SWAT officer would respond to the deadly force of a firearm with the nondeadly force of a Taser (Alpert report, ¶24).

Comparing the interviews of Sergeant Brown's initial statement to the statement he made to Detective Columbus on the scene of the incident reveals yet another striking contradiction by your officers that serves to further illustrate that Brown is making this all up as he goes along. Sergeant Brown stated at the scene that Officer Campbell shot the Taser, yet at his interview a few days later, Brown claimed he fired the Taser himself. Detective Columbus, after Brown's interview with the sheriff's office, was asked by the sheriff's office if he was "positive" that Brown told him that Campbell discharged his Taser (p. 11 and 12, Detective Columbus interview, date), and his answer was, "Yes. Yes. Yes."

Furthermore, Brown made absolutely no mention to Detective Columbus about his melee with Samuel at all! These contradictions are far too abundant and far too pertinent to be passed off as simple errors in the mind of anyone trying to cover up a bad shooting. Undoubtedly, the press and your constituents will have a veritable field day with them. In all likelihood, the contradictory statements by the shooter as to who fired the Taser relate to issues far too central to the case to have overcome.

Defending a civil suit already severely corrupted by the tangled web your officers have weaved would be an irrational waste of taxpayer dollars. Juries in police shooting cases come into court these days already influenced by the current social atmosphere as it exists by virtue of such widespread police violence against African Americans and the backlash against government in general. Against that backdrop, there just is no upside to ripping off the scab that has formed over this incident for the city through the passage of time by ushering it into the limelight once again. Why would you do something so harmful to the community after having made it past the difficult days and nights that came after your officers killed David? Just to pour the half a million dollars or more it would cost to defend the case down the drain?

Additionally, the discovery process and trial are certain to involve discussion of the mass exodus of officers from the department around the time of the incident. Perhaps Sergeant Brown's lies as to who fired the Taser contributed to five officers resigning from the department within a week of the shooting. I suppose it may also have had something to do with the absurdity of Brown's belief that Mr. Samuel had a third hand. Regardless, the salient issue is not as much the cause of the mass exodus from the department but rather that this incident already has raised so many serious issues for us to investigate through discovery.

We intend to seek recovery of all damages available at law for Mr. Samuel's wrongful death, including the value of his support and services to his surviving family members, their loss of companionship and guidance, their mental and emotional pain and suffering, and the loss of net accumulations. Accordingly, we demand $8.5 million on behalf of David's estate. However, if we are forced to try this case, we will be seeking $15 million in damages. As referenced above, we will be filing a complaint in short order. We plan to serve it after giving you a chance to evaluate our demand and, if you desire, discuss this matter with us at this juncture, either informally or through formal settlement discussions.

Each of the city commissioners was copied, and the city braced for the lawsuit to come. In the meantime, lawyers began negotiating. The city decided in short order that it was in their best interest to settle this suit prior to even the first deposition. While the Samuel estate received some money, it was a pittance of what was initially proposed.

CHAPTER 23

Conclusions

While I was not allowed to reach conclusions while conducting administrative cases, now that they are over and I am no longer with the agency, I have a few observations. I know that for the most part, public confidence in law enforcement is higher in general than those who would cast doubts upon the profession. Unfortunately, there are the Than Campbells in the job who cause the rest of us to suffer. Any police officer reading this knows the personality I am referring to, namely, the glory-seeking, self-aggrandizing, bullying, never-wrong liars who took the job to seek their fortune. Those kinds just do not belong. It is the job of the supervisors and managers who work with those types to ferret them out of the organization before tragedy strikes, or suffer their fate when the inevitable occurs (like Sergeant Brown).

Yes, Sergeant Brown got his job back and was "made whole" by the organization. Yet he must carry the weight of having shot an unarmed man for the remainder of his life. Knowing the bonds he developed with members of the SWAT team, there was no way that Brown did not know that Campbell chose to ignore orders and carry unauthorized equipment. The sergeant chose to overlook those indiscretions, which only emboldened Campbell to continue to push the envelope. Campbell was so incensed by his demotion from lead training officer and placement back on the street in patrol that he was on a mission to prove he was the police (I have seen it too often).

That personality can be a really bad day for any civilian who would dare challenge such an officer's authority. To be sure, both Brown and Campbell stepped outside of their training allowing their complacency to lead them into deadly circumstances. Officer safety in law enforcement is not just a course; it demands unparalleled and consistent observation in following training. Always vigilant while remaining professional with the public. Always seeking to defuse the situation, and avoiding placing oneself in harm's way.

I did not fail retirement the second time. Chief Truth asked me if I would stay if she made me a deputy chief of police, and I politely refused the offer. The real boss (my wife) said I was needed at home. To be sure, I have the credentials to seek a chief of police job anywhere in the United States. I have been close enough to the top to know that I do not have the stomach for it. Given today's environment in law enforcement, I could not imagine returning to a job wherein each day is a challenge to avoid the pitfalls that can end with you in civil court, administrative hot water, or even jail. At one time, I thought the profession was honorable and worthy of my best efforts. While I still believe it is honorable and I did give my best every day I was involved, I have developed multiple stress-related health issues that will likely put me in an early grave. I intend to enjoy however much time I have left in this world and return to my community as much as I can through volunteerism.

ABOUT THE AUTHOR

Bob Country retired after thirty years in law enforcement in the state of Florida. His highest level of education was a master's degree in public administration. He graduated from the University of Louisville's Southern Police Institute, receiving the Director's Award for Academic Excellence in the graduate program (awarded to the highest grade point average). He taught in the police academy at his first agency, in the classroom at the University of Phoenix, and for an online college during his law enforcement years. He has been married to his beautiful wife for over thirty years, and they have two wonderful children as well as three grandchildren. Bob spent his first two years of retirement building his mother-in-law's house on the back of their property one "stick" at a time. Bob loves to fish and play golf (when his back will allow). Bob is a member of his local Kiwanis club, where he gives back to his community regularly.